STEPHE

Stephen Gregory was born in Derby in 1952 and was educated in North Wales and at the University of London where he read law. After eleven years teaching in Britain and abroad he left the profession to concentrate on writing. His first novel, THE CORMORANT, won the Somerset Maugham Award for 1987 and the Welsh Arts Council Young Writers' Prize for 1986.

sceptre

Stephen Gregory

THE WOODWITCH

sceptre

First published in Great Britain in 1988 by William Heinemann Ltd.

Sceptre edition 1989

Sceptre is an imprint of Hodder and Stoughton Paperbacks, a division of Hodder and Stoughton Ltd.

British Library C.I.P.

Gregory, Stephen, *1952*
The woodwitch.
I. Title
823′.914 [F]

ISBN 0-340-50803-5

Printed and bound in Great Britain for Hodder and Stoughton Paperbacks, a division of Hodder and Stoughton Ltd., Mill Road, Dunton Green, Sevenoaks, Kent TN13 2YA. (Editorial Office: 47 Bedford Square, London WC1B 3DP) by Richard Clay Ltd., Bungay, Suffolk.

FOR JAN AND BRIAN
at
Tros-y-gol

I

SOMETHING WAS dead in the forest. The dog could smell it.

However, for the whole of that autumn afternoon she had been lying in the long grass, in a patch of sunlight which fell through the branches of the silver birch, watching the man at work with his bow-saw. It was a golden day, and the man was working in his shirtsleeves, sweating as he sawed rhythmically through the limbs of a fallen mountain ash. The dog lay and watched. When the breeze changed direction, she lifted her delicate face to meet it, and it was then that the smell of death came to her, the smell of something dead in the forest. Sometimes she rose lazily from the grass and went to the stream to drink, or else the man would rest for a while and amuse himself by throwing sticks for the dog to fetch. He threw them into a deep pool of clear brown water, where the dog sprang and swam repeatedly until the water was no longer clear. And when the man was tired of the game, he dropped the stick and directed his dog to lie down again in the soft grass. She did this, after she had shaken vigorously from head to tail and sent a rainbow shower of droplets into the still sunlight of the glade. 'Good girl, Phoebe. Stay there.' The man returned to his tree. It had fallen, but most of it was still alive, for there were clusters of shining red berries dangling from its branches. However, one of the branches was quite dead, the man was sure, for it had not a single berry on it and the wood was dry and brittle beneath the bark. The sheep had sheltered there, gnawing the bark away and stripping the greenery. So the man felt justified in taking his bow-saw to the tree. Now he had completely severed the branch, dragging it into the sunlight, and for the rest of the afternoon he had been removing the smaller sections and sawing the wood into manageable lengths which would go into the wheelbarrow he had brought with him to the side of the stream. As the afternoon wore on, he saw that his work would result in one good barrow-load of timber for the fire, and this made him happy, to feel that aching in his shoulders and to wipe away the sweat from his face, looking forward soon to wheeling the barrow down the track to the cottage, where he would stack the logs in the little stone outhouse.

The breeze changed direction. Turning her face into it, the dog sniffed. Her nose wrinkled and she lifted her lips in a silent snarl which showed her perfectly white teeth. The man did not notice her snarling, for he was just then arranging the lengths of wood in the barrow, but he felt the breeze and realised that soon it would get cooler. He shivered, reaching for his pullover from the branches of the mountain ash which were still alive and fruiting, tugging it over his head. As his face emerged from the inside of the pullover, he glanced upwards through the fine sprays of the birch trees to see that already the sun was slanting and would shortly vanish behind the hillside. The moon had risen, a massive white disc against the darkening blue of the sky. And there was Venus, the man wondered, a single brilliantly silver spark which made the whole of that autumn afternoon feel tired, a spark in the sky which made the man shiver again and realise that his afternoon in shirtsleeves was over. The sun itself now touched the black horizon of the mountains, throwing up splinters of light as though it had shattered on impact with the cold rocks, and, as the man watched, the sun slipped down and went, in quite a matter-of-fact and unspectacular way, to leave the sky suddenly much darker. At the same time, the moon and Venus were brighter and bigger, launching themselves higher and claiming what the sun had left behind. It was an evening in October, with the moon as big and as heavy as it could be. There might even be a frost that night. It was time to return to the cottage and light the fire. The man put the saw on top of his logs. He went to the fallen tree and knelt down by the fresh white stump where he had sawed away the dead branch. Pulling up a tuft of grass, he rubbed the stump with soil until it was no longer white. He smiled to himself, that he was something of a countryman and a poacher who could survive the cold autumn nights by pilfering fuel from someone else's land, and he turned to the barrow and manoeuvred it away from the stream. The floor of the glade was white with sawdust, as if that frost had already bitten, so the man scuffed it about with his wellington boots until it was hardly noticeable. It was getting dark quickly. Then he pressed forward with the wheelbarrow, calling out to the dog to follow him. When he glanced around to check that she was there, he saw that she was not. The man was alone in the twilight.

The dog watched all this from an outcrop of rock in the silver birches, some fifteen or twenty feet above the man's head. Just as the sun went down beneath the horizon, as though that was some sort of a signal to her, she moved noiselessly from her patch of soft grass and sprang higher up the hillside. Behind her, where the woodland of birch and oak and mountain ash finished, there began the endless acres of the fir plantation, a bristling black blanket of larch and pine, hundreds of thousands of trees packed densely together and covering every feature of the land like a shroud. Even in the brightest sunshine, the plantation was a place of gloom and shadows and silence. Now, with the sun just a memory of warmth and colour and light and the flutter of small birds among bright red berries, the forest was simply black. Nothing much lived and moved inside it. Only its tracks and clearings were picked out like threads of silver by the trembling moonlight.

And in the forest there was something dead which the dog could smell. She looked down and watched the man. 'Come on, Phoebe, where are you?' he called out to her, and then he whistled his customary whistle. At this, the dog barked once, a high clear sound like the bark of a fox, so that he looked up and saw her. She barked again and sprang away further up the hillside, to the very edge of the forest, and she continued to bark until he put down the wheelbarrow and began to scramble up the path towards her. Seeing him approach, the dog cavorted with excitement, one moment lying in the grass and beating it with her tail and then spinning round and round and yelping. The sound was pure and light, echoing a little from the surrounding hills, but then it was absorbed into the deadening mass of the plantation. It was the only sound, for not a raven or a jay was moving that evening, with the dark blue sky leaning more heavily on the horizon, with the moon quite silent and almost opaque in its luminosity. The twilight was still. The trees did not move and even the streams were muffled and oiled to a kind of whisper. But the dog increased the intensity of her barking so that it rang against the darkening bowl of the sky and would not be obliterated by the forest. And the man was soon there with her, stroking her glossy black head and wanting now to follow her urgent beckoning. The dog stopped barking. In a few seconds, she was sprinting alongside the barbed-wire fence which ran around the perimeter of the plantation, to the nearby gate. She leapt over it and stood waiting on the forest track while the man climbed carefully over. 'Hang on, Phoebe, wait for me.' He came down heavily on the other side, the big black boots slapping against his calves. The dog lifted her face and sniffed. Then she turned like an eel, such was the silken movement of her blackness in the enfolding blackness of the forest, and the man saw only a disappearing blur of a shadow along the moonlit track. But he walked on, hearing the rhythmic slapping of his boots and the accompaniment of his own breath. Also he could hear the patter of the dog's feet. He could hear her running on ahead and then her stopping and waiting for a second before she turned and retraced her steps to see that he was following. And once or twice, picked out in the moonlight which made the footpath bright but which could not penetrate the trees themselves, he saw the glimmer of her teeth or the reflection of Venus in her eyes. So he continued to follow her, concerned to stay with her but quite content to go further into the plantation because there was no one at home in the cottage who was waiting for him or who might wonder where he had gone.

Deeper into the forest went the man and the dog. It was only a hundred yards, but the matter of depth inside the plantation could not be measured in feet or yards or miles: to be inside it on a cool clear moonlit night was to be entirely cut off from the gentle shadows of the silver birch. In the plantation, there was only blackness in the trees, only metallic white moon-colours in the tracks and the clearings, and nothing in between. The edges of the shadows were sharp and cruel. The man's moon-shadow was simply another man who went striding up the track, a rippling black oil-shadow on the ground. The shadow of the dog was another dog, which flickered like a guttering black flame. It was this shadow which turned suddenly from the track and was eclipsed by the blackness of the trees. The dog disappeared.

The man whistled faintly, somewhat winded by the pace of the climb. Standing very still and listening, he was exasperated at first to hear only the thudding of his own blood in the back of his head, until it relented and was replaced by the creaking silence of the forest. He called out to the dog. His voice clanged into the shadows. Above him, the moon was massive and seemed to pulse with the clanging of his voice, as though by crying out in the stillness he had drawn some resonance from a huge silver gong. Then he could hear the dog, and he ducked quickly from the track into a deep dry ditch, a drain along which he could stumble beneath the low branches of the trees and aim towards a pool of moonlight ahead of him. He felt with his hands for the twigs which were brittle and sharp and which tore at his hair, and he trod cautiously with the boots through a carpet of needles. There was the dog, in a clearing. Her coat shone brilliantly in the moonlight. But now, instead of her silent, determined pursuit along the ditch, she was drawing from within herself a series of long pathetic howls which began as moans and ended as sobs, as the dog stood still in her silver floodlight. She closed tight her eyes and lifted up her face to the moon. The man shivered, stopping to catch his breath. He watched the dog along the tunnel under the trees and his scalp prickled at the intensity of her almost human cries. Then he burst noisily from the drain. As he clambered into the brightness of the clearing, he stumbled on something and fell sprawling on the lush long grass. The dog retreated from him with her lips raised, snarling a long, high-pitched snarl. It sounded as loud and as keen as a chain-saw. The man sat up and looked around him.

He was in the centre of a small clearing which had been created by the falling of a tree. The tree had been taken away, but the stump remained and was overgrown with grass and mosses and lichen. The deep drain joined another drain there, and with the sunlight and air and the moisture which the clearing had enjoyed through the summer, something of an oasis had appeared, surrounded by the arid shadowland of the plantation. And in the clearing there was the dead thing which the dog had scented through the brightness of the afternoon. The man saw it at his feet, for he had stumbled over it when he burst from the ditch. Now he grunted with surprise and recoiled from it.

The dead thing was a badger. It lay in the direct beams of the moon, the size of a good pillow, on its back so that the grin of its muzzle was bright and hard as the jaws of a steel trap which had sprung and were clenched tightly together. It had died slowly, reluctantly, unwilling to surrender its grip on a long and dour life. Entwined around its hind quarters were strands of barbed wire. The man looked closely. His dog had withdrawn to the edge of the clearing and continued the buzzing snarl, her lips curled at the blossoming smell of dead flesh. The badger must have blundered into a derelict fence somewhere on the perimeter of the forest, where the wire had been left to sink slowly into the bogs and the marsh grass. The wire was rusty, almost rotten through, but the animal had somehow entangled itself in it, by turning and twisting to free itself, and now it formed a kind of corset around its body. The badger had managed to bite through the wire with its powerful teeth, except that the wire had become inextricably tightened around its hind legs and fatally hampered its ability to find food. The animal was emaciated, an empty sack of skin and bones and bristle and teeth, an ancient beast which had crawled deeper and deeper into the forest, along the tunnel of the drain, drawn by a desire to reach that pool of light and life in the clearing. Finally the badger had dragged itself with its forelegs out of the ditch. There, in the soft grass around the tree stump, it had rolled on to its back and ground its teeth together for the moment of extinction.

The man stood up. 'Good girl, Phoebe,' he said. 'Just what we want for our little experiment.' With one boot, he turned the animal over, raising a roaring cloud of flies from it. The broad black and white stripes of the badger's face were a startling caricature of everything in the forest that night: impenetrable shadows and silver light, the one crisply delineated from the other so that there was no blurring or smudging, and the tip of every bristle on the animal's back was a tiny tingling spark, iron filings pricked out by the unblinking eye of the moon. The wire had cut deeply into the flesh. There was a great deal of raw bruising and the workings of putrefaction.

Kneeling closer, the man was struck by the force of the smell which the dog had caught on the wind from outside the plantation. The corpse was over a week old, he thought, for it was ripe with maggots and in the surrounding grass there were scattered the dull brown pupae. Nevertheless, since he had turned it on to its belly, a little blood had started to ooze from between the animal's teeth, quite black in the monochrome forest. Furthermore, both eyes were intact, untouched by the chisel-beaks of ravens, but they were glazed, suffused with a milky blur, so they would not accept the brilliance of the moon. In spite of the increasing cold which was clamping down on the hillside, the man took off his pullover. He tucked it and bound it around the strands of barbed wire, to form a secure grip for him to hold, and he tested the weight of the animal. He could lift it easily. Grimacing at the smell, he swung it up and on to his back, so that it hung head downwards behind him like a sack of coal. The dog increased the volume and the menace of her snarls, repelled by the sight of the man and the swinging corpse of the badger on his back, but she trotted at his heels when he ducked with his load into the dry drain. Bent double to avoid snagging the dead animal on the overhanging branches, the man went painstakingly through the tunnel, hearing the beat of his own blood and his shortness of breath. The dog was behind him, now and then releasing a snarl of disgust at the scent of the dead thing. Or else she paused to avoid the dripping of blood and maggots from the badger's snout.

Together they emerged from the ditch, on to the forest track. The man went quickly down the hill, for the path was brightly lit, his burden was a comfortable weight which pressed him easily onwards and between the black trees, and he could hear the movements of the dog behind him. When he reached the gate at the edge of the plantation, he swung the badger over it, on to the grass on the other side, before he climbed the wooden bars. The dog slid silently over the gate. She stopped her snarling and went running on ahead, as though pleased to have quit the claustrophobic confines of the forest, and she disappeared down the steep hillside before the man had heaved the badger again on to his back. He went carefully through the glades of birch and oak, and there, from an outcrop of rock, he could look down and see his wheelbarrow, all stacked with logs, with the bow-saw on top of them, in a clearing by the stream where it seemed that the frost had quickly clenched its fist, for the ground was white over. He smiled then, warm and happy from his exertions with the saw and with the weight of the old badger bouncing between his shoulder blades. The dog was waiting by the barrow. When the man arrived, he gently eased the corpse down on to the stack of logs. It lay there on its back and smiled its steel smile at the moon.

The barrow was quite heavy. Its wheel went bouncing along a narrow track across the hillside, where the sheep had worn the grass away. The moon was floating overhead, so that the shadows of the man with his barrow and the dog which trotted on ahead were black puddles which sucked noiselessly around their feet. It was much colder in the open, but the man had left his pullover entangled with the barbed wire around the body of the badger and he pressed on faster to reach the cottage. It was not far away, just a little further down the hillside from where he had spent the afternoon dismembering the mountain ash. And there it was, the bulk of it like a big black boulder hunched under the cliffs and trees of the valley. The man wheeled swiftly past, although his dog had automatically turned in towards the front door, expecting to be let inside, and he gathered speed with the barrow so that he could use the momentum to push it up a slope to the ramshackle outhouse in which he stored his fuel. There he stopped, leaving the barrow while he walked to the cottage. The dog was waiting furtively by the door; her elation at leading the man to her prize had been eclipsed by her distaste for the man's manhandling of the dead thing, and now she was cowering from the man and the moonlight as though both were repugnant to her. She slunk inside when he unlocked the door, going directly to her basket and lying down. Ignoring her, the man took a torch from the mantelpiece and returned to the outhouse with it. The dog remained inside.

While the man had been in the cottage, only long enough to fetch the torch, a single unspectacular cloud had risen from behind the mountains and travelled like a gigantic moth to the candle of the moon. It was suddenly much darker on the hillside. The man fumbled for the padlock, unlocked it and opened the door. Ducking into the outhouse, which was constructed of stone and slate but had been much neglected for a decade, he felt about his head for a hook he knew was hanging there. He found it and set it rattling as he brushed it with his hand. Then he switched on the torch. Its beam lit up the neatly stacked logs along one wall, a few planks and buckets and coils of rope, the litter of paint pots and brushes, a few tins of fuel, paraffin or turpentine, relics of the days when someone had taken an interest in the condition of the cottage. There were four meat-hooks swinging from the timbers, about head height as the man stood in the little shed, and he tugged on one of them to test that it and the rafters were strong enough to take a weight. Satisfied, he set the torch down on the logs so that its beam shone upwards. He stepped out to the wheelbarrow, where still the brightness of the moon was smothered, and he hefted the corpse of the badger in front of his face, lifting it with his hands in the folds of his pullover around the rusted strands of barbed wire. Then, turning into the shed, straining to hold the weight and the smell away from his body, he managed to summon the strength to raise the badger to the hooks. He was lucky first time: the confusion of wires which had buried themselves in the flesh of the animal now snagged on a hook, and as the man stepped backwards he left the badger aloft, swinging its head downwards, rotating gently so that now the mask of the jaws was grinning at him and then it was the milky eyes which stared blindly into his. The man was breathing hard. But he was pleased with what he had done and to think of what it would produce, and he thought of this as he took the logs from the wheelbarrow and stacked them regularly against another wall of the outhouse so that they would dry quickly. When he had done this, he stood and regained his wind, happy to be in his little shed with the ranks of timber which he himself had cut and with the hanging corpse. 'You're perfect,' he said quietly to the badger. He removed his pullover from it. The light from the torch was soft and warm on the walls and the wood, and it made golden sparks of the animal's bristles; it made the awful fixity of the mask relax, as if almost the warmth of the light could restore some life to the badger and unclench its gritted teeth.

The man turned out the torch, locked the shed and went back to the cottage. As he did so, the single cloud moved on and the land was once more flooded with moonlight. There was silence, not the breath of a breeze to move the trees, nor the cry of an owl in the forest. Only, in the woodshed, there was the dripping of blood from the mouth of the dead thing, forming a crimson stain on the new white wood of the mountain ash, and the tumbling of maggots from its nostrils.

*

The man's name was Andrew Pinkney. Phoebe was a little collie, no bigger than a fox, crossed with some other indeterminate breed, and in the eyes of Andrew Pinkney she was the prettiest dog alive. Predominantly she was black, her coat was long and very fine, and she was vigorously brushed after every walk and every plunge into the streams, so that she shone more beautifully than any other dog. Her tail was a great black plume, almost as long as her body, which she could raise like a banner. She had a long delicate face, all black except for a pair of patches of tan, one above each eye, and these patches were like another pair of eyes which stared from the dog's head even when she was asleep. Her real eyes were liquid brown with rims of white, and

Phoebe used them to get whatever she wanted from her master. When she drooped her tasselled black ears and melted those eyes at Andrew Pinkney, at the same time resting her face most gently on his knee and then lifting a paw to touch his hand, he knew that he could do nothing else but submit to her, whether it was simply to reassure her of his presence by caressing her velvet black head or to take her out on to the hillside, in rain and wind and darkness. Outside, she would run away and always turn to see that he was there, returning if he stopped, to nuzzle her face into his hand and to gaze up at him with those beseeching eyes. Under her throat and on her chest she was tan, and so were her paws and her belly. She could run and swim for as long as the man was prepared to walk with her or to lob branches into the pools for her to retrieve; she looked with a kind of disdainful curiosity at the sheep, as though they were imbeciles, but she was not inclined to pursue them, which was a great relief to her master who knew that the local farmers did not hesitate to shoot any dog which stampeded their flocks; she stayed healthy on her regime of long walks on the hillsides and through the forests, on a good diet and painstakingly groomed every day, so that her coat gleamed and her eyes were clear and frank; and she was the only close companion of her master's life, always nearby with her face on his knee, always there with her eyes looking directly into his, seemingly as grateful for his companionship and love as he was for hers. In a nutshell, he relied on her affection. He knew that, while he sat in an armchair and dangled one hand from it, or while he stood on the hillside and waited with one hand hanging by his side, he would always, yes, always be comforted soon by the touch of Phoebe's face against his fingers. And then he could look down and meet her enquiring eyes, knowing that she would hold his gaze and never glance carelessly away.

Andrew Pinkney was a man of twenty-five who looked younger. He was big and blond, with a hairless face and blurred features. Talking of dogs, if he had been a dog instead of a man, he would have turned out as a big, soft, golden labrador with a name like Bumper or Bruno, patient with children, adored by the elderly, always ready with a smile or a long, beseeching yawn, whichever was appropriate to the situation. In spite of his size and weight, for he was six feet tall and heavily built, he gave an impression of tenderness, as though he were a great blond baby, a man-sized toddler, with his fine blond curls of hair which fell over his forehead and over his ears, with his downy cheeks all pink from walking the hills or from sitting too close to the fire, and with that look of baffled vulnerability in his eyes. He wore glasses with thick lenses and black rims, and these gave the only real definition to his face. Not that he was really a tender child: he was as strong as his height and weight suggested and was becoming harder with more recent exercise, and he was capable in his own way if left to use his initiative as well as a kind of dogged perseverance. These days he did not speak much, except to Phoebe, but he had a soft flat voice which could be curiously persuasive. He was an articled clerk in a small firm of solicitors in the south of England, before his move to Wales a few weeks previously, and in the office he had proved himself to be diligent, organised and able. He was valued by his employer. People liked him, especially when he gave them the benefit of his sudden, instinctive smile. And then they thought that Andrew Pinkney was something like a big old labrador dog, all soft and smiling and indiscriminate with his affections, incapable of a hard word or of inflicting a wound of any kind. He would have thought this himself too, until he did what he had done which resulted in his sudden removal from his job as a budding lawyer and brought about his visit to Wales.

It was like this. There had been a colleague of his in the office, a young woman called Jennifer, who was gradually charmed by the softness of Andrew Pinkney's smiles. Some years older than Andrew, she was fully qualified as a solicitor and might soon be invited to join the partnership. She was no beauty, as they say, for she resembled one of those caricatures of a lady librarian which appear deceptively in second-rate films: rather fearsomely bespectacled, her long dark hair drawn too tightly back into a knot behind her head, her boyish figure hidden somewhere beneath a plain skirt and cardigan. Her smiles were white and thin, like those of a reptile. But, like the lady librarian, she was transformed when her glasses came off, when they were taken off by Andrew, and she became quite an attractive and yielding woman. She was only yielding, however, to a certain point which meant that she would allow herself to be kissed (after Andrew had removed her spectacles) and then she would wriggle free, smacking her lips and wincing as though she had been forced to swallow some unpleasant medicine; she would hurriedly tie up the heavy mass of her hair which she had allowed Andrew to release, complaining that now she looked a mess, and she would have to tidy herself scrupulously with mirror and comb while Andrew watched her and wondered about her boyish figure. But he became very fond of her.

She grew to like Andrew. Furthermore, she approved of Phoebe. Every weekend they were out together in the Sussex countryside, throughout the seasons of the year, for there was so much to see and for Andrew to learn from Jennifer. She had a profound and genuine love of the outdoors, supported by a knowledge of it and its wildlife which greatly impressed Andrew. They left Phoebe in the car while she led him breathlessly through the woodlands of Alfriston. There they stood silently in the twilight of the trees until, before their very eyes, only yards away, the enquiring young head of a fox cub bobbed up from the ground and the animal emerged to roll and sniff and to groom itself, quite oblivious of their presence, and then to trot suddenly into the enveloping gloom of the forest. With the badgers, it was Jennifer's gentle boast that she never went in search of them, to watch them, without success: evening after evening, in different locations, she and Andrew held hands in the shadows and enjoyed the spectacle. The badgers and their cubs tumbled shamelessly in the moonlight, everything bathed in a silvery glow which was generated by the scree of chalk from the badgers' set, until the moon would vanish and reappear to find that the animals had gone. Her speciality was owls. To Andrew, who had often listened to owls and wondered about their secret shifting as he lay in bed at night before he drifted into an owl-inhabited dream, it was simply magical that Jennifer could show him so much so easily. One frosty Sunday morning in January, she had him drive her very slowly across the Pevensey levels, until, even as she told him to pull into the verge and stop, the lovely wafting shape of a short-eared owl rose moth-like from the rushes. It blew away down the frost-covered fields. And then it sat on a broken gate, dipping its head and writhing the cat-mask of its face in the direction of Andrew's car. '*Asio flammeus*,' whispered Jennifer. 'Beautiful . . . ' Andrew answered, the Latin name quite out of place on the ice-encrusted marsh. There were celebrations which resulted in the removal of Jennifer's glasses and the untying of her hair, before she was shoving away Andrew's hands to sit up and smack her lips. Andrew breathed heavily while she put up her hair again. Phoebe watched keenly from the back seat. On another expedition, Jennifer produced a little owl ('*Athene noctua*') in the churchyard at Bishopstone, a bobbing hissing gnome of an owl which sat obligingly on a headstone, and there was even a long-eared owl ('*Asio otus*') in a hawthorn hedge near Arlington reservoir. It stood motionless in the deepest, most impenetrable thicket of the hedge, with its eyes shut. Andrew peered through the twigs until his own eyes ached, to make out the upright shape of the owl while it roosted there in a state of torpid stupefaction. But never, even after the long-eared owl, did Jennifer's yielding yield more than a flurry of tight-lipped kisses. And then there were nightingales in the bluebell woods; golden plover and snipe among the clods of earth in winter fields; woodlands pungent with fungi; hedgerows which boiled with the flocks of fieldfare and redwing and the mistle thrushes which stripped away the berries before rising in a dense, vociferous mass to forage somewhere else . . . The year was a treasure-house for Andrew which Jennifer unlocked for him and taught him to explore, although her insistence on Latin labels seemed to place an unnecessary barrier between him and the creatures he loved to watch. He became fonder of her, wishing ruefully that he had some area of expertise of his own to offer her. She liked him. And gradually he wanted more and more for her to yield to him, to give up to him something of herself which was more than a teenage fumble in the car. He needed her, and he told her so. Eventually, that dogged perseverance, which characterised his work in the office and made him such a valued employee, was rewarded with success, of a kind . . . And a failure which led to his sudden departure from Sussex to the hillside cottage in Wales.

It was a painful affair which can be recounted in a few words. Andrew's perseverance, bred from a real fondness for Jennifer, took them to his bed-sitting-room in

Newhaven. There was a brief skirmish on his sofa. Clothes were very quickly shed and strewn to all the corners of the room, once it was established that the removal of glasses and the loosening of hair was not the only yielding which would take place that afternoon. And in the ensuing encounter, perhaps because of the delay before Andrew had been allowed to manifest his affection for Jennifer in such an unequivocal way, perhaps because Phoebe was following their efforts with such a keen and noisy interest, he could not kindle any spark with which to prove his love . . . They fell apart, panting heavily. 'Was that it?' the woman asked. That was it. 'Heavens! What a lot of fuss about nothing!' Jennifer covered herself quickly with the clothes which came to hand, while Andrew sat naked on the sofa and scowled shortsightedly at that piece of him which had let him down. She dressed, angry and disappointed now that she had dropped her defences. And then she made her big mistake: she looked at Andrew's desolate figure and in particular at that unprepossessing thing which lay white and flaccid between his thighs, and she started to laugh. At first it was only her reptilian smile, then a smothered giggle. But it grew and grew and she disguised it no longer. She broke into a braying guffaw. Phoebe began to bark. And Andrew Pinkney forgot that he was a harmless old labrador dog, all soft and slow and golden blond, for he crossed the little room in one leap to land the woman a heavy punch in her mouth. 'You bitch!' he shouted. She went down in a heap. Andrew groped for his glasses. 'Jennifer? Jennifer? Oh Jesus Christ . . . ' A brief inspection revealed that she was unconscious. The dog had retired to her corner, from where she looked on and smiled, as though the whole affair was one baffling but marvellous game.

Andrew telephoned for an ambulance and the police and had time to dress before they arrived. Only minutes had passed between their fiasco on the sofa and Jennifer's hasty removal from the room, and the ambulance was gone in a blur of lights and sirens. Andrew was mortified to be faced by policemen who knew him as a young lawyer from his regular visits to Lewes magistrates' court. While he was detained for questioning in Lewes police station, two important developments took place: first, it was soon established that Jennifer was not seriously hurt and that she had swooned from the shock as much as from the force of the blow. There was no damage which a little dentistry could not repair; hours later, she was alert enough to prevent the police from pressing any charges. And secondly, the influence of Andrew's employer was invaluable in securing Andrew's release; the solicitor's reference was considerable enough to impress the police that their detainee was a man of impeccable character who had suffered a momentary aberration. Andrew was released, Jennifer was discharged. Neither of them seemed much the worse for their experience. But their employer, who valued both of them as conscientious members of his firm and did not want to lose either, saw that they would not straightaway be able to work together, so he offered them the option of taking an extended break from the office. The woman bridled at this, stung by the implication that she might not be ready to take up her duties after her injury. But the man, far less volatile now that he had once more assumed his role as a mild and malleable old labrador dog, accepted the offer immediately. His employer, the senior partner, had a holiday cottage in north Wales: Andrew could use that if he wanted, for a month or two months, right through the autumn. And then he could come back whenever he liked, refreshed and wholly recovered from the shock he had had.

Thus, a week later, Andrew drove north and west, followed the winding but scenic route from Shrewsbury to

Llangollen to Betws-y-coed, and arrived at the isolated cottage he had been lent. Naturally, Phoebe came with him. Apart from a few clothes and a radio, he brought only his paintings to enliven the cottage and to give him some permanent visual link with the woman he had struck: for they were watercolours which Jennifer herself had painted and given to him. Mostly they were landscapes of the Sussex countryside which she loved and knew so well: she had captured the flat and featureless expanses of the Pevensey levels, more sky than land, with the glinting of frost in the air and on the fields. Andrew could almost sense the cold in the prickling of his nostrils. There were golden plover, geese and a smudging of snipe. From the downs, she had painted the sinuous estuary of the Cuckmere river, a silver snake which wound its way to the metallic sea. One of her paintings caught the clutter of the moorings behind Denton island, the view from Andrew's bed-sitting-room, something of the untidiness and accumulated debris of boats and their tackle against the mudflats of a tidal river. All Jennifer's watercolours were of sunshine. But Andrew's favourite was her watercolour of Phoebe. From a series of preliminary sketches, she had conjured the quintessence of the dog, her alertness and good nature, somehow a combination of the persuasive powers of her eyes with the vitality of her shining frame. Phoebe was smiling an affectionate, feminine smile. This was the picture of Jennifer's which Andrew Pinkney admired most.

But it was quite unlike the chain-saw snarls and the abhorrence on Phoebe's face when she recoiled from the dead thing in the moonlit forest.

*

The man and his dog slept soundly. They were alone in the

cottage. The woodlands of birch and oak and mountain ash were alive throughout that night, with the movements of the moles and voles, the leathery clicking of bats, and the padding panting footsteps of the fox. The brown owl was gorged on beetles and had swallowed the sweet body of a shrew, so that it sat stupid against the trunk of a tree until dawn, when it retched a smooth wet pellet of fur and bones and chitin on to the ground below. The night was a place of hunting and killing and eating, where little lives were snuffed out with nothing but a whimper or a swiftly silenced squeal. And then there was a splintering of bones, like the tinkle of icicles. It was cold. The first rime of the year lay faintly on the grass, just a beaded breath of ice to warn of the winter to come.

But in the plantation it was warmer, under the cover of the heavy black blanket. Things grew in the clammy moisture of drains. On rotting tree stumps, in the decay of needles which were warm and wet and which could not breathe under the smothering of the forest, fungi grew. They were white things, dank and mucous like the flesh of something very sick. They pushed up quickly through the soil, forcing their way like fetid fingers through the beds of needles, white and somehow luminous in the muffled shadows. They gave off a powerful pungency of rotting meat. The stinkhorn thrust upwards its globose head. Its perfect phallus was erect in the silver lights of the forest, erect in the darkness too. Where the badger had been before the man came to take it away, the stinkhorn grew. From the earth which had been first warmed by the body of the dying beast, then dampened by the rising of moisture to meet the heat of the body, from the spores of the bruises and the poisoned flesh and the rusted barbed wire, there rose a fine new stinkhorn. It stank. It was putrid through and through. It dripped a green-black slime which drew dung-flies to feed there. But for a short time, a matter of hours, it was the phallus of a corpse, the perfect expression of rigor mortis.

Not far away, the dead thing which had fostered such a bold erection swung slowly on its hook. No more blood dripped from its teeth. The crimson stain was dry on the mountain ash. And when that night dissolved to dawn and the frost no longer clung to the long grass, more flies came to the woodshed. They came to the blossoming stink of the badger, and when they found its wounds among the wire they laid more eggs on the purpled flesh. They laid their eggs in the dead thing's ears, they tunnelled through the congealed blood in its nostrils and into all the secret places of its head. Only a fly could penetrate the gritted trap of teeth: the flies did, and then there were more eggs in the badger's mouth.

In every part of the corpse, things were working. The ripest of the maggots were developing now into pupae, dropping from the badger and landing gently in the earth and the sawdust below. The dead thing which Andrew Pinkney had hung in the woodshed was really not dead at all.

II

THE COTTAGE was easy to find but hard to reach. That is to say, Andrew followed his employer's meticulously drawn map, which was to conduct him from Betws-y-coed to the cottage, and was straight away able to recognise the building from the road. He had driven some five miles from Beddgelert, through hills which folded into the mountains of the Snowdonia national park, through a number of villages made up of dismally grey terraced cottages. The road became narrower and more winding. It was a nondescript day early in October, under a sky the colour and texture of corrugated iron, when at any moment it seemed that the windscreen of Andrew's car would be spattered with the spittle of an irritable squall. But it did not rain. He drove very slowly, consulting his map, until it was quite obvious that the angular white cottage he could see high up on the hillside to his left must be the one he was looking for and which he was going to inhabit for the following weeks. It crouched in the shadow of a beetling bulge of mountain. Splendid, he thought, and he reached out to Phoebe, who was dozing on the passenger seat. She sat up straight and looked grandly ahead of her, with that delicately cultivated expression of unconcern which driving instructors wear so fixedly on their faces. 'Over there, Phoebe, that white one, that's where we're going . . .' He noticed as he spoke that the fields were speckled with the grey shapes of the sheep which his employer had warned him of, and he reminded himself that it was imperative to keep the dog most carefully under control if she were to survive the ready shotguns of the local farmers. Phoebe peered into the distance, cocking her ears at Andrew's voice but perfectly oblivious to the reason for his enthusiasm. He stopped the car at the gate which was indicated on the map.

It then took him twenty minutes to negotiate the quarter of a mile from that first gate to the cottage. He drove very slowly across the field, following a track which was rutted so deeply that the long grass and thistles in the middle of it hissed and screeched along the bottom of his car. The track rose sharply and dipped, to reveal the river ahead, as marked on the map. There were two bridges across it. The first was the old railway bridge, completely derelict, simply a rusted skeleton which had remained since the mountain railway had been closed some fifty years before. The sudden sharp rising and falling in the track was the remains of the embankment. The second bridge was made of concrete which was laid directly on to the bed of the shallow river, shot through with a number of great iron pipes which took the water on its way, and Andrew was exasperated to see that just now the level of the river ran smoothly over the surface of the bridge, overflowing in a curtain of silk, undisturbed by a single snag. Stopping the car, he got out and changed into his wellington boots, for at the other side of the bridge there was a second gate into another field. He drove carefully on to the bridge and stopped the car, while the water ran smoothly underneath it, only an inch or two in depth. Again he left the car, the water flying in fountain sprays from his boots as he waded to open the next gate, drove through, shut the gate, returned to the car and continued into the second field. He was beginning to see that his employer's cottage was indeed a refuge from the pressures of a busy solicitor's office. Here the track was even more deeply rutted. The sheep rose so reluctantly from it that Andrew had to stop and wait before he could drive on, while they squatted and squittered a spatter of shining brown droppings. Phoebe watched them with an air of haughty disdain. The next gate let the car into a farmyard, and this time he accomplished the business of opening and closing the gate and getting the car through very briskly, encouraged by a wild-eyed sheep-dog on the end of a leash which kept the animal only narrowly at bay. He drove on. Once more the track rose sharply and continued to climb, through a fourth gate they went with only the sheep to contend with, and then the car was slithering its way upwards, closer and closer to the cottage, to stop gratefully on the steep hillside in front of it.

The cottage was old, hundreds of years old by Andrew's estimation. As he unlocked the front door and went inside, his nostrils were assaulted by the smell of the damp. There was another smell too, of soot and decomposing meat, which combined with the damp to give the overwhelming first impression that he was stepping into a dungeon. The building was on one floor, a sitting-room leading directly into a kitchen, a bathroom and two bedrooms. Everything was clammy and dark. Wherever Andrew put down his hand he felt moisture, something sticky with wet soot. He moved quickly from room to room, drawing back the curtains and flinging open the windows, leaving open the front door, and soon, as he went backwards and forwards to and from the car with his few belongings, there was some welcome circulation of air through the building. Pausing on the path outside the front door, he realised that, notwithstanding the cottage's dank interior, it enjoyed the most beautiful sweeping views down the valley, to the distant road and across to the opposite hillsides. Behind the building there rose a steeper hillside, green at first and mottled with a woodland of oak and birch which was quickly quenched by the dark monotony of a fir plantation. Above that there was barren rock, a towering cliff all grey and glistening, until the clouds concealed the mountains. There would be time later to explore the surrounding country. The first priority was to make the cottage habitable as soon as possible. So he attacked it vigorously with sponges and dusters and powders, with anything available in the kitchen cupboards, and before the afternoon was over he had made the place more welcoming. After all, there was only himself and Phoebe, for a month or so. There was no need to be meticulous, as long as the rooms were reasonably clean. The dog waited patiently outside while Andrew bustled from room to room. He had tied her lead to a drainpipe, from where she sniffed her face into the building, recoiling from the unfamiliar scents, and then she concentrated her attention on the sheep which had strolled closer to the cottage. She sat still and stared at them, flashing her benign smile.

After a while, Andrew was reasonably satisfied with the state of their temporary home. He had spent hours, once the rooms were cleaned, searching for the source of the smell of dead flesh, without success. It lingered above the freshness of the new air which had been allowed in, it obscured the scent of disinfectant. Phoebe wrinkled her nose at the whiff, but she settled into her basket in a corner of the strange new room, rummaging with her paws into her blankets, rearranging them over and over again as though these familiar things with their familiar smells were a great comfort in a time of upheaval. Andrew shifted cupboards, he flashed his torch into that abyss which harbours nameless things behind the cooker and behind the refrigerator, he pulled out the wardrobe in the bedroom and he tottered precariously on the back of a chair as he pushed his head into the dusty cobwebs of the roof space. The torch lit up the glistening darkness of a roof which had had no attention for many decades. But there was nothing to explain the putrid odour which permeated the cottage.

Until, in the evening, he lit the fire in the front room. He had found, as his employer had told him, that there was some coal and a few pieces of firewood in the little outhouse by the side of the building, enough for a week, and after that Andrew would be entitled to scavenge for fuel from the surrounding hillsides. He inexpertly laid the fire, unused to doing so, accustomed to the instant heat from the electric fire in his bed-sitting-room. But the wood was dry, there were the desiccated spars of gorse which crackled instantly into flames, and soon he was adding pieces of coal to form a dome over the blossoming core of heat. Thick blue smoke went puthering up the chimney. Andrew reclined in an armchair and smiled at the success of his handiwork, and straight away Phoebe was there beside him with her wet black nose against his fingers.

But she sprang away in disgust when the smoke stopped pluming up the chimney. Dense clouds came billowing back. Andrew cried out and beat his way to the front door, flailing his arms through the smoke. In seconds, the room was thick with it, and it continued to pour from the fireplace in a stinking black wave. The smoke boiled from the hearth until it was impossible to see across the room.

While the dog escaped into one of the bedrooms, preferring that to the unknown darkness outside, Andrew searched in desperation for the broom he had been using in the kitchen. Wielding this, he forced himself forwards to the grate, where he knelt on the rug, gagging and retching on the fumes, and he thrust the handle of the broom as far up the chimney as it would go, in a wild attempt to clear some imagined blocking. The broom handle struck something. Showers of soot cascaded on to the fire, exploding into short-lived but spectacular flames as they landed on the coals. Rubble came down too, crumbled pieces of brick from the lining of the chimney. Still the smoke came writhing into the room . . . Until the broom handle broke through the obstruction. A wreckage of debris crashed on to the hearth and spewed outwards over Andrew's knees. With this avalanche there issued a nauseating smell of rotten meat, as though the chimney had vomited into the room the remains of some disgusting meal. Andrew staggered back. But as the fire regained its composure, it exhaled its smoke through the piles of soot and half-bricks, through the filthy stuff which now lay all over the rug, and the smoke went sweetly upwards to vanish in an unbroken wave into the maw of the chimney.

It was a bird of some kind which had died up there. The stink of its putrefying corpse now filled the room, quite eclipsing the smell of the soot. Phoebe had started to howl in the bedroom, sobbing in a resonant high-pitched voice. Whatever the bird had been, it was reduced to this, a chaos of filthy black feathers from which there protruded a pair of shattered legs complete with claws, clenched into tight fists, and a beak of weighty black horn. The compacted remains of its frame were pulsing with maggots. Andrew, no longer so blond nor so good-natured as he was generally reputed to be, rolled up the hearth rug into a temporary coffin and hurled the whole thing from the front door. The smoke swiftly dissipated. When Andrew had been through the room once more with his sponges and cloths and had manhandled an antique vacuum-cleaner across the carpet, Phoebe consented to being led from her hiding-place in the bedroom. The fire drew beautifully, blooming a tremulous golden flame. It sent the smoke up the chimney in one co-operative plume.

*

Andrew kept the cottage warm in the evenings and he left it to be aired in the daytime, while he and Phoebe scouted the countryside. It seemed to him that there were two distinctly contrasting sides to the cottage, in outlook and appearance: the front of the house was painted white and from it there were open views of light and air; the back of the cottage was painted black, and to walk up the hillside behind it was immediately to enter a darker world. There was a stiff climb into the gentle dappled shadows of the silver birch, a place of pungent autumnal scents where the leaves had fallen and matted into a perfumed carpet. Clusters of berries had dropped from the mountain ash, and they lay like jewels in the sweetened dampness. A stream ran swiftly through the woodland. Where it hurried over boulders which were thick with sponges of moss, it tossed up a spray so fine that only the sunlight could see it, and in the invisible mists of moisture there gathered throngs of tiny insects. Cobwebs of grey lichen had grown and covered the branches of the trees. It was an underworld of little creatures living little lives: the creeping of a wren among the dead leaves or the ticking of a tree-creeper in the fractured bark of a birch were somehow appropriate, a shrew might hurry past the columns of toadstools with the writhing coils of a worm wrapped round its face, but it was a place which must for ever remain a mystery to anything bigger than a hedgehog. The fox and the badger and the ubiquitous magpie could use it as their larder, raiding it for a feast, and then the darkening clouds of fieldfare in their hundreds could strip it of its fruit, but it was not their place as it was the place of the vole and the pipistrelle. To be sure, the woodland was a joy to Andrew Pinkney, but it could never be more than a whispering jungle of mystery to him, where he went trampling in his big black boots and where he would come with his saw and his wheelbarrow. To Phoebe it was a playground. She splashed ecstatically into the stream, she sprang out again in an explosion of spray, she chased the scent of every hot-blooded creature which tickled her nostrils, but the only things she caught were the sticks which Andrew flung for her, deep into the dying bracken.

And then, higher up the hillside, the darker world closed in. The man and the dog trod silently into the silence of the fir forest.

Nothing much moved there, but a few stray sheep. And even the sheep were different in the fir forest. They stood quite still as the man and the dog went by, staring in a pop-eyed, manic way, quivering with tension, staring and staring like mad, humourless women. Clearly the dog was puzzled by them. There was a big black sheep which appeared round a bend in the track, to sneeze loudly and stamp its feet, sudden explosive sounds which were amplified somehow by the prickling shadows of the plantation. Phoebe strained on her leash, recoiling at first but then tugging towards the sheep and triggering her dangerous snarl. The black sheep had a patch of pure white above each eye. And it was these false eyes, like empty, staring sockets, which followed the man and his dog as they hurried along the track, as they felt the bristling sides of the forest forever closing in on them. From time to time, in this place of darkness peopled by a flock of moody mad women, the air was ripe with the stink of decomposing meat. Somewhere in the gloom, it seemed that something had crawled away to die and now was being dismantled by the silently working teeth of the maggots. The smell arose like a vapour exhaled by the earth itself, and then it was gone again, as if Andrew had imagined it, as though the stink were conjured in the darkest recesses of his own mind, to appear and disappear like a memory. It was difficult for him to restrain the dog as she pulled him rapidly upwards and onwards to the clearer air of the mountain. Suddenly the plantation stopped. There was a barbed-wire fence, rusted and broken in many places, and the man and his dog emerged from the forest to find themselves beneath the sheer cliffs of a great crater. There were no more trees.

Andrew and Phoebe stood at the bottom of a gigantic bowl which a glacier had gouged from the mountainside many thousands of years before Andrew had struck Jennifer in his moment of humiliation. The rocks rose sheer around them, glistening black slabs on which nothing could grow but a patina of moss. On a fine day, when the man and the dog burst thankfully from the stale blanket of the forest, they could peer upwards and imagine they saw the ridge of the mountain. It was never entirely clear. Twists of mist had caught on the highest crags and had blurred their definition. But when Andrew and Phoebe climbed to the crater on an afternoon of drizzle, when even the forest twitched like the coat of a mangy old hound, the rim of their bowl was obscured by a boiling broth of cloud. The crater became a cauldron which overflowed with steam. Somewhere around the shrouded cliffs, a raven circled and croaked, and when it passed close overhead its wingbeats were the regular pantings of some exhausted beast. The clacking of jackdaws echoed from the sides of the crater. These sounds and the moaning of the wind were funnelled around and around the mountainsides, they were joined by the bilious cries of the sheep in the forest and by the perpetual whispers of water: for the crater was the source of all the streams and drains and ditches which cut through the plantation and ran more gracefully among the woodland below. It gathered every droplet from the snagging clouds and sucked them into its steep-sided bowl, until the walls of the crater were coursing with water which was soaked up by the sponge of the mountain. The man and the dog stood silently and were wreathed by the lowering mists, they waited respectfully in the desolate place of water and rock, sensing that it was appropriate to be still in the bowl of the crater. Andrew, listening to the raven and to the diminishing thuds of his own blood, was tired but exhilarated after the rapid climb through the plantation. Phoebe let her mouth fall open and her tongue loll out. She thought back to the big black sheep and the way it had followed her with its eyeless sockets. Her nostrils still tingled with the lingering scents of the forest, the clammy shadows and their hidden repositories of putrefaction.

And then they were aware of another sound, a sound which was so much a part of that empty place that it registered slowly, gradually, as though the slabs of the rocks and the seething white mists had produced the sound themselves and were reluctant to let it go . . . The baying of hounds . . . It was like the wind at first, it blurred with the wind and was part of it, until it swelled and grew into a sound of its own and was unmistakable. The first time they were there and they heard it, both Andrew and Phoebe were afraid. Together they stared around them, cut off by the plantation from the open world of air and light and sunshine. They were in the crater, with a smothering of cloud pressed on them, surrounded by walls of rock and the inescapable murmurings of water. A single howl untangled itself from the movements of the wind, it was joined by another and then another until the winds and the water were simply an accompaniment to the overwhelming music of the hounds. The crater took up the sound, echoing it from wall to wall and amplifying it, and soon the crater was the bell of an enormous trumpet which rang out its fanfare to the sky above. The mountain was struck like a gong by the baying of the hounds.

Andrew pulled Phoebe with him across the marshy ground, the man wading carelessly through the quag while the dog sprang from one clump of tough grass to another. They pressed on, with the silent forest below them, with the reverberating cliffs above. Ahead of them, looming through the drizzle, there were buildings and a large muddy area enclosed by a high wire fence, wooden sheds from which the cries of the hounds were coming. Andrew stopped. Phoebe waited, standing delicately on a green boulder. She was cowed by the proximity of so many dogs, and she tucked her tail tightly between her legs so that its plume disappeared among the long fur of her belly. Her ears drooped. She looked up at Andrew with her most beseeching expression. 'All right, Phoebe, we're not staying. Let's just have a closer look,' and he led her reluctantly nearer to the sheds. It was raining harder, no longer a drizzle but a driving, drenching mist which flattened Andrew's curls into a golden helmet, tight and cold on his skull. His glasses quivered with globules of water. He wiped them with his fingers, and he could see a figure moving quickly from shed to shed, appearing and disappearing from one building to another, carrying a bucket in each hand. Someone was feeding the hounds, someone they greeted with their chorus of howls. The figure emerged from one shed, completely shrouded with a rainproof green coat, the hood enveloping the head, a shining green figure which went purposefully around the compound in the submarine gloom. Andrew raised his arm, wondering if the figure would lift its head and see him and the dog against the background of the drowned crater. And the figure paused, just long enough to put down one bucket and to hold up a hand for a second before vanishing once more from sight.

*

In this way, Andrew Pinkney and his dog, Phoebe, spent the first week of their stay in Wales. They went for hours, morning and afternoon, through the woodland glades around the cottage. The steep sides of the hill which were clad so beautifully that autumn by a covering of deciduous trees, predominantly by the graceful shade of the silver birch, repaid more thorough exploration. The ground was very steep, but the man and the dog scrambled among the trees, the man often falling on his hands and knees in the aromatic carpet of leaves. And he found what he could easily have missed if he had stayed on the beaten tracks, that the hillsides were riddled with shallow caves, mere slits and hollows in the rocks in most cases, but there were some which he and Phoebe could penetrate for a few yards. They had been used by the sheep, as shelter, so the floors of the caves were trodden bare and were covered with droppings. Hidden high up among the tallest branches of the silver birch, Andrew sat with Phoebe in a particular vantage point, the best and deepest of the caves, from which he could gaze across the top of his cottage and for miles down the valley. He imagined the cave used by a hermit, in the days when the remote fastnesses of Wales were more popular with the religious recluse than with solicitors from Sussex, for he found in the cave that he was quite aloof from the valley below and was completely hidden. He went there often, to his hermit's cell, to sit and think of what he had done to bring him to Wales . . . And to think of what he had not done, what he had not been able to do, what had provoked the derision of the woman . . . This troubled him more than the fact that he had knocked her unconscious. After all, he knew from his legal studies that such outbursts of violence were commonplace. What was the name of the case, almost analogous to his own? What was it? Ah yes, every law student remembered it with a chuckle because of the inappropriateness of the appellant's name: Bedder versus the Director of Public Prosecutions, sometime back in the fifties. Bedder! The man had found himself incapable of consummating his business deal with a prostitute he had hired, on account of his sexual impotence, and had been so enraged and humiliated by the woman's laughter that he promptly stabbed her to death. What was the judgment? Bedder had tried to plead that he had been provoked by the prostitute's jeering, that his impotence rendered him uncommonly vulnerable to such ridicule; he had appealed to the DPP that the charge should be reduced from murder to manslaughter. No such luck. The appeal was dismissed and Bedder was hanged. Andrew brooded on the case. Jennifer's laughter at his failure had provoked his uncontrollable violence, and now he was banished for it. Thinking of Bedder, he tried to brood less. Both he and Jennifer had escaped lightly in comparison, if there was a comparison to be made. At least they were both still alive, only angry and bruised.

He pondered the notion of his impotence, until he sprang again from his cell to walk and walk with Phoebe, to dispel the thought by trudging endlessly through the woodlands. And, in spite of the melancholy darkness of the fir forest, they pursued those shadowy tracks as well, in the sunshine of a splendid autumn and as it deteriorated into mists and drizzle. There was something magnetic in the gloom of the plantation which drew the man to it almost every day. Higher and faster they climbed, the dog tugging remorselessly on her lead, with the bristles of the black trees closing in on them. Slap-slap-slap went the wellington boots on Andrew's calves, and that was often the only sound in the forest. Phoebe's feet were noiseless on the grass and needles, there was her rasping breath as she strained against the collar, and then there was always the sudden appearance of that black sheep, the maddest woman of all the flock, which materialised like a shadow from the shadows of the trees, detaching itself from the darkness. It would stand quite still on the track ahead of them, utterly black, fixing the man and the dog with the only whiteness of its fleece, those staring blank sockets which had never been eyes. With a sneeze and a stamp, the sheep was gone. It melted back into the forest, while the man was left to wonder if he had imagined it there in the increasing gloom of late afternoon, while the dog switched on her chain-saw snarl. Faster and higher they climbed, pausing to adjust their nostrils to the pervasive stench of death which assailed them from some dank corner, accelerating as they sensed the open air above, until the forest lay silently behind them. It was only then, when they emerged into the crater of rocks, that they caught the baying of the hounds. And several times Andrew saw the green figure going from shed to shed of the kennels with its buckets, and he was able to elicit a wave as he stood some distance away with the reluctant Phoebe.

More often than not, Andrew would return to the cottage laden with firewood. He became used to taking the bow-saw with him on their walks, for there were always broken and fallen branches to be cut. Most of the available timber was in the deciduous woodland. He found a silver birch which had recently come down; its roots had never dug deeply into the earth because of the rocks, but had splayed in all directions around the tree trunk, only inches beneath the soil, clawing desperately for a grip. When the winds came, the weight of the trunk and its nodding branches had been too much on the sloping roots, and the tree had toppled. The roots protruded like a great plate of soil radiating from the base of the tree. Andrew had soon sawed right through the thickest part of the trunk. Although he was unaccustomed to heavy exercise, more used to his wills and conveyances in the office, he was strong and big and his weight behind the saw made short work of the slender birch. Through the rest of an afternoon, while Phoebe watched him and waited impatiently for the man to take her walking, Andrew moved from branch to branch until the tree was cut into sizes he could fetch with the wheelbarrow. There were ancient dead trees too, still upright. Uneasily aware that Jennifer would not approve, he tested the sturdiness of such trees by leaning on them, and if they groaned and teetered sufficiently he would exert more weight until they came crashing down. 'Even dead and rotten trees are invaluable to the ecology, you know . . .' he could imagine Jennifer saying in her prim librarian's voice, 'they provide shelter and food for countless thousands of useful insects, which, in their turn, are food for countless birds and . . .' Andrew pushed, while Phoebe watched, and gradually the little stone outhouse was stacked with logs for the fire. To supplement this, he contacted the local coalman, recommended by his employer. Andrew observed through his binoculars as the coalman approached from the road: it was a Land-rover which heaved its way to the river bridge, a man in wellington boots who got out to open the gates. Clearly the coalman knew what to expect and had come properly booted for the overflowing river. His vehicle lurched up the track, four times the man stopped to open and close the gates, and when he arrived at the cottage he was appropriately irritable. Andrew beamed at him, pushing back the wave of flopping blond hair from his forehead. 'You made it then? Quite a track, isn't it!' The man went slowly about his job, muttering to himself in Welsh. Andrew wondered whether it was a good idea to offer some help in manhandling the sacks from the back of the vehicle, especially as he was somewhat bigger than the coalman, but he did not. Wanting to be genial, he added a few more pounds to the cost of the coal, which the man was tipping against the side of the woodshed, and he pressed the extra coins into the coalman's blackened hand. 'I wonder if you can tell me what this means,' he said cheerily, as much to be friendly as genuinely curious, and he gestured towards the sign on the front of the cottage. 'How do you pronounce it? Clogwyn Ceiliog? Something like that?' He was delighted to see that he had improved the man's humour by asking, because the sooty little Welshman first grinned an unnaturally dazzling grin and then broke into peals of high-pitched laughter. But he jumped into his Land-rover and drove away, still laughing, without offering a translation.

The woodshed filled up. Andrew and Phoebe searched the hillsides for dead and fallen trees. The trunk of a recently up-ended larch would ooze and grip the blade of the saw, until sometimes the man would have to resort to brute force to free it; then he would wrench on the limb of the tree until it splintered, until a long white wound appeared from which the saw could be extricated. Cutting the trunk of a dead rowan was like cutting a French loaf with a breadknife, the blade went easily through and shed the dry crumbs of sawdust on the ground. He wanted to gather as much fuel as he could before the weather worsened, and he was satisfied to see the walls of the woodshed gradually hidden by the stacks of logs. Indeed, with the open fire lit in the evenings, he could make the cottage warm, arranging a bed of coal and laying his timber on it, happy to see the fruits of his afternoon labours burst into flames. But unquestionably the cottage was damp. He would recommend most strongly to his employer, when he returned to Sussex, that some drastic structural work be done on the building before it deteriorated beyond repair. The place had only been used as a summer retreat, never in the autumn or winter months. From time to time, someone had slapped a coat of whitewash on the walls inside and outside, and that was all the maintenance it had received. Blooming through the whitewash, in every room, were the mouldy green blossoms of damp. From the floors upwards, these areas of moisture spread and crept like the lichen which grew on the woodland trees. Somehow, the warmer the living-room became, as Andrew banked up the fire each evening, the more clearly the bruises of green stood out against the whitened walls. Condensation trickled down the windows into the rotted paintwork of the sills, the walls themselves oozed vapour like the cold stale air of a crypt, and Andrew thought he could see the gossamer mists of water floating around him. He was not too concerned: it was not his property, he and the dog were there for a matter of weeks. He built up a comfortable fug in the living-room and sat in front of the fire, with Phoebe curled on his lap like a blanket, uninterested in the condition of the old cottage as long as he and Phoebe could stay warm and dry for a while.

Over the mantelpiece, Jennifer's watercolours hid some of the worst patches of damp, her sunlit souvenirs of Sussex blotting out a growth of virulent green. Her visions of air and light and sunshine were a façade behind which the mildew bloomed.

As the weather closed in, Andrew thought of Jennifer a good deal. There was so much more he could have seen in his walks up to the crater if she had been there with him. It was she who had opened up the countryside for him on their expeditions in Sussex, with her twilit vigils in the forests where the fox and the badger gingerly moved, with her conjuring of the owls, her magic with the nightingale when the woods were a trembling mist of bluebells. Wherever Andrew and Phoebe walked, either behind the cottage where the world grew darker, or below it, across the fields and down to the river, he was picturing Jennifer beside him and imagining her reaction to all there was to see. He was exasperated to feel that, however much he thought he was appreciating his unfamiliar environment, he was probably missing so much more which Jennifer would have pointed out to him.

One evening, by the fire, he started to write a letter to her. Perhaps he could mend their relationship by writing, by trying to share with her something of this new place; maybe, in spite of the indelible fact that he had knocked her senseless, he might bring her round again, raise her to a consciousness of his own condition by offering a gift. 'Dear Jennifer, Just a scrawled bulletin from my banishment in the wilderness of Wales . . .' But a picture of her unconscious face as she was carried away on a stretcher kept swimming into his mind, so that he screwed up the letter and put it on the fire, where it exploded into a flame as big and as bold as a chrysanthemum. He wanted to tell her about the bush of wild privet which was blossoming outside his window: gnarled and knotty though it was, it was just then abloom with tiny white trumpet-flowers, like the blooms of a bindweed, and to these flowers there came a host of red admirals to probe with their long tongues. A flock of long-tailed tits blew into the privet one morning, but the butterflies returned when the birds had gone. He wanted to describe his heron on the river, for Jennifer liked the heron; she would be thoughtful, chewing her lips and quite abstracted when she watched her Pevensey heron, and Andrew was pleased to spot his bird most mornings when he and Phoebe went down to the bridge. It stood like a statue in the reeds, a grey hunchback, a frozen fisherman, until, at the sight of Phoebe, it came miraculously to life and flapped heavily upstream. Why then did it suddenly jink and dive in flight, as if under attack from a falcon, when there was no such bird in sight? Was this some vestigial ploy it practised, something bred deep in the heron's memory? Andrew watched, and he knew that Jennifer would know the answer to his questions if only he were to write to her. Why was the rowan so thick with berries, for weeks before the redwing came? When the fieldfare arrived, the sky was dense with their flocks: scores upon scores of them filled the air with their clucking; big handsome thrushes which had flown all the way from Scandinavia to Andrew's cottage, so that they could gorge themselves on the mountain ash. He stood on the hillside with his binoculars, as Phoebe gnawed a stick in the long grass, and he watched the murderous skills of the sparrowhawk (*Accipiter nisus*, for Jennifer's benefit) which had noted with a welling of blood-lust that the winter thrushes had come: the hawk went hurtling through the woodland, fast and as lethal as the jets which howled from Anglesey, and it sent a whirling cloud of fieldfare from the trees. Easy pickings for everyone, thought Andrew . . . The thrushes were sated on the clustered red berries, and the sparrowhawk killed at random, for the man and his dog to find the shattered remains of its meals on the forest floor. Jennifer would have been thrilled. Andrew picked up a pellet from the foot of a tree, the regurgitated wad of matter which some bird of prey could not digest, and he took it back to the cottage to dissect. Imagining Jennifer's approval, he dismantled it with tweezers: the pellet was an inch long, three-quarters of an inch in thickness, black and dark brown, containing the chitinous remains of fifteen beetles ('one dor beetle, that's *Geotrupes stercorarius*, and fourteen leaf beetles, or rather, *Chrysolina staphylaea . . .*'), assorted grass, and seven quartz pebbles up to a quarter of an inch in size. Why? Why the pebbles? To aid the digestion? Surely, on a diet of tiny beetles, an owl or a hawk wouldn't need to pick up pebbles for this purpose? Jennifer would have known the reason, and she would have been able to deduce which bird had produced the pellet. A kestrel? A merlin? A little owl? He had begun to pose these questions in his letter, before consigning it to the fire. Jennifer was recovering from some complicated dentistry. She might not be in the mood for owl pellets.

Meanwhile the weather worsened. In the sloping fields, the bracken changed suddenly from bronze to black, the bracken which had been so tough and elastic lay now in blackened spars, like the charred remains of a devastated city. A few contrary foxgloves stood up, survivors of the wreckage. In the sodden grass, the armoury of thistles grew tall. Morning after morning, Andrew awoke to the enveloping blanket of drizzle on his windows. The surrounding mountains were erased by cloud. The air was warm and dense with moisture. He continued to walk the woodland, through the plantation, high up into the seething cauldron of the crater, where he and Phoebe recovered their breath to the accompaniment of the hounds' wild chorus. And Jennifer was on his mind throughout this time, a ghost who shadowed his footsteps when he climbed to the hermit's cell, a ghost who laughed him to sleep. Always, night after night, he heard her laughter, and he felt again the shame and the anger which it had provoked. It had broken over his nakedness like a bitter cold wave. He squirmed at the memory of his flaccidity.

*

All was not flaccid in the fir forest. There was nothing nervous or reluctant about the stinkhorn. In the shadows, from any bed of warmth and damp, the stinkhorn thrust its lewd erection. Throughout the plantation, the phallus stood up, white and firm, crowned with a swollen head which ejaculated its viscous seed.

But the stinkhorn was tired. It was nearly finished. It would be time for even this erection to be unmanned.

Until Andrew Pinkney arrived . . .

In his walks through the forest, he had smelled the stinkhorn many times. From the dark trees there was wafted that whiff of rotting flesh which Andrew knew was no such thing. Phoebe may have been deceived, or else she was simply unnerved by the scent in the clinging clamminess of the plantation, for she lunged onwards, pulling the man towards the open air of the crater. It was the dog which was reluctant to linger, so Andrew was whisked from the fetid corners of the forest. But he recognised the smell. Jennifer, of course, had shown him her selection of fungi in the sweeter woodlands of Sussex, delighted by the fairy-tale umbrellas of fly agaric which decorated the glades of silver birch. There were blewits and blushers and crumble caps. In passing, with a grimace of disgust on her mouth, she had gestured into the gloom of Alfriston forest and mentioned the stinkhorn. 'Filthy things . . .' she muttered. 'Come along, Andrew, come away from them . . .' It was one of her tricks to stop dead suddenly on a woodland track and to sniff the air excitedly, twitching her nose like a hamster. 'Fox?' she would whisper to Andrew. 'Fox? *Vulpes vulpes*? Can you smell it?' And Andrew would raise his eyebrows and nod his head, although he could never smell anything different at all. To make up for this olfactory incompetence, he cultivated a routine of his own, which involved taking Jennifer by the elbow, stopping her abruptly as they walked along, to inhale long and loudly through his nose before hissing an exaggerated stage-whisper: 'Stinkhorn? *Phallus impudicus*? Can you smell it, Jennifer?' She was amused by this at first, pleased that Andrew was copying her techniques albeit facetiously, but for her the joke wore thin when he started to work the same routine in the office. Nevertheless, he could pick up and recognise the putrid odour of the fungus whenever he and Phoebe made their breathless way up the hillside, although he did not stop to investigate more closely.

It was the big black sheep which induced him to do this, one dark afternoon that October.

For once, that day, the sheep would not move from the track. It had drifted from the trees, as Andrew had become used to seeing, almost invisible in the gloom, to take up its position some fifty yards ahead of him and his dog. The sheep had slipped out of the shadow and was now a heavy black smudge on the lighter strip of the path. Phoebe strained on her lead. As the man and the dog drew closer to the sheep, Phoebe started to yelp, emitting a strangled yip-yip-yipping against the tightness of her collar. Andrew yanked her back to him, irritated that he was being taken for a walk by his dog, angry that the pace of the walk should be dictated by her. But she increased the intensity of her barks, fusing them into one unbroken wail. The sheep fixed its unblinking white sockets on the dog. It remained still. Once more Phoebe lunged forward, until she received the unmistakable signal from the sheep that it was not going to give way this time. Some magic through the air-waves was transmitted from the big black animal, impassive and silent on the forest track, to the smaller hysterical creature which came noisily closer . . . For the dog suddenly stopped lunging and barking. Instead she tucked her tail between her legs and froze. The two animals eyed each other for a further second, sniffing, quivering. And then the sheep strolled casually towards the dog, slowly and inevitably like one of those big mad women who assume the right of way with their supermarket trolleys, while Andrew found himself stepping meekly aside and tugging Phoebe with him. The sheep passed by. Phoebe was stunned by the insolence of it. She gazed in disbelief at the waddling creature, which now squatted as decorously as a duchess and extruded a single glistening turd on to the track, before drifting back into the darkness of the fir trees. Only then did the dog recover her wits. Shrugging off the hypnotic effect of the sheep's stare, Phoebe wriggled from her collar, somehow writhing her head free from it. She flew into the forest in pursuit of the animal.

There followed five minutes of confusion among the densely packed trees. Andrew ran up and down the path, shouting hoarsely for the dog. Her lead, with the collar attached to the end of it, dangled uselessly from his wrist. The sounds of a frantic chase were all around him: at first to one side there was the splintering of branches as a number of animals stampeded riotously through the undergrowth, and then on the other side of the track he heard Phoebe's manic cries. She was beyond his control. Now that the sheep were running ahead of her, there was nothing he could have done, nothing he could have shouted to bring her back to him. Around and about him, as though the animals were deliberately describing a series of circles through the plantation, with the big blond man aghast in the middle, Andrew heard the blundering progress of the sheep; the snapping of brittle wood, the trample of hooves through dead bracken, the scrambling of heavy bodies through muddy ditches . . . everywhere the plantation echoed with the breaking of ground and vegetation to make way for the sheep. Piercing high and clear above all this, there rang Phoebe's joyous yelps. More and more sheep which had strayed into the forest were now swept into the pursuit. Bunching together for the security of numbers they had learned from their previous experiences with dogs, they blundered in blind panic from end to end of the plantation. As Andrew waited, his hairless face blenched with fear and his eyes expressionless behind the heavy lenses of his glasses, he leapt with the shock of seeing a dozen or fifteen sheep go haring across the track higher up the hill, appearing and vanishing from one side to the other. And behind them there was Phoebe. She sped through the forest, very low to the ground, gliding between the trees as swiftly and easily as an otter in the green depths of a pool. Black, shining, volatile, she went snaking like a shadow and there was nowhere for the sheep to hide.

Then the forest was shaken by a deafening explosion. Very close by, there was the boom of a shotgun. It was followed by a ghastly, welling silence, more abysmal than the silence of an empty cathedral. No more cracking of branches. No more bleats of terror. No more yelps of simple joy from the dog. Nothing moved. Nothing was heard to move. Andrew was frozen still, as the crash of the gun dissolved its echoes into the blanket of trees. He listened to the layers of silence settle one on top of the other, until he was buried under the weight of the hush . . .

The first sound then was Andrew's voice. It came out,

faint and disembodied, and all it said was, 'Phoebe? Phoebe?' like the call of a rare bird of passage which had been blown by a storm into that unwelcoming place. There was no answer. Louder this time, the call went out, 'Phoebe! Phoebe!' and still it sounded somehow lonely, the cry of a lost and solitary bird. But it was answered by the movement of footsteps, human footsteps, high on the track above him, the noises of someone striding away up the steep path. Andrew shouted an indeterminate word and began to scramble upwards. His breath came short, his wellington boots slapped loudly as he ran and slithered from bend to bend, and when he stopped to listen for the footsteps they were always receding, higher and higher towards the lowering clouds of the crater. He ran on. His head was pounding when he reached the top of the plantation. The mists were so low into the bowl of the cauldron that he saw nothing of the sheer walls. He stood still, taking long and rasping breaths to settle his pulse, again and again pushing back the flopping curls of hair from his face, and he peered dimly around him. He cried out an incoherent sound which clattered on the slabs of wet rock. A party of jackdaws beat through the cloud, clucking like chickens. The only other sound was the ubiquitous whisper of water down the cliffs. As his heartbeat settled, he thought he heard the rhythmic splashing of footsteps through the quagmire of the crater, and again he called out. But by the time he had smeared away the droplets of mist from his glasses, he had missed any chance of sighting that person who now strode quickly away. Nevertheless, Andrew waited for a minute in the darkness of an evening which had crept unnoticed over the mountain. And he was rewarded by the sound he expected to hear, the pealing chorus of the hounds which rose suddenly into the gloom. Cursing at this, a single crisp expletive, he wheeled round and returned to the forest, his bulk moving rapidly downwards and downwards, drawn into the twilit bowels of the plantation.

The light was fading fast. However, Andrew found the spot from where the chase had begun, marked with the turd which was losing its sheen as it cooled. Now there was no time for timorous cries if he were to find Phoebe before the forest became too dark. Over and over he shouted the dog's name, no longer like the plaintive notes of a bird, but a bellowed enquiry. The trees rang with it, they tried to absorb the ringing into their clustered needles, failing as the man persisted, while he paced the track upwards and downwards from the turd. When he paused to listen for a movement or an answering bark, that benumbing silence took hold, infecting the forest with a kind of fatal torpor. He paused for breath and strained to catch a sound. There was none, except the clamour of the blood in his own head and the rasping hoarseness of his throat. He held his breath. From somewhere in the serried darkness, there came a voice, very small, but a voice which echoed his shouts. 'Phoebe?' he said quietly, as though to himself, and he heard that little voice again, hardly more than a mew. Repeating his gentle call, he plunged from the track into the trees, burrowing on his hands and knees through the tangled network of twigs. They tore at his face and his hands, they snagged in his hair, but he leaned more heavily into the clutches of the undergrowth and writhed further into the ranks of the forest. Drawing him on were the insistent whimpers of the dog, somewhere ahead. The ground fell away in front of him when he came to a drain, so he dropped gratefully down where he could move more easily beneath the branches. There was a thread of light too, from the thinning of trees above his head. And, shining faintly in a clearing, where the gloom was relieved by some silver slivers of sun which the day had left behind, there lay Phoebe. She had forced herself tightly under the up-ended roots of a fallen sapling, and there she crouched, whimpering for the arrival of the man. 'Phoebe, Phoebe, Phoebe . . .' he murmured, continuing to repeat the word like a charm as he knelt by the dog and took her head in both his hands. 'Let me see, Phoebe, let me see what's happened to you . . .' He ran his fingers around her face and neck. The dog was shuddering with terror. Every part of her, as Andrew felt along her sides and up and down her legs, every piece of her was trembling. 'You're all right, Phoebe,' he whispered, his voice catching in his throat with the realisation that she was uninjured, 'come on, girl, come to me . . .' And at this, the terrified creature crawled on to the man's lap and buried her head as deeply as she could into the folds of his jacket.

Together, the man and the dog remained enfolded in the swelling silent darkness of the clearing, entirely cut off from the world outside the plantation, from the silver birch below and the crater above, embedded in the core of the fir forest.

Andrew closed his eyes. The beating of the dog's slim body relented while he held her close. There was no sound at all, no light, he tasted nothing, now that he had swallowed the rank saliva of his fear . . . No sensation whatsoever, except for Phoebe's diminishing tremors against the pit of his stomach. He was cocooned from the persistent demands of his own senses . . . until he inhaled one long draught of the evening air, and the unmistakable stench of the stinkhorn jolted his eyes open.

'Stinkhorn?' he whispered. The dog lifted her head from his jacket, looking quizzically up at him. 'Yes, Phoebe, stinkhorn. Can you smell it?'

Surrounding him and the dog were a score of the pale fungi. They seemed to possess a light of their own, for they glowed faintly like phallic devotional candles, lit by pilgrims in a hushed cathedral. Confidently erect, they pushed up their tumescent heads and exhaled a powerful smell of rancid meat. They were horny with desire, quite brazen in their own rigidity. Their covetousness, their itch was upheld in the most cavalier way, which made that clearing in the forest a shrine to lust. And in the middle, uncomfortably like a winsome madonna encircled by candles, sat Andrew Pinkney, whose itch had not sufficiently itched, whose covetousness had not been covetous at all, whose own candle had flickered and gone out. He gazed around him. All this way to bloody Wales, he thought, all the way from Sussex to create a breathing space, to clear the air after that failure and the subsequent disgrace, and here I am buried in the deepest Welsh forest where no one could ever find me . . . surrounded by the most vivid and explicit reminder of my successlessness! Surrounded by these lewd phalli! 'Jennifer, oh, Jennifer,' he started to say, 'is this something you arranged? Part of your magic, along with the owls and the badgers?' But he knew that the stinkhorn was not part of her repertoire. He was forced to smile, and then he felt a chuckle beginning to grow until it erupted and became a laugh, that same braying guffaw which Jennifer could not resist, and that little clearing shook with Andrew's laughter. 'Splendid, splendid!' he chuckled, while Phoebe grinned and pricked her ears and began to bark. He laughed and laughed at the irony, inhaling the fetid pungency with the sensual relish of an opium addict. He forgot the mayhem of the dog's mad chase after the sheep, and for a while he forgot that explosion from a shotgun which had rocked the forest and begun a frantic search for Phoebe. As he sat and cuddled the beloved dog, he thought of Jennifer, her love of the countryside in which she had so thoroughly instructed him, and he started to spawn an idea which might help him to mend the rift in their relationship. The stinkhorn were still erect. But it was October. Their emasculation was inevitable. Soon they would flag and falter and fail, as other erections had failed before. Unless? Unless he, Andrew Pinkney, could postpone their wilting and return to Jennifer with a phenomenon of his own amateurish creation, signifying nothing but a joke against himself which might endear him to her once more. At last, he might be able to claim his own area of expertise.

It was an idea which he cuddled to himself as he cuddled the dog, while he carried her tenderly through the dense undergrowth, shielding her from the needles. The idea started as a wry joke. Slowly, carefully, for they were both weary from the trauma of the afternoon, the man and the dog went down the track and emerged from the forest. Andrew pondered. He followed the nodding plume of Phoebe's tail along the path, through the less hostile shadows of the birch wood. He pondered the idea which might occupy his time constructively over his weeks in Wales, and which might raise a smile of forgiveness on Jennifer's face when he returned to Sussex. That was all he wanted. Save the stinkhorn, he thought, and then he tested the slogan out loud to anyone or anything which might be listening in the woodland. 'Save the stinkhorn! Save the stinkhorn!' he sang, chanting it like a spell. The sibilance of it lingered in the leaves. They rustled as a shiver of cold cold wind ran through the tree tops. Andrew shuddered violently and glanced over his shoulder at the dense blackness of the forest. He hurried back to the cottage.

Save the stinkhorn . . . Save the stinkhorn . . . sighed the breeze that night, long after the man and his dog were sound asleep.

III

THE SPORES of the stinkhorn are dispersed by flies. So the badger in the woodshed was preparing to play its part in Andrew Pinkney's little game.

Only a few days after Phoebe's unnerving experience in the forest and Andrew's subsequent discovery of the stinkhorn clearing, the dog had led him into the plantation on the scent of the dead badger. Now that he had suspended the corpse in his woodshed, he could leave it there for the maggots to proliferate while he gathered the other essential ingredients for his project. Whereas he had become used to glancing into the outhouse because of the simple satisfaction he felt in his accumulation of wood, now he found himself ducking inside twice or three times a day in order to inspect the condition of the badger. The morning after he hung it there, he caught the rising odour when he went to the outhouse. He smiled excitedly at the dead beast. It grinned back at him. He saw on the freshly cut logs their crimson stigmata, and in the air of the woodshed, mingling faintly with the sweetness of congealing sap, there was the powerful whiff of putrefaction. Andrew spun the badger slowly, he turned it on the corset of barbed wire, inspecting the bruises which now turned black and the seeping wounds. 'You're perfect,' he said. He was pleased to see the tiny white eggs of the flies inside the badger's nostrils. Bending close to the animal's body, he listened carefully, expecting almost to hear the murmurings of industry from inside, imagining the myriad workings of gases and juices with the maggots which were breaking down the dead flesh. He saw that the pupae had fallen into the sawdust at his feet. He listened to the silence and he thought of the countless millions of organisms which would play their part in the decomposition of the badger: it reminded him of a radio debate he had heard not long before, about the decommissioning of a nuclear power station. Someone had protested that it was all very well wanting such stations to be closed, but what of the jobs of the people who worked in them, the hundreds of people who would be made redundant? There was a simple answer: the decommissioning of a nuclear power station took years, involving the work of many more people than normally worked in an operative station. There would be plenty of work for plenty of people ... And here was Andrew's badger, being decommissioned. Dead, it was busier than it had ever been when it was alive.

He made a rapid trip to Caernarfon, where he sat in the noisy little library long enough to get a picture of what he could do to bring off his surprise for Jennifer. He thought of her fondly and often, now that he had set himself a harmless and interesting task, the sort of inexpert experiment she approved of; she liked to think of herself instructing Andrew in the patterns of wildlife, showing him things which were alive in their natural environment, and Andrew guessed that she would muster her wry, crocodilian smile at his schoolboy enthusiasm. That was all he wanted. If she could smile and shrug, even ridicule his silliness with her schoolma'am manner, then he might have mended something. He wanted to show that he could make a joke at his own expense. And, for a change, he could be the pundit, he would be able to instruct her in his new field of expertise. Furthermore, after a fortnight in the cottage, although he did not want to return to Sussex yet, he saw that there was a limit to the satisfaction he could derive from his solitary walks and the long dark evenings alone with the radio. He was pleased to have stumbled across a game to occupy him and inform him as the autumn closed down. It would be something to do.

After a brief exploration of Caernarfon, where he admitted grudgingly to himself that the castle beat any castle that the south of England had to offer, and after exercising Phoebe on the sea-shore, he returned to the cottage; sometime, he thought, when he needed a rest from the suffocation of the mountains or when the stinkhorn let him down, he would go back to that sea-shore. The estuary was busy with waders on the sand flats, along with gulls and terns and cormorants; in five minutes with Phoebe among the rock pools of low tide, he saw fifteen or twenty species of bird, and again he felt the presence of Jennifer at his side, the lingering appeal of her enthusiasm. Yes, when he needed the sharper sting of the salt air, just as he and Jennifer had needed sometimes the tingle of the frost on Pevensey levels, he would return to the estuary.

But now, having gleaned from the library all the information he wanted, Andrew was eager to be busy. Equipped with wellington boots, he made short work of the river bridge and its silken curtain of water. He shouted and gestured in the face of the sheep-dog in the farmyard, having established from the safety of the car that the snarling beast was on its leash, and he slithered the car up the track to the cottage. Furthermore, in the library, he had not forgotten to glance into a Welsh-English dictionary for a translation of the name of the cottage: Clogwyn Ceiliog, the sign read, which signified something hilarious to the coalman. 'Clogwyn': 'Cliffs' . . . appropriate enough with the steep hillside and the crater high above. 'Ceiliog': 'Cockerel'. Therefore, something like: 'Cockerel in the cliffs'? Was that anything like a good translation? Andrew was mystified, whereas the coalman had been greatly entertained. He could think of no reason why the cottage should have such a name, putting it down to some distant chapter in the building's past when perhaps a farmer lived there with his stock. The only bird he had encountered in connection with the place had come tumbling down the chimney with a choking cloud of soot. A cockerel? More likely a jackdaw which had been trapped there in the summer. He put it out of his mind.

It was easy to find the clearing full of stinkhorn, except that Phoebe had to be practically dragged there. In spite of her gleeful return to the plantation when she had found the badger, when all her memories of her terror seemed to have gone, she was reluctant to go by the spot where the confrontation with the big black sheep had taken place. Andrew kept her carefully on the lead, in case there were stray sheep in the forest again. Phoebe had been allowed free before, precisely because Andrew gathered there would be no sheep in the plantation. Now, having seen the derelict state of some of the fencing and realising that stray animals came and went as they wished, he was alert for the sound of sheep among the trees. Along the track, they came to the single big turd, now powdered with the cottony mould of coprophilous fungi. The dog raised her lips and recoiled from it. 'Come on, Phoebe,' Andrew said, tugging her with him into the cover of trees, 'no sheep today, and no guns either.' Together they dropped into the drain, and Andrew's squelching footsteps preceded the delicate patterings of the dog as he led the way through the darkness, towards the daylit clearing ahead. Before they reached it, he sniffed the scent of the stinkhorn. It tunnelled at him down the gloomy corridor, it felt his face with fusty fingers. When he emerged, still crouching, into the light, he was obliged to pull Phoebe after him or else she would have fled from the malodorous place. Andrew bent sharply to seize the scruff of her neck, preventing her just in time from slipping her head again from the collar. And to his surprise, she struck at his hand so fast that the movement was invisible, nipping him keenly with her teeth. He swore at her. It was the only time she had ever bitten him. Angry, he used both hands to hold her head and he heaved her out of the ditch.

'Come out of there, you bastard!' he yelled at her, squeezing tight to prevent her striking a second time. He spun her across the clearing. There, releasing her quickly, he took the lead and tied it twice around a branch of the fallen tree. Phoebe rolled on to her back, to lie there in her most pathetic pose, hind legs splayed apart, forelegs raised and trembling, her ears flattened against the sides of her head and with her eyes pitifully rounded. 'That's all right, girl,' the man whispered, kneeling to console her, for he could see that she was aware of her guilt in biting him and needed consolation. 'All right, Phoebe, all right . . .' and he put out his hand to touch her belly. She lifted her lips in a high-pitched snarl. Andrew stood up, withdrawing his hand an instant before she writhed from her back and shot out a second raking flick of her teeth. 'You bitch!' Instinctively he thrust out his boot. It caught her under the mouth and there was the sharp click of her jaws closing together. A few flecks of blood flew from her tongue, rubies in the long grass. Sorry for what he had done, but not prepared to make another gesture of consolation, he turned to see what the clearing could offer for the benefit of his experiment.

There were the stinkhorn, in different stages of their erections, growing around the base of the fallen tree. The collapse of the tree had permitted more light into the area, enabling the growth of lush grasses to take place. The ditch, running through the clearing, promoted the burgeoning profusion of mosses, and among the litter of needles in the damp grass the stinkhorn pushed up their heads. Andrew squatted, examining the honeycombed crown of a fine example, to dab it with a finger and feel the stickiness of it. He turned to another which was weeping its glutinous juices. Two big green dung-flies rose heavily from it, intoxicated by the sweetness. The pungency was sweet to the flies, but not to Andrew, whose mouth went dry as he inhaled it, as though his tongue were powdered with the mould which flourished on sheep droppings. But he probed with his fingers into the soft earth around the fungi, gently feeling through the needles, until he found what he was looking for.

'Here we are, here we are . . .' he muttered, and he levered from the ground a pale round object, not unlike the egg of a pigeon. It was the fruit-body or 'egg' of the stinkhorn. Unlike a bird's egg, it was soft, as though there was a layer of some jelly or spongy substance beneath the flexible shell. A number of roots dangled from the bottom of it, fine strands which were not much more substantial than hair. In the ground around this first egg, Andrew found more, until he had four of them lying on the grass beside him. Wrapping each one individually in a piece of tissue paper, he put them into the pocket of his jacket. Satisfied that he had found enough eggs, he then produced a plastic bag from another pocket and filled it with handfuls of earth and needles from where he had dug up the eggs. That was all he needed.

'Let's go, Phoebe. Come on home,' he called to the dog, which was sulking on the other side of the clearing, and he undid her lead from the tree. She made no objection to this, indeed this time it was she who led the way along the drain, eager to quit the unwholesome place. Perhaps she could sense that, for the first time on their walks, there was something which interested and preoccupied her master more than she did, and she was jealous. Once they were back on the track, she leapt and wheeled so hysterically at the man's slow pace that he grew irritated with her. Against his better judgement, thinking guiltily about the incident with the sheep, he unleashed her and watched her go streaking away down the path. She disappeared around a bend without a backward glance. She would be all right, he felt sure, she would run all the way back to the cottage and be waiting for him by the door when he arrived. Nevertheless, as he trotted through the plantation, he listened carefully for the movement of sheep or indeed the sounds of human footsteps which might precede that appalling explosion of a shotgun. But nothing else was moving in the forest that day. When Andrew approached the cottage and whistled the whistle which Phoebe knew, she dashed around to meet him, waving the banner of her tail and beaming as though they had had no difference of opinion in the plantation.

'Now, this is what we do . . .' Clearing the table in the living-room, he prepared to plant the stinkhorn eggs. He unfolded them from the paper, put them gently on the table. From the kitchen he brought the empty jars he had mustered for the job, large coffee jars whose screw-on caps he had already pierced with two or three small holes. At the bottom of each jar, four of them, he laid a wad of tissue paper which he then dampened by pouring in a trickle of water. He took the plastic bag he had used in the forest and added to each jar a handful of the soft, moist earth, to a depth of about an inch. Using a kitchen fork, he dug over the soil to be sure that it was fine enough, leaving a hole in the centre, and there he planted an egg, with the roots or hyphal strands at the bottom. He tenderly arranged the soil around it with the fork, so that just the top of the egg was still exposed. Then he screwed on the caps of the jars. These jars he put on the mantelpiece, to adorn the room alongside Jennifer's watercolours of Sussex.

That was it. There was nothing more that Andrew could do, not yet, having followed step by step the instructions he had found in the library book. The stinkhorn would grow, and he would have a grandstand view of their erection. *Phallus impudicus* was their name, 'the lewd phallus', and lewd they would be . . . no longer reserving their arrogance for the denizens of that wasteland of a plantation, for the unappreciative stares of a few sheep, but rearing their tumid heads in his sitting-room! He smiled. In suburban Sussex, suburban people were watching their televisions from the security of their armchairs . . . In Wales, Andrew Pinkney, having failed dismally in his last attempt to rear a home-grown erection, could sit back and enjoy these surrogates as he relaxed beside the fire.

Before his eyes, the stinkhorn would grow. That was the easy part. Andrew's plan was to prolong their cultivation past the usual time, well into the winter, and this would be somewhat more difficult. He did not know whether his trick would work.

Stinkhorn did not smell so unpleasant simply to aggravate passing ramblers, it was not just a practical joke which nature played on the human nose, to imitate the smells of dead meat. It was intended to deceive the flies, to encourage them to visit the stinkhorn and to feed on the glutinous ooze which dripped from their swollen heads. The flies then carried away spores on their bodies and also released more spores, unharmed, from their digestive systems when they defecated. In this way, spores were communicated from site to site. Apparently, one single fly speck, carried from an oozing stinkhorn, could contain several million spores of the phallus. In the natural way, the onset of winter would limit the activities of the flies and cut short the transmission of spores, until the following spring. Andrew Pinkney's idea was to promote the continued cycle by introducing a fresh and eager supply of flies to a new generation of the fungus in his living-room, so that he could return to Sussex with an unusual present for Jennifer: the proudly erect phalli of the stinkhorn, completely out of season in the depths of winter, as highly prized and as exclusive as Christmas strawberries . . .

*

Andrew's living-room was developing perfectly as a nursery for his fungi. As he worked harder to keep it warm, by lighting the fire earlier in the afternoons, settling in sooner against the onset of the darkness which crept more quickly over the valley, so the blooms of damp increased their disfiguring hold on the walls. The fire drew perfectly now that he had cleared the chimney, but, within minutes of lighting it, the first breath of condensation formed its film on the windows. Shortly afterwards, the film was a sheet of vapour on the glass, which trembled as the moisture put on weight.

Heavy droplets of water broke in trickles down the panes and ran into the rotted woodwork of the frame. The walls wept. The ceiling, a botched affair of plasterboard and paper, began to sag: big bubbles inflated themselves behind the paper as the moisture gathered and loosened the adhesive, occasionally a few drops of water wobbled from the ceiling before landing with a click on the carpet. Since its last coat of whitewash, slapped willy-nilly on top of the existing growth of fungus, the room had blossomed again. At first there was a spot of green on the white wall, a spot which grew overnight to the size of Andrew's hand, and then it became a crumbling powder of rot, a mixture of new moss and decayed whitewash which spread like blood on tissue paper. Like ink on blotting paper, the blooms grew. At night, Andrew slipped reluctantly into a cold bed, where he slept without moving a muscle lest he turn his head on to the clammy cold of his pillow. He would wake to find himself curled up like a foetus, huddling the warmth of his own body, exhausted from the effort of sleeping. The rooms were not cold, but they were damp, and the damp was harboured in the sheets of the bed and in the clothes which Andrew hung in the wardrobe. Flecks of grey mould appeared on any clothing he left for a few days. There was a smell of decay, in spite of his efforts to air the cottage in the day and to heat it at night.

Now that the sun had fallen lower in the sky, it never touched the building from morning to evening, but passed it by, travelling its course behind the ridge of the mountain which loomed above the fir forest. There would be no more sun until the spring, but five months of the year when the cottage clung dankly to the dark side of the mountain and never felt a touch of warmth, never saw a beam of light. Andrew shuddered when he thought of this. He thought of the open sunshine of Sussex, where there were no great slabs of glistening, slime-covered rock to blot out the light. There, even in the deepest gloom of January and February, he and Jennifer could find some air, some dry air which did not cling like a rot to the insides of their mouths, there was somehow always a glimmer of light on the downs or the tingle of frost on the levels. Now, near the end of October, in Wales, he was festering sweatily in a cottage which had seen the last of the sun for nearly half the year. It had crawled like a toad under the rock, a toad in the sweltering clamminess of its own body, or a slug under a brick, where no light or air could get in. Warm and damp, the cottage withdrew beneath the blanket of the fir plantation, cowered against the wet walls of the crater. It was shunned by the sun.

Phoebe spent more hours in her basket. In the first week in Wales, when they had enjoyed an Indian summer as compensation for a poor summer in Sussex, she had cavorted like a puppy through the bracken and through the woods. For hours, afternoon after afternoon, she had been hurling herself into the streams and tumbling through long, unfamiliarly scented grasses. But now she retired earlier to her basket, to rummage violently in the blankets which had started to chill with damp. She lay for hours and licked her paws. When Andrew went to bed he carried her basket into his bedroom, for she was used to sleeping in the same room with him, and before he dozed fitfully between the cold sheets, he listened to the rhythmic slapping of her tongue on her feet. She would not, however, allow him to inspect her paws, but would snarl with the venom of a stoat when he tried to take a closer look. Andrew watched her, and he wondered that she was changing in the darkening atmosphere of the mountainside. She had bitten him once and had attempted a second bite. Now she skulked in her basket, lifting a quivering lip when he knelt to comfort her. Still she came to his dangling hand when he was sitting in the armchair, reading or listening to the radio, to nuzzle her fine face into his fingers, and on their walks she was as buoyant as ever. Only, when he approached her in her basket, or when she felt the encroaching shadows of the forest press tightly around her, Phoebe reeled off that buzzing snarl and wrinkled her muzzle. There was a growing germ in her mind which triggered this reaction, more and more often, as though, with the spawning areas of damp on the walls of the cottage, with the enveloping darkness which was earlier each day, she too was infected by her surroundings.

Andrew studied the watercolour of her which hung over the fire, above the four jars on the mantelpiece. In Jennifer's painting, Phoebe was beaming affectionately, showing her teeth in a disarming smile. There was no spark of ill-temper in her eyes. But, when he looked closely at the picture, Andrew was alarmed to see that a few droplets of condensation had formed behind the glass. And, peering also at Jennifer's landscapes, he saw the mist of moisture there as well. It clouded over the sunshine of her views. They were no longer so clear and bright . . .

*

By the end of October, Andrew Pinkney and Phoebe had been in the cottage for three weeks. During this time, the man had stocked the woodshed with more than enough timber to last throughout their stay in Wales, he had stumbled on the stinkhorn and planted their eggs into jars which he arrayed on his mantelpiece, and he had suspended the decomposing corpse of a badger above his stacks of logs, with the intention of cultivating flies for the continued promotion of the stinkhorn. His interest in the stinkhorn had really eased his brooding. He spent less time reflecting in his hermit's cell, that shallow cave on the hillside. At night, notwithstanding the dampness of his bed, he slept tolerably well without thinking too long about Jennifer, although he awoke each morning as torpid as a toad. He pondered less on the subject of his impotence, which was surely temporary: he knew that it was not such a rare occurrence for a man to fail like that if he was nervous or preoccupied, that the normal thing was a complete recovery, that he would be able to consummate a sexual relationship perfectly satisfactorily in future. To be sure, it had never happened before, in his student days. He must have been unduly apprehensive, after many long months of hesitation and the repeated fumblings with Jennifer in the car. If only she had not laughed at him! If only he had not struck her! Certainly he was not the first man to react with violence under such provocation, as he thought again of Bedder and the Director of Public Prosecutions. Thinking this, he brooded less. Soon he would return to Sussex, invigorated by his weeks in Wales, to laugh off the pettiness of his failure by presenting the stinkhorn, to resume life as though nothing odd had happened.

As for human company in those three weeks, Andrew had had none, apart from a few chance conversations in the village shop. Twice a week, no more, he and Phoebe walked down from the cottage towards the river and then followed it upstream to the village. It took them about a quarter of an hour, depending on whether the heron was there or not. If it was, then Andrew watched it until it flapped off, which departure coincided with the limits of Phoebe's patience; for she quickly tired of waiting while the man peered through his binoculars at a scrawny bird, and she would only have to jump and bark for a moment to have the heron flee. Andrew bought supplies in the little shop; they were more expensive than they would be in a Caernarfon supermarket, but he did not want to trail into town for shopping, opening and closing all those gates to reach the road, wading across the flooded river. The lady shopkeeper, a gently courteous little soul, asked where he was staying, when he had been into her shop a few times over the course of a fortnight. He told her the name of the cottage. 'Clogwyn Ceiliog,' he said hesitantly, wondering at his pronunciation and expecting her to laugh. 'It belongs to my boss down in Sussex. He's just letting me use it for a short while, for a month or so.'

The lady smiled, but did not laugh, such was the tender old-fashioned politeness of the young Englishman. She waited as he continued. 'I've looked up the name of the cottage in a dictionary,' he said, 'so I know what it means. Something about a cockerel, a cockerel in the cliffs. Is that right? Where does the name come from? Do you know?' And he smiled his labrador smile, all blond and ruddy, awaiting her reply.

The little Welsh lady pursed her lips and pushed back a strand of greying hair. 'Yes,' she answered. 'I know what it says on the sign outside your front door. But it's a mistake. I've met your boss in here several times, he comes in for his newspapers, but I never wanted to point out his mistake. I didn't want him to think I was being impolite or anything.'

'A mistake?' said Andrew 'But what's wrong with it? What should it say?'

'Well, you're right in your translation,' the shopkeeper went on. ' "Ceiliog" does mean "cockerel". Your boss must have misheard or misread the correct name somewhere and got a few letters wrong. It should be "cellog", that's c-e-l-l-o-g, which means "cells" or "caves". Nothing to do with cockerels at all!' This time she laughed. 'You see what a difference a few letters make to the meaning! But once your boss had had that slate sign made up, quite expensive, no one in the village wanted to tell him he'd made a spelling mistake. Nothing to do with cockerels at all! What it really should be is "Clogwyn Cellog" . . . something like, "the caves in the cliffs" or "the cells in the cliffs". It's difficult to translate it directly into English, you know.'

Andrew joined in with her laughter, remembering the coalman's laughter too. 'I'll look forward to telling my boss when I get back,' he said. 'No, don't worry, I shan't let on where I found out! But, the caves, or the cells . . . I think I've found them already. Those slits and holes high up in the rocks, in the woodland? Is that what the name refers to?'

And the lady smilingly confirmed this. She liked the young man, so polite and friendly, not at all stand-offish like his employer, not at all like the snooty Sussex solicitor who only used the shop as a convenient place for his mail and the newspapers. She hoped other people in the village would be friendly with him too.

Along the road from the shop, facing across the river, there was a hotel which Andrew's employer had mentioned as a place to have a drink in the evenings. It was big and white, not a pub, but a family hotel with an ordinary drinking licence for non-residents. From the road, it looked to Andrew like an old-fashioned prep school, with rolling lawns in front and a number of horses standing like statues under a chestnut tree. The building itself seemed somewhat weary with wear. The season was over. There would be no more residents until Christmas and the New Year. Looking around at the few houses which made up the village, at the shop and the derelict chapel, Andrew wondered where the custom would come from, to drink in the hotel lounge over the dreary months of autumn and winter. He and Phoebe walked from the shop to the foot of the hotel drive. Yes, he thought, just like a prep school, the day after the end of term: empty and echoing, the corridors scented of floor polish and the whiff of old dogs; maybe from upstairs the humming of a vacuum cleaner, or the maid's transistor radio . . . and from the headmaster's study there would float some idle tinkerings on the piano, the audible expression of someone's loss now that the term was over. Indeed, Andrew heard a random arpeggio as he and Phoebe turned and walked away.

The same evening, he decided he would end his self-imposed retreat, with a visit to the hotel for a drink or two.

He left Phoebe behind in the cottage. She had been playing an annoying trick throughout the evening, while Andrew was bathing and changing. Every quarter of an hour, heaving a colossal sigh, she would drag herself listlessly to the door and sit there, as if she wanted to be let out. 'All right, Phoebe, want to go out? Go on then . . .' he muttered as he tugged open the door, but by the time he had done this, the dog would have slunk back to her basket, where she lay in her most craven pose, rolling those desperate eyes and splaying her legs. Andrew shut the door. 'Don't go out then. Just stay there . . .' When, the first time, he good-humouredly crossed the room and bent to caress her exposed belly, for that was surely what she was inviting, she writhed up at his hand, snapping and snarling. 'Bastard!' he exploded. 'What the hell do you want then?' And periodically she padded to the door, from where she gazed out at the drizzling darkness and snuffled at the draught which came through the rotten woodwork. She whimpered like a child. But, before Andrew could reach the door and open it, she returned to her basket, tail between her legs, ears flattened against her skull. Henceforth, she started her high-pitched snarl whenever he passed by her corner, as he went from bathroom to bedroom and back again. 'You're bloody well staying here on your own tonight, Phoebe. Make sure you're in a better mood when I get back . . .' Out he went, with his anorak and wellingtons and torch, to go down the hillside to the village.

He was quite wet when he walked up the drive to the

hotel. It was the first time he had been down there in the dark and he was surprised how easy it had been to lose his way across the fields with only the torch to guide him. Occasionally he had blundered into the bracken, or rather the blackened remains of it, and then it was hard to find his bearings again and return to the track. His trousers were soon wet and he felt the drizzle clenching its cold hand around his scalp. From time to time he paused to wipe the raindrops from his glasses. But, having stumbled to the river, from there it was a simple thing to follow its course upstream. He was astonished to see, around a bend in the darkness, that the white hotel was brilliantly floodlit, so brightly that he was forced to shield his eyes from it while he felt his way over the uneven path. His boots slapped against his calves as he splashed through the sodden meadows of the riverside. He was glad to be walking on the road through the village and past the shuttered windows of the shop, through the pitch-black shadows of the chestnut which had been thrown into greater relief by the glare of the floodlit hotel, and across its gravelled drive. Standing outside for a moment, he flicked some water from his hair and wiped his glasses again. There was one vehicle parked there, a dilapidated black van, its wheels and its sides spattered with mud. Andrew looked down at his boots. He wondered whether he could go into a hotel lounge in such a state, so he went to the verge of the drive and drew the boots repeatedly backwards and forwards through the long grass. Then he stepped into the hotel.

There were three people and a dog in the little bar. The dog, a spaniel with a raw bald patch on its rump, was lying in front of a blazing log fire, not asleep but watchful, for it flicked its eyes up and down, from Andrew's smeared boots to his dripping blond hair, as he entered the room. Satisfied, it thumped its tail twice and closed its eyes. 'Hello,' said

Andrew quietly, flashing his instinctive smile at the three people. He stood foolishly at the door. 'Sorry about the boots . . . Are they all right or shall I take them off?'

The woman behind the bar peered sternly over, following the dog's example by examining Andrew from head to foot, before smiling and saying, 'You'll do. Come on in and take off your coat.'

He struggled out of the wet anorak. The woman, he thought at the same time, was the image of that headmaster's wife he had conjured up when he had been looking at the hotel that morning; she was tall and finely built, and he thought of Jennifer's heron too. He imagined her sitting at a piano in her husband's study, her long languid fingers stroking a melody from the keys, he could imagine her feeling sorry that another term was over . . . Meanwhile, he took out his wallet and paid her for the drink she put on the bar for him. She smiled an elegantly exhausted smile. Andrew watched the cords in her hands and in her throat. She was fifty, he thought, as grey and as thin and as dignified as a heron, but she smiled wearily as though she was relieved that he had come in. Her other two customers sat on stools at the bar. They were a teenage couple, spectacularly untidy in matching denim jeans and jackets and wearing high black leather boots. Their clothes were frayed and dirty, smudged with oil, mud and other indistinguishable stains, and Andrew smelt the odour of stale sweat as he reached forward to take his drink. The youth grinned at him, gulped his lager and smirked at the girl. They were both small and dark, with dirt in their fingernails, but it was the boy who smelled more strongly. The girl's hair was clean at least, and when she looked at Andrew her smile was less overtly insolent. She had small, white, very pointed teeth. She also was drinking from a pint glass of lager, snorting with laughter when the boy said something in Welsh, laughing so explosively that she had to wipe her mouth and nose with the back of her hand. When she could control her outburst, she slapped the boy playfully on the shoulder and replied in Welsh, with a gesture of her head in the direction of Andrew's boots. Andrew smiled gently at her. She blushed and looked down, running her hands up and down the tight denim of her thighs. 'Bit wet out there,' he suggested, which made the couple laugh again, but the woman behind the bar said, 'Where have you walked from? Are you staying in the village?'

'Not exactly,' he answered. 'About a quarter of an hour's walk away, up on the hillside, across the river. A little cottage with a peculiar name . . .' and he went on to explain how he had found out about the spelling error from the lady in the shop. 'I'm just staying for a month or so, a bit of a break from work. I'm really from the south of England.'

'Bit isolated up there, isn't it? Are you on your own?' the woman asked. The teenagers had listened in silence to his description of the cottage, exchanging glances as he spoke.

'Well, there's me and the dog. She's good company most of the time, but I thought I'd leave her this evening. I'm up here to do a bit of walking and otherwise relaxing, getting away from the office,' and he told her in his gentle, humorous way about the confines of his bed-sitting-room in Newhaven. 'A lot more space up here, isn't there?' he smiled, including the young couple in his remarks. 'You live here, I suppose?' he said, raising his eyebrows at the girl.

'Not far from your place,' she replied, addressing her half-empty glass. 'In fact, we're probably your nearest neighbours, the farm on the other side of the forest. Seen you walking up there a few days ago, I seen you with your dog a few times.' Glancing up at the boy, she added with another snort of laughter, 'I suppose that is a dog anyway . . . more like a daft little toy to me . . .' And the two of them continued in Welsh, their banter punctuated with staccato sniggering.

Behind the bar, the woman summoned another weary smile. 'You've got to be careful around here, with a dog,' she said, over the girl's giggles. 'With all the sheep around. Is yours all right with them?'

Andrew hesitated. Both boy and girl drained their glasses, as though suddenly overwhelmed by thirst. The girl glanced away. The boy stared straight at Andrew, waiting for his answer, but then spoke before Andrew did. 'Good idea to keep it on a lead, all the time. No such thing as a dog what won't chase a sheep. They can't help it. But round here there's people with guns what'll shoot on sight if they see a loose dog . . .'

'She's not so bad, so far,' said Andrew carefully. 'I'll keep a good eye on her. We go up through the plantation usually and hardly ever see any sheep at all in there. But we've never got as far as a farm. We never go much further than that sort of crater at the top of the forest. Where did you see us?' he asked the girl.

'You seen me too,' she answered. 'At the kennels. I'm up there feeding the hounds every afternoon.' She looked coolly at him and went on. 'Seen you up there waving at me, like somebody lost. With that sort of dog as well. We might be coming down past your place tomorrow, got to run a couple of hounds round the forest and get them sorted out. And then we'll be out hunting soon, right the way past your cottage . . . What's it called? Something about a cockerel, isn't it? Clogwyn Ceiliog . . .?'

This reduced the boy to a state of hysterical giggling. The woman refilled their glasses, while the spaniel stood up from the fire and started gnawing frantically at its threadbare rump. Andrew managed to join in with the laughter.

'Cockerel Cottage!' he proclaimed. 'The best-known

spelling mistake in the valley! Hey, I'll get these . . .' and he took out his wallet again. 'What's that? Two pints of lager, and another pint for me, please. Are you having anything?'

The woman declined, turning her attention to the spaniel as it chewed more fur from its coat. It settled down as the boy stopped laughing and the woman put the glasses on the bar.

'Cheers. I'm Andrew Pinkney.' This announcement amused the boy once more, who went out of the bar, wiping his face with the fingers of an oily hand.

'Cheers,' the girl said, raising her glass. 'I'm Shân, and that idiot's my brother, Huw. Hope you enjoy your stay in Cockerel Cottage.' She was quite pretty then, holding up the glass towards the light, with an open smile and an ordinary face which relaxed as soon as her brother had gone. She sipped her drink. 'Hang on to your dog if you see me coming with the hounds tomorrow. Personally, I couldn't care less about the sheep, the stupid things, but Huw's a bit trigger-happy. Right?'

'Right,' said Andrew. 'Thanks for the warning.' And they exchanged a glance over the rims of their glasses which seemed to seal their understanding.

The boy returned and applied himself to the drink, without acknowledging Andrew. There were a few moments' silence, as though there was something sacred in the sharing of beer, as though Andrew and the two teenagers were sealing a kind of pact. The brother and sister sat closer together and spoke in Welsh. Andrew made some small talk with the landlady, who was English too, who had moved to Wales from Cheltenham eight years before. She had been to Newhaven, she remarked, as everyone did whenever Andrew mentioned the name of the town, to catch the ferry to Dieppe. So the conversation ran its usual course: seasickness, cheap wine, the threat of rabies and the quarantine of animals, soccer hooligans on Channel crossings . . . until Newhaven had had much more coverage than it deserved. 'And have you had a good season with the hotel?' Andrew enquired. Having asked the question, he paid little attention to the woman's answer, but peered over the top of his drink at the girl. She was a child, certainly no more than sixteen. She must have just finished school in Caernarfon, at the end of last term maybe, and now she was the kennel-maid for the local hunt. Andrew watched her drinking, saw the tip of her tongue go deeply into the lager, saw her run it pinkly around her lips after every mouthful. He swallowed hard. She was listening to her brother, nodding in agreement and sometimes smiling. Then she laughed, a bark like Phoebe's barking, sudden and high, and they both looked over at Andrew. Andrew smiled back at them, and the girl reddened once more. Her tongue appeared, pointed and pink like a sea-anemone, and then disappeared between her tiny teeth. 'It'll be very quiet now,' the woman was saying, 'right through to Christmas. There should be a few more in here tomorrow night though . . . We're having a bit of a party for Hallowe'en. Coming for that?'

Andrew tugged his gaze away from the girl. The mention of a party silenced the two youngsters, who looked around at the woman. 'You two will be here, won't you?' she said to them. 'Hallowe'en's tomorrow night, 31st October. Were you here last time?'

The boy nodded, but the girl simply grinned and answered, 'Too young, me . . . not allowed to things like that. Anyway, I'm frightened of witches and ghosts and things.' Her brother guffawed at this, spilling some of his lager on the girl's jeans. Andrew watched the stain grow across her thigh. She just laughed, showing her wet teeth, while the woman went on, 'There'll be a bit of soup later on, and the beer will be cheaper too. Maybe a few people will dress up a bit, make it more fun.'

The brother and sister were getting ready to leave. Still giggling, they left the stools and moved towards the door. 'Thank you, Mrs Stone,' the girl called across the room, ignoring the renewed efforts of the spaniel to gnaw away more of its fur. 'Maybe see you tomorrow.' She seemed even younger now, in her big boots and tight jeans, immersing herself in a green waterproof coat which came down almost to her ankles. Pulling up the hood, so that now she was hidden except for the childlike smiles of her face, she said to Andrew, 'Do you recognise me now? See you at the party tomorrow . . .' and together they went out. There was another outburst of laughter, both of them engulfed with mirth, followed by the boy's raucous imitation of a cockerel's crowing. More peals of hilarity, the churning of a reluctant engine and the sounds of their van crunching down the gravelled drive . . .

Andrew went home too, or rather, he returned to the cottage whose name was the source of so much amusement in and around the village. The rain had stopped. He followed the yellow torchlight, a wavering pool on the ground in front of him, flashing it occasionally on the slow moving waters of the river. The darkness of the fields was heavy and dense around him. The floodlights on the hotel went out and left a bottomless black hole where the building had been, leaving the entire valley blanketed under the weight of the night. Andrew paused and urinated into the bracken. His torch was the only light, there was not another single pinprick to be seen, and he shone it on the glistening toe-caps of his boots and into the wet grass. The hillsides with their covering of woodland, the oppressive mantle of the fir forests, then the steeper slabs of rock which rose up to the mountain ridges . . . they all merged into the dark skies, where not a star could pierce the clouds. Andrew turned off the torch. It was then a darkness like no other darkness he had ever seen (and here he felt that he really could see it, a positive phenomenon rather than the mere absence of light), as though the valley had been flooded with one enormous liquid shadow. And he, Andrew Pinkney, possessed the only antidote, he felt the power and responsibility of holding the torch in his hand. But when he switched it on, he realised how puny his little light was, when everywhere he looked there was only the heavy black oil of night. He continued walking. Here and there, a sheep stood up from the grass and limped away, squatting and then dropping a patter of droppings which shone bright as the berries of the mountain ash when Andrew touched them with the beam of the torch. As he drew nearer to the cottage, he ran the light over the low white shape of it, an oyster fungus, pale and luminous, blooming on the dead wood of a fallen beech. To the right, there was the stone outhouse, and this was where he headed, the slapping of the boots and the regular sounds of his breathing suddenly louder against the side of the building. Before he went in, as he undid the padlock, he smelled the ripe rottenness of dead meat which was to him like incense from the gloom of a cathedral, and he composed himself by steadying his breath and clearing some condensation from his glasses. He inhaled the sweetness. Then he opened the door and ducked into the woodshed. In the torchlight, the badger seemed to be moving as the light moved, it swung slowly on its hook, wearing only its truss of barbed wire and its immovable grin. From it there rose an almost audible stench of decomposing flesh. The beast had swollen with the workings of gases in its belly, and Andrew grinned back at it, amused by the irony that now it looked sleeker and healthier than when Phoebe had found it emaciated in the forest. Now, this time, as he tendered one ear closely to the grey bristles of the badger's side, he was sure he could hear the machinery of countless jaws, busy in the tubes and organs and cavities which death had tried to silence, and he ran the torch lovingly from the stub of the animal's tail to the mask of its hanging muzzle.

'Good boy,' he whispered in the quietness of the woodshed. 'You've been busy.'

He left the woodshed in darkness again, tiptoeing out as though he were leaving a confessional and wanted no one to see that he had been there, and he let himself into the cottage.

Phoebe started to snarl before he could step across the room and reach the light switch. She remained in her basket, wild-eyed, baring her teeth, dazzled by the sudden glare. 'Calm down, Phoebe, it's me,' he said to her, but he did not approach her and soothe her as he was used to doing when he could see that she had just been woken from a deep sleep. As she unwound herself from the basket, got out stiffly and stretched each joint of her back with a cat-like languor, Andrew could smell the warmness of her fur and the dampness of it. She stopped snarling and rearranged her dishevelled coat on the hearthrug. He bent to feel her blanket: it was hotly moist, as though she had wet it as she slept. He took it out and draped it across the back of an armchair, to air a little, meanwhile fetching another one for her from the next room. Everything in the cottage was unpleasantly clammy. It was when he came inside from the clean air that he could almost taste the stagnation of the atmosphere on the roof of his mouth. He threw down the new blanket for Phoebe, who was vigorously slapping at her paws with the length of her tongue. He straight away thought back to the tiny pink tip of the girl's tongue, the faint aroma of her sweat as he had leaned across her lap to take his drink. 'What's the matter, Phoebe? Let me see . . .'

and he knelt by the dog to inspect her paws. She rolled automatically on to her back, as she always did, and this time she was soft and consenting, the Phoebe he had known before, who moaned a long pathetic sigh as she allowed the man to press his fingers between her pads. Had she been hit by a few pellets of shot? Maybe, he wondered, a shotgun fired through the dense cover of the plantation would diffuse its pellets into a fine, less incapacitating spray. Perhaps this had saved Phoebe from the direct blast (most likely fired by the girl's rancid brother), but the dog could nevertheless have sustained a slight wound. But he found nothing to explain Phoebe's persistent licking, putting it down to her cleaning out splinters from the forest or washing off the sickly scent of sheep droppings. He stood up.

Turning to the mantelpiece, he inspected the four glass jars. One of the eggs of the stinkhorn had split open, there was a scar across its fleshy whiteness. None of the other three seemed any different from the eggs he had planted into the moist soil. Next morning there might be a proud new erection when he awoke . . . He was suddenly very tired.

'Out you go, Phoebe,' he said, and the dog went obediently from the front door. Andrew watched her circling the area of light which fell from the cottage on to the hillside, slipping sometimes from light into shadow and back again. Then, near the privet, finally satisfied that she had found the spot she was searching for, she elegantly lowered her haunches and trickled a brief golden thread into the grass. She held up her long face into the breeze. There was a dead thing close by. She could smell it. Something emphatically dead swung silently in the same breeze which blew its stink to the dog's nostrils. And this brought first a wrinkle to Phoebe's face, then a quivering of her lips, until she started her electric snickering snarl. 'Come on in, girl, come on,' the man called from the open door. The dog ran to him, glancing into the darkness in the direction of the dead thing. When Andrew bent to stroke her, to greet her return to the cottage, she slithered past his proffered hands with a leering of her teeth towards his fingers. She slunk to the corner and dropped instantly into the blanket of her basket.

Andrew closed and locked the door. One last look at the splitting egg of the stinkhorn, then he was going to bed. The egg stared at him through the glass of the jar, a gaping, sightless eye, slit across and seeping a mucous tear. He shivered, for the room was chill, and he switched off the light.

*

That night, above the mantelpiece and its gallery of unborn phalli, the watercolour of Phoebe was changing. While the man slept, the mist of condensation on the glass had increased, forming droplets of moisture. The droplets grew, they quivered under the mounting pressure of their own weight, and soon they trickled down the inside of the frame. The paper puckered and creased. The colours started to run. The dog's affectionate grin distorted, the line of her lips was changed about her teeth. And then there was something different in the set of her eyes.

Slowly and secretly and silently, through the hours of another night, the smile became a snarl.

IV

ANDREW PINKNEY woke late the following morning and dragged himself to consciousness. He had had a dream, he realised as he lay still in bed and gathered the shreds of images and sounds which had troubled him through the night. In the dream, he was being chased by a great flock of sheep, bleating and crying in one unrelenting cacophony as they pursued him through the trees of the forest; the noise rose and fell, he was whipped by the tough branches of the plantation as he fled in a panic and forced his way among the trees, everywhere around him were the rasping cries of the sheep, the splintering of undergrowth, a labyrinth of shadows and darkness with that flock of manic, mad-eyed women behind him. Whenever he twisted to face his pursuers, when he was trapped in the clutches of the trees, there was the big black sheep staring him down with its empty white sockets, stamping its feet and lunging towards him. Time and again he would wriggle free. And then the hunt would begin once more. He was flayed by twigs, scored by needles, and always behind him came the swelling chorus of the sheep as the flock drew ever closer, and then there was the black sheep which separated itself from the shadows and made its charge . . . On waking, Andrew lay still, weary from sleeping. It was late, nearly ten o'clock. He crawled out of bed and padded through to the living-room.

Phoebe hardly stirred when he pulled back the curtains. The room was lit by a grey metallic gleam, the feeble sunshine which was reflected from the opposite hillside. The air was heavy with condensation. The dog opened her eyes and watched, without lifting her head from the blanket, as Andrew moved vaguely around the room. He found his glasses and went straight to the mantelpiece.

In three of the four jars nothing at all had happened. The eggs of the stinkhorn remained pale and round, just peering from the soil. They had not split. But in the fourth jar, the fungus had risen and fallen overnight. It was over, the erection was over. However jaunty it may have been in the smallest hours of darkness, Andrew had missed it. Now the phallus lay limp against the sides of the jar, a clammy shrivelling thing whose head slipped slowly down as the white column of its body deflated. Perhaps, thought Andrew, he had not allowed enough air into the jar, so that, although conditions were right for a rapid and spectacular erection, the surfeit of moisture in such a confined space had caused wilting just as quickly. And, of course, there were no flies to feed on the glutinous secretions which had oozed from the honeycombed head. No pungency lingered. Well, there were three more jars on the mantelpiece for him to watch. As yet, the eggs showed no sign of hatching a cocky new horn. He might still be able to find more eggs in the forest, for further experiments. Andrew drifted thoughtfully to the bathroom, pleased that one of the stinkhorns had worked, sorry to have missed it. The atmosphere in the cottage must be ideal for their growth, the clinging damp combined with the warmth which he managed to generate from the fire. In the bathroom, moisture ran unashamedly down all four walls. The mirror was fogged with condensation; Andrew wiped it with the heel of his hand and studied his face. He needed a haircut, the blond curls fell heavy on his brow and his ears were hidden. But for the hillsides of Wales it was somehow appropriate, he thought, that he was becoming shaggy and dishevelled, that he should become more a part of the untended, glowering landscape. He was no longer an articled clerk in Sussex. He was in Wales to rear a clutch of pulsing erections on his mantelpiece, to cultivate the seething of maggots in the rotten sack of a dead badger . . . there would soon be a crop of phalli in his living-room, and he would move from jar to jar to feed each one by hand, releasing dung-flies to gorge themselves into a state of stupefaction on the stinkhorns' seed . . . No, you don't need a haircut, Pinkney, he thought, leave it to fall like a mane over your ears and down your neck. The mirror misted again, and he watched the familiar genial features become clouded into something different, something he had not seen before. He removed his glasses and washed, avoiding the face he had just seen in the mirror, uncomfortable whenever he met its altered glance.

The day passed under a lowering mist of an unhealthy dun colour, not the drizzling grey which Andrew was becoming used to, not the shifting silver sheet which filtered through a little watery light, not a series of clouds with any individual shape or characteristics, but a thickening brown fog whose weight pressed dully on the hillside, like a bruise. It was as though the world were being lagged by a conscientious guardian, wrapped around with a thick, soiled blanket to protect it from the hard colds of an approaching winter, smothered in folds of fusty wool. The ravens rowed over the mist, invisible, croaking, panting with their wings through the clutches of the air. The sheep drifted past Andrew's window, to nibble at the grass outside the cottage, to stare fixedly into the distance as though they could pierce the fog with their protruding eyes. Andrew peered out over the rim of his coffee cup, and he imagined he was marooned on an island, surrounded by the rolling vapours which the ocean exhaled . . . not an island with jungles and parakeets, but a barren outcrop of rock which was peopled only by himself and these barmy women, who loomed from the surrounding fume to nibble and pee, to pee and squitter, to nibble and squitter, a flock of deranged women who had escaped from an asylum or a nunnery and had been washed up on Andrew's island . . . On a morning like that, it seemed that the world was inhabited by the man and his dog and the ubiquitous sheep, overseen by the dark invisible birds, and by nothing else.

Andrew took the bow-saw and went to the woodshed. He hardly glanced at the badger, although the smell of it was stronger still. There was a stack of logs which he had brought back on the wheelbarrow in lengths of three or four feet, and he heaved them out of the shed, ducking under the badger's dangling snout, and carried them over to the cottage. There, wedging the logs between a pair of heavy boulders, he set about sawing them into small sections suitable for the fire. The wood had dried just a little since he had retrieved it from the forest, allowing the blade of the saw to cut more smoothly through without the logs sappily gripping. Soon, as he worked throughout the morning, there was a growing drift of sawdust on the ground, white and fragrant, something which was fresh in the suffocating staleness of the mist. The logs fell into a pile and then Andrew returned to the woodshed for the wheelbarrow, going slowly and methodically from the cottage to the shed and back again with loads of fuel. He stacked the wood neatly against the walls, tremendously satisfied to see the little building fill up, to smell the scent of resin which hung in the air and tried in vain to eclipse the pungency of the dead animal.

Phoebe strolled out of the cottage to watch. Sniffing the privet, she squatted and strained until a pool of yellow slime bubbled from her. She turned and inspected it, before sitting down and dragging herself through the wet grass to wipe her backside clean. A slick of the slime glistened where she had slithered. For the rest of the morning the dog lay still, gnawing the bark from a stick, but she limped away again, and a third time, to strain more froth from her. 'Poor Phoebe,' said Andrew soothingly. 'What've you been eating?' But he suspected he knew the answer already, having found the chewed remains of a toad near the cottage the day before and wondered whether she had had it in her mouth. He knew (because Jennifer had told him at some length when it was toads which preoccupied her for a short while instead of owls or foxes) that these unattractive creatures secreted a poison in the glands of their heads, a toxin which was released in times of stress. If Phoebe had picked up a live toad, she would certainly have been adversely affected, and even the skin of a dead toad exuded the poison. 'Is that it, Phoebe? Have you been at that toad? Well, you won't do it again, I bet, not after the first time. It'll teach you a lesson . . .' and he reflected that both he and the dog had come from suburbia with only a smattering of experience and knowledge of the country; here, on their Welsh hillside, on Andrew's desert island, they were learning each day that there was a big difference between Jennifer's expeditions into the ordered, comely Sussex woods and now their climbs through the plantation. Wales was different. The forests were wet and quickly dark; pop-eyed females stepped from the shadows and then vanished again; shotguns crashed away the silence and made a greater, more terrifying silence; a cauldron of mist boiled over, it sunk the world into a place of fumes where hounds cried out and ravens panted . . . Thinking of these things and watching as Phoebe wrung more poison from her, Andrew continued to saw. He stopped and looked around when he heard a shout from the hillside behind the cottage. It was the kennel-maid, ploughing through the bracken.

Andrew put down the saw and moved across to Phoebe. Remembering the girl's warning about the hounds, he sent the dog inside the cottage. She obeyed immediately, as though she had already scented the approach of the hounds. When he went back to the corner of the building where he had been at work, he saw that there were three hounds with her, big white leggy creatures, rangier than the hounds he had seen in England and with heavier coats. They danced around him, perfectly harmless and affectionate, just wanting him to touch their heads and stroke their lovely velvet ears, and he was crouching down to greet them as the girl trotted breathlessly to him.

'Hello,' he said. He had forgotten her name. Glancing past the grinning faces of the three hounds, he saw that she was wearing the same waterproof green jacket, the one he had seen her wearing around the kennels, baggy green trousers tucked into black wellington boots, and a man's flat cap. Her face was flushed with the effort and exhilaration of following the hounds. 'You're looking very rosy,' he added. 'Giving you a bit of a run, are they? Aren't they lovely dogs . . .?'

'Hounds . . .' She panted the single word, grinning as frankly as her three animals. Regaining her breath, she went on to correct him. 'Your little pet is a dog, Andrew, just about. These are hounds.'

'Oh yes, of course,' he smiled, straightening up again. 'My mistake. A typical townee, aren't I? And I didn't really catch your name last night either.'

'Shân,' she replied. 'That's s-h-a-n, with what we call a little roof over the "a". Where's the little beast then? Snoozing in her basket, I expect . . .' And she looked pointedly around for Phoebe.

Andrew squatted once more to fondle the head of the most affectionate hound. 'Yes, Shân, you're dead right in actual fact. She's got the runs, some sort of bug she's picked up, so she's inside, feeling very sorry for herself. Do you want to come into Cockerel Cottage for a cup of tea or something?'

He was surprised then to see the girl's face quickly redden, first of all on each cheek as though she had been slapped quite hard, and then across her forehead. 'What do you mean "or something"? You cheeky man! I might have to tell my big brother about you when I get home again!' And she tried to cover her embarrassment by bursting into a fit of giggles. Andrew laughed too, but felt his own cheeks begin to glow. The kennel-maid, no more than a schoolgirl really, put up her hands to her mouth until her blushes faded, and after that he watched her tiny tongue slip out and slide across her lips. 'He was watching you last night, you know, my brother was. He's not as daft as he looks, fortunately! Very protective of his little sister, he is.' Andrew shrugged and said nothing. 'No, I'm not coming in for a cup of tea, or anything else for that matter, thank you,' the girl went on. 'Unlike you, I've got work to do, running some sense into these three buggers . . .' She pulled her cap on more firmly, her short dark hair as ragged as a boy's beneath it. 'Come on, you three, let's go . . .' and she moved to set off down the hillside, through the mist, towards the river.

Without thinking, Andrew called after her, 'Going to that party tonight, are you?' at which she spun round and shouted, her face split in two with a grin like a stoat's, 'I dunno, Andrew. Will you be there? Watch out for my brother, you naughty man!' By which time, the hounds were loping ahead of her and she trotted after them, calling in Welsh.

Andrew watched her go. As she went, she became more and more like a child, a boy, smaller and slighter and jauntier, until she dropped out of sight into the trees on the riverside. Seconds later, the grey ghost of the heron rose wearily into the air, as Andrew knew it would. It flapped upstream and banked three times, swerving from an imaginary attack, for the girl had awakened it from its recurring nightmare and now it flinched, still dreaming, from the shadow of an imaginary falcon. Andrew's meeting with the girl, Shân, lasted no more than a minute or two, and then she was gone with her hounds. He remained still, his boots powdered with sawdust, and caught himself thinking of Jennifer, imagining her here on the hillside. Guiltily, he thought of her as almost an alien being . . . utterly out of place in the mist, in the sawdust, in the company of the imbecilic sheep, in the brown bruises of the mountains, in a country of quag and fog, in a land which was toxic with toads. Jennifer, dear Jennifer, he thought (and the name itself rang wrong, too prim and starched), what would you say to the mossy walls of the cottage, to the eggs on the mantelpiece as they prepare to erupt, to the badger in the woodshed? What could you say to the kennel-maid, a child as frank and inviting as only a child can be? Jennifer, he whispered to her (thinking of her pinned-back hair and the way she grimaced at his kisses), Jennifer, even the heron here is different from your heron in Sussex . . . yours is a powdered old spinster, stiff and upright, peering around as gimlet-eyed as a headmistress, but mine in Wales is a ghost which inhabits its own self-inflicted nightmare, a nightmare in which it is relentlessly haunted by a falcon, so that it flinches like a spastic from any passing shadow . . . Jennifer, what would you think of your watercolours now, your scenes of sun and colour, all smudged with the drizzle and the mist? Did you misjudge Phoebe, to portray her as you did? Now she's cowering in her basket, her belly inflamed with poison, her face a-quiver with snarls . . . Andrew licked his lips. His mouth had gone very dry. He thought of the kennel-maid giggling, the spreading of her blushes over her face and down her throat, and he saw the tip of her tongue go wetly around her mouth. Yes, he might go to the party, instead of celebrating Hallowe'en alone with an ill-tempered Phoebe.

He returned to his sawing of the logs, while the day, like the dog, nursed its own particular sickness. There was very little light, only the dun-coloured drabness of the clouds, until the evening came. Then the clouds rolled away and revealed a night as clear and crisp as the day had been stale.

*

'Yes, this time you can come with me, Phoebe,' Andrew said, preparing to go down to the hotel. She flapped her tail at this, sensing from the tone of his voice that they were about to leave the dampness of the cottage for the clarity of a fresh evening. 'Want a walk? A bit more cheerful tonight, are you? Good girl, Phoebe . . .' and the dog rose stiffly from her basket to stretch herself and lick away the dishevelment of her coat. It was half-past eight. Andrew, determined to enter into the spirit of the occasion, was working in front of the bathroom mirror, crudely painting his face into what he thought might be a passable likeness of a vampire or a ghoul.

He had some shoe-whitener, which he daubed all over his cheeks and chin and forehead until he was ghastly pale, and then he found a black felt-pen with which he outlined his eyes and the corners of his nose, before blacking in a cruel moustache and goatee beard. Unfortunately, his vampire still had blond curls and a pair of heavy spectacles, but there was not much he could do about that; at least he had made an effort. Rummaging around the living-room, searching the pockets of his jackets, he eventually found a red ball-point pen and sketched a trickle or two of blood from the corners of his mouth. That was the extent of his disguise. As for his clothes, he had only brought with him to Wales a suitcase full of casual shirts, a few baggy pullovers and some waterproofs, hardly the wardrobe of a bloodsucking fiend, so he merely wrapped a scarf around his throat and put on his customary anorak and wellington boots.

Phoebe watched with an almost human expression of puzzlement on her face. 'Come on then, you hound,' and she leapt with her old enthusiasm towards the door at the idea of a walk. 'You're part of the outfit tonight, Phoebe, one of the hounds of hell, black and satanic and ready to spring at the throat of any passing virgin . . . Come on, you great fierce beast!' She was jumping and wheeling and yapping as he spoke. Good, he thought with a glance at the watercolour of the dog which was baring its teeth through a mist of condensation, that's more like my old Phoebe. His eyes went automatically down to the mantelpiece. Still the other three jars were unchanged, the eggs like dirty golf balls plugged into an unplayable lie. And in the fourth, the phallus was more like a garden slug, just a smear of slime which had slithered to a standstill on the wet soil. Andrew was ready to go out. Having built up the fire to survive, he hoped, until he returned, he fixed the guard in front of it and checked that everything was switched off. He took the torch from the table. As soon as he opened the door, Phoebe shot out, scrabbling with her claws for traction in her eagerness to be off. 'Bloody hell, Phoebe, wait for me . . .' and he followed her away from the cottage.

Outside, all was clear and still. Every shred of the shroud which had mummified the day had gone. A gibbous moon hung like a medal on the deep blue uniform of the sky. The hills and every scar of them, all the tumbledown walls and the stitches of the derelict tin mines, each wound of scree which had clattered down and grazed the ground away, the heaps of spoil from the slate tips, every sheep which dotted the valley like crystals of quartz in a granite boulder . . . all of this was lit by a clear light. Andrew turned back to see the cottage. Its whiteness had become silver and even the running stains of rust were erased. From the chimney, a pillar of smoke rose perfectly straight, an exclamation mark of pale blue against the mass of the mountain. Ahead of him, the dog ran and stopped and stood, shining black and finding a moonbeam wherever she moved. She waited for him to catch up and then together they walked down the hillside towards the gleaming ribbon of the river. They trod quietly among the trees which leaned softly on each other and whispered, conjuring their own breeze, and soon the floodlit hotel appeared before them, ugly in its brilliance when the rest of the landscape was so splendid, a dazzling white block of fluorescence, brazen and vulgar. Beneath the chestnut trees which lined the drive, the horses froze solid in their stillness and then shifted their weight from hoof to hoof with a massive sigh of resignation, oblivious to the man and the little black dog which went crunching over the gravel. 'Wait now, Phoebe,' he called softly, 'you're going to need your lead on. Come on, come here.' She trotted obediently to him and consented to his attachment of the lead to her collar. He felt nervous, with his face made up.

The skin of his forehead and chin had gone dry and tight, he sensed that the ink and whitewash might not be suitable for application as a cosmetic. Nevertheless, now he had arrived he would go in, with Phoebe. It was only a bit of fun, a few pints and a bowl of soup. Inhaling a great draught of the clean night air, he opened the front door of the hotel, turned from the lobby and stepped into the bar.

His senses were struck by three immediate impressions as Phoebe pulled him into the room. First of all, his glasses steamed up at once so that he could see none of the faces in the crowd; he was aware only of a number of people gathered closely together in the confined space of the hotel lounge. Secondly, after his lungful of air as he and the dog stood under the moonlit chestnut trees, his nostrils were greeted by the combined odours of cigarette smoke and human sweat. And the third impression was that the room, which had been a hubbub of voices and laughter heard from the lobby, suddenly fell silent. Andrew halted, restraining Phoebe. It was like a dream, where the senses are disarranged and disoriented, where events are a sequence of inconsequences. As he reached for his glasses with his free hand, before he could clear his vision, someone shouted the single word, 'Pinkie!' and the room itself seemed to burst into laughter, since for him there were no individual mouths and faces but simply a smoke-enveloped blur of laughing people.

'Pinkie, come on in!' the voice rang through the din, the voice of the kennel-maid. 'Don't just stand there . . .' and by this time he had wiped the lenses of his glasses so that suddenly her bright and candid face appeared before him. 'Bloody hell, Pinkie, what have you done to yourself? Come on and show yourself to the others . . .' He felt her hand on his, and she led him from the door towards the crowd of people at the bar. Phoebe baulked at this, tugging in the other direction and snarling, but the girl bent suddenly to the dog and yanked her along by the scruff of the neck. 'What's its name? Phoebe? Come on, Phoebe, you frightened little thing, you're all right with Shân. I won't hurt you . . .' To Andrew's surprise, because he was about to save the dog from the girl's rough handling, Phoebe stopped her snarling and trotted with the girl, her tail wagging like a feathery black banner. There, at the bar, he was dismayed to see that not one other person in the hotel had taken the trouble to put on a Hallowe'en mask or any sort of costume. No wonder the conversation stopped, he thought; who told me it was going to be a costume party? But then the girl was pressing a pint of beer into his hand and slipping Phoebe's lead from his other wrist. 'There you are, Pinkie, or is it Count Dracula? Not sure that the wellies are really suitable for a vampire though . . . Cheers!'

All around him, the conversation was buzzing in Welsh. He took several long mouthfuls of beer, grateful to the girl for her brisk intervention and prepared to forgive her use of a nickname he had not heard since his schooldays. There were not as many people as he had guessed from his first impression of the room, no more than fifteen pressed around the bar, but the smoke and sweat and perhaps the meaninglessness of the chatter made the sensation of clamour more powerful to Andrew. Glancing across the lounge, he was pleased to see that Phoebe was sitting contentedly in the middle of a circle of admirers, who seemed to be complimenting her on the gleam of her coat. In any case, she was grinning up at them, languishing in the caresses they lavished on her. 'She's all right, no need to worry about her,' Shân was saying. 'Everyone here's like me, we're all used to having lot of dogs around. I'm always a bit rough with them, 'cos I know that's what they like best. Even your little lap-dog would respond better to being shoved around a bit. Soon get her used to the sheep, if she knew she'd get belted for chasing them . . .' Her voice trailed off, and Andrew watched a blush blooming over her face.

'Chasing sheep?' he asked her innocently, eyeing her over his beer glass. 'She hasn't been after the sheep, has she? I hope not . . . I wouldn't want any trigger-happy farmer taking a pot-shot at her.' Her brother materialised beside her, and Andrew caught his bitter scent. 'Hello, Huw,' he said, feeling the painted skin of his cheeks pulling tightly as he smiled. 'Your sister was just saying something about . . .'

But she interrupted him with a shove and a 'Shut up, Dracula . . .' so he shrugged and turned the smile into an elaborate grimace. 'She was just saying how much she liked my vampire make-up. What do you reckon, eh? Reckon this would frighten the sheep more than anything, don't you?'

The youth said something smartly to his sister, in Welsh, at which she blushed again and replied in English, 'You mind your own business, Huw. I can look after myself, thank you. Can't I, Pinkie?'

Andrew smiled genially, raising his glass to the two teenagers and saying, 'Cheers, to a charming brother and sister! Happy Hallowe'en!'

The boy drifted off and the air cleared, except that the staleness of his clothes was straight away replaced by the clinging sweet smoke of cigarettes. The girl seemed both relieved that her brother had gone and, at the same time, uncomfortable in the presence of the older man. She feigned nonchalance, swigging at her pint of lager and looking around the room as though Andrew were not there. 'Was it you who said this was a fancy dress do?' he asked, as much to get her attention as to elicit the information. 'I feel a right charlie with this stuff on my face. I thought lots of people would be dressed up.'

Affronted, she lifted her eyebrows and answered, 'No, it was not. I never said anything about fancy dress. It was Mrs Stone,' gesturing at the woman behind the bar and raising her voice in mock outrage that she was responsible for his embarrassment.

Mrs Stone, the languid lady who was to Andrew a hybrid of heron and headmistress, inclined her grey head at the sound of her name and beckoned him closer to the bar. She drew him closer still. 'Congratulations, young man,' she whispered into his blond curls, 'you win the prize for the best costume of the night. Yes, I know,' she laughed, in response to his indignant look, 'the only costume of the night and not much of a costume at that!' She lowered her voice again, so that Andrew strained to catch what she was saying. 'I knew none of the locals would bother, except that they're suddenly all here for the cheap beer. Bastards!' Andrew blinked at the unexpected expletive. She ushered him nearer again. 'That's a pretty little dog you've got. Keep your eye on her, and keep an eye out for that bastard Huw. He may be the result of chronic in-breeding, but he's cunning with it . . .' Then she was busy serving drinks, with just the time for a cryptic nod in his direction.

Andrew turned his attention back to the girl. 'You're very pretty tonight,' he said to her. 'I'd hardly have recognised you.'

She countered his deadpan look. 'Charming, I must say. I don't always look scruffy, you know. Just like you don't always wear make-up. Although we hear all sorts of rumours about you southerners . . . Don't know what kind of things you get up to down south, especially in London, but if it's anything like they say in the papers, I dread to think . . .' She was wearing jeans again, except that, unlike the ones she wore the previous evening, these were clean. They were just as close-fitting as the other pair. Over a plain white blouse, she had on a loose blue pullover, very soft and comfortable, something she might have borrowed from her older brother and thoroughly washed. She wore white training shoes. The overall effect would have been that she was a schoolgirl, scrubbed clean and fragrant with talcum powder, but she had applied a little pale lipstick and had painted some metallic green liner on her eyelids. Nevertheless, Andrew thought, those adult touches were restrained enough to render her still fresh, rather than coarsening her childlike features. 'Oh, I lead a very boring life in the south,' he was saying. 'Don't believe those newspapers, Shân. I get up and go to the office (without make-up by the way). I slave away at my desk, go home and watch TV, and then go to bed. At weekends, it's walks in the countryside, a few drinks in the evening, and back in the office on Monday morning. Another drink? I don't think I can keep up with you, knocking back your pints . . .' He took her glass with his own and had them refilled.

Meanwhile, as he and the kennel-maid exchanged more harmless banter by the bar, her brother kept a watchful eye on her and on the Englishman who had painted his face. Andrew knew he was looking. Occasionally, deliberately, he peered over to the boy's corner, and whenever he met his scowling glance, he winked grotesquely and felt the dried ink around his mouth crinkle with the wrinkles. Then the boy looked away. The girl drank quickly and talked more; it was easy for Andrew to keep her talking, with a few questions to prompt her about her hounds and the work at the kennels, a subject on which it seemed she could enthuse at length. Content to let her go on, he allowed his eyes to wander over the room, wondering, while he half listened to her, that there was no one, no boy apart from her brother, who objected to her being cornered by a complete stranger, furthermore by an Englishman decorated with ink and whitewash. From time to time, he found that Mrs Stone was watching him with the girl, and then the woman would smile and nod at him as though to seal their private remarks, to reinforce their Englishness, she and Andrew alone in a hotel full of Welshmen conversing in Welsh. Phoebe had manoeuvred herself into a position in front of the open fire, where she lay outstretched and basking in the heat, her eyes forever on Andrew. When he looked down at her, she thumped her tail and he would smile.

'You're not listening to a word I say, are you, Pinkie?' chirped the girl, her blush no longer transitory. Her face was suffused with drink. 'Not very flattering, you know, for a girl to be talking to a bloke who's more interested in a bloody dog, is it?' But she was amused by his distraction.

'I'm sorry, young lady,' he blustered, affecting the pomposity of the magistrates he was used to observing, 'of course I was listening to your every word. Most interesting, most interesting. Please, go on, do . . .'

She started to giggle and to shove him with her little white hand, until a few slops of lager spilled on to the carpet. And it was when she was giggling that Andrew watched her wet mouth, the way her tongue slipped out and made her painted lips glisten. He felt his stomach go light, as though he were descending rapidly in a lift. She had spilled her drink once more on her jeans, and Andrew watched the stain diffuse across her narrow thigh. The lift accelerated, plummeting downwards, or so it seemed to Andrew's stomach. The girl controlled her giggles. Catching his look, she suddenly flinched from it as if she were stung by what she saw in his eyes. And there, across the crowded room, her brother had noticed too, for he was fixing Andrew with a stare which said he had recognised the game even from a distance. Mrs Stone was drying glasses, watching, missing nothing, as sharp as a heron. Andrew concentrated on his drink, although when the laughter in the smoke-filled room rose and fell and there was a squall of female shrieking, he was haunted by a memory of Jennifer's laughter at his impotence; he was troubled by the proximity of the kennel-maid and he juggled uncomfortably with a persistent image which plagued his mind . . . that of the wilting stinkhorn, with its deflated head slithering wetly and meekly down the inside of the jar.

The evening increased its volume. He did not drink much, but he watched other people drink a great deal. Opposite him, Shân was sitting on a bar stool, with her back against the wall, and the effect of the drink on her was to loosen her features so that her cheeks sagged and her mouth fell into a pout. In spite of her efforts with the make-up, she now looked younger again, because her face resumed the softness and blandness of something which was far from finished. Instead of chattering to Andrew, she smiled a permanently vacuous smile and stared around the milling throng, her cheeks flushed with the smoke and alcohol. Shifting away from the bar, where the traffic had suddenly increased and where Mrs Stone was busy, he detached himself as far as he could from the festivity of the occasion, saddened by the irony that he, the only person in the hotel to have made any effort to match the mood of the evening, was furthest removed from the atmosphere of drunken hilarity. He stared at his wellington boots. Somewhere down there, at that level, somewhere in the lounge was Phoebe, not asleep of course, but stretched out and spectating the uproar in a state of bafflement at the noise and the smells and the press. And instinctively he felt a great surge of envy, that she was no part of this and could never be, however hard she tried. He touched with his fingertips the dried crust of whitewash, the plastic smoothness of the ink on his face, he recalled the idiot-mask he had presented in the mirror in the bathroom, he remembered vividly that instant shock of silence when he had entered the bar and the explosion of mirth which followed, and he envied Phoebe so passionately her detachment from all of this that he felt a prickling of angry tears in his eyes . . . The fiasco with Jennifer on the sofa! All the stupidity and indignity of removing clothes just so that two white and ordinary and unappealing bodies could tangle for a minute of fumbling ineptitude! Then the disentangling of inexpert limbs, the avoiding of each other's eyes, reaching for clothes which smelled suddenly different and anyway were inside-out from being hurriedly peeled off! All of this applauded by Jennifer's crowing laughter and the excited accompaniment of Phoebe's barking . . . No wonder, he thought, mouthing angrily and silently to his boots, no wonder Phoebe started to bark! She was laughing too, at the absurdity of the whole charade, at the incompetence of the whole operation, and most of all at the bogus significance which the players attached to it. Why hadn't they just got on with it, one afternoon in the forest? Why didn't they rut vigorously and briefly in the twilight, while they were waiting for the badgers to come out? What was so important and holy about it, that they should approach it with such breathlessness in the tiny bed-sitter and afterwards think it was worth the effort of coming to blows? He stared at the muddy black wellingtons and envied Phoebe her present separateness, her undisturbed vantage point on all this shouting and ribaldry and inhaling of fumes and farts . . . She was down there somewhere, on a different plane from all the baying voices, from all the wet mouths and addled tongues, from eyes which now were shot through with blood and from the features of people which were coarsened and heavy with drink . . . He looked at the kennel-maid. Oh yes, she was pretty, in a childish unfinished way, and yes, when he saw her thin thighs wet with beer he felt the buckling of his stomach. Yes, he could see the evenness of her tiny teeth and the bubbles of saliva on the secret pinkness of her tongue . . . But now she was slack with drink, as if the bones in her neck and her spine and her narrow pelvis were dissolving in alcohol.

'What you looking at me like that for, Pinkie?' she managed to say, leaning right forward to put her hand on his shoulder. Her face bobbed in front of his, pale and moist and white, like something washed up on a beach, something from which all the colour and texture had been bleached by the sea. 'Why you looking at me funny like that? Call my big brother if you're not careful . . .' Then she reached up her mouth to his, not to peck him with a kiss, but, before he had the wits to recoil, to run her tongue across his lips. He felt her tongue slip all around his mouth, from the right corner and along his upper lip and more slowly over the lower, pausing there a split-second to flicker upwards and downwards like the fluttering tongue of a snake, before it moved on and returned to its starting point. Mesmerised, he inhaled the scent of talcum powder and the faintest odour of her body and her hair while her face brushed on his. All around him, in spite of his sobriety, the noise of shouts and laughter welled up, as though she could conjure a renewed intensity of sound by holding herself close to him. Someone blundered by, stumbling against Andrew. The girl fell back to her position on the wall, her eyes closed, her lips sealed in a snake-like smile. She looked up and released an arpeggio of a giggle at the remarks of the man who had knocked into Andrew, remarks which Andrew did not understand, and there was then a great deal of lascivious winking from man to man and to the girl, with Andrew surrounded by a hilarious mob. He essayed a nonchalant smile, but felt the skin tighten on his cheeks and forehead. The scent of the girl lingered on him, and as he licked his lips he tasted her metallic flavour. The men roared to see him uncomfortable, that he had been sucked into the bottom of a crater of braying faces, faces which were red and blotched and puffed with the heat, all of them discharging their unintelligible cries.

As more of the crowd assembled at the bar, Andrew decided to take a breather away from them. Unable to make himself understood by shouting against the sudden up-surging of voices, he tapped the girl on one knee and signalled in the direction of the toilets. She responded with a vacant grin, which she then obliterated by fixing her glass of lager once more to her mouth. Andrew manoeuvred his way through the circle of people, having manipulated his features into what he imagined was a buoyant smile, and he shot out of the room.

It was blissfully quiet and cool in the hotel toilets. He urinated at some length. Then, as he washed his hands, he studied himself in the mirror. He saw the same grotesquely painted face he had decorated in the bathroom of the cottage, the crude ink and whitener quite ludicrous behind the spectacles and under his flopping blond hair. Jesus, what a stupid mess! he thought, while the eyes which met his from the mirror seemed to narrow with contempt for his efforts to ingratiate himself with the local people. What would Jennifer have thought, he wondered, if she had seen him like this, just a little tipsy but not drunk, daubed with make-up in an attempt to entertain a bunch of Hallowe'en revellers for whom the only significance of the occasion was the reduction in the price of beer? And if she had seen him flirting with the kennel-maid, a little schoolgirl of fifteen or sixteen with an electric tongue and thighs as narrow as a boy's? He could still taste that wet kiss. How long would it take him to remove the ink from his face? Was it supposed to be waterproof, indelible?

Angry with himself for the silliness of his appearance, angry too because he could not control the stirring of his stomach as he tasted the tang of the child's tongue on his lips, angry because he was getting angrier, he spontaneously tore off his glasses and prepared, there and then, to try and wash the paint away. He filled the basin with warm water. Muffled now, the sounds of more raucous hilarity rose and fell in the hotel bar, and at the core of the general laughter he heard the cock-a-doodle-doo of the girl's brother, his falsetto rendition of the cock's crowing. Bugger them, he mouthed into the mirror, watching the painted face mouthing back at him, appalled by the moist blandness of his eyes now that he had removed his glasses and placed them between the taps . . . Bugger the peasants who could make such mileage out of his foolishness and the spelling mistake on the cottage! If their lives were so humdrum that they needed that sort of banal stimulation, then let them continue their crowing . . . But the eyes in the mirror, wet and unappealing as a pair of pale slugs, stared back, unblinking. They would not excuse him such feeble self-pity. 'Don't be so pathetic, Pinkney!' he said in a clear crisp voice. 'Have a laugh and a few drinks and stop feeling sorry for yourself!' So, blotting out a renewed eruption of mirth from the bar, a great uproar of shouting and baying, he plunged his face into the water and started to attack it with both hands.

Suddenly, the door of the toilet was flung open behind him with such force that it banged loudly against the wall. He straightened up from the basin, spluttering and blowing like a sea-lion. He had no time to reach for his glasses to see if there was any improvement from one attempt to remove the ink, but he squinted into the mirror, blinking at the stinging of soap. All at once, there were three or four people in the room with him, arriving with a tremendous shout and clamour, such a sudden turmoil that Andrew spun around to try and see what was going on. 'Hey, what's . . .?' he began, and was barged and bumped by the youths, forced backwards against the basin by their shoving. 'Come on, you lot, what are you . . .?' But their hands were on him, on his wrists and elbows, under his arms, three or four pairs of sinewy hands which wrenched him forward and manhandled him to the door. The shouts rang hard on the bright tiles and porcelain of the room, cries in Welsh from one assailant to another, their clanging urgency more frightening in a different language so that Andrew, practically lifted from his feet, could not possibly judge the cause of the struggle to remove him from the toilet as quickly as possible. All he knew was that he was being half-carried, half-hustled to the door and through it by an indeterminate number of strong youths, one of them the kennel-maid's brother whom he could recognise by smell. This youth, doing most of the shouting (jabbering like a chimpanzee, for all that Andrew could understand), had his head so close to Andrew's face that Andrew twisted away from the scent of sweaty hair which brushed his cheeks, from the indefinable sweetness of something animal and rank. 'Hey, put me . . .!' but then, amidst louder shouting and more shoving with knees and shoulders and hips, he was borne out of the room. Someone pushed open another door in front of them, and there he was deposited in the bar again, his face running with water and dissolving whitewash, without his glasses, surrounded by a now silent crowd of people. The gripping hands fell away from him.

The operation of removing him from the wash-room to the bar must have taken less than half a minute. He stood there, panting and squinting, flicking soap and water from his eyes, unable to ascertain the mood of the attack, unsure of how to respond. He straightened his jacket, tucked his shirt into his trousers. His mind raced as the silent faces spun before his myopic stare. Was it a continuation of the joke, and so should he now laugh and buy a round of drinks? Had he just been rescued from some appalling danger, so should he now thank his saviours? Or had he been brought in to answer some charge or other, and, if so, when would someone tell him what he had done wrong? Sensing from the sullen silence that the last scenario was the most realistic, hearing only the shuffling of feet on the carpet and the heavy breathing of the youths who had now drifted into the crowd of onlookers, he exhaled sharply and then asked, 'Anything wrong? Did someone want me?' There was no reply. 'Shân? What's the matter?' He could distinguish the shape of the girl, that she had moved away from her bar stool and was now over by the fireplace. 'Is it Phoebe? What's up?' And he walked towards her.

The girl said simply, 'Yes, it's fucking Phoebe. Take the fucking thing home.' She brushed past him to the bar again, which signalled the instant resumption of animated conversation from the entire party, as Andrew went quickly to where the dog was lying.

The renewed talking became a snigger which threaded its way through the room, in and out of every pocket of people, running from group to group like an electric current. Andrew knew why as soon as he knelt on to the hearth rug beside the dog. His knees sunk softly into a pool of slime which was still oozing from the dog, seeping like lava through the fine plume of her tail, a spreading pool of yellowish liquid excrement which the dog was unable to control. 'Hey, Phoebe,' he whispered down at her, and she managed to flick her tail in response, splashing it twice in the stinking hot mess. 'Phoebe, Phoebe, Phoebe . . .' eliciting a flap of the tail for each whisper of her name, 'hey, Phoebe . . .' and all he could do was to stroke her head and down her neck to her belly. There, when he touched her stomach, she snickered like a weasel, showing her teeth and starting her mournful wail. This provoked another current of sniggering. Andrew experienced a rush of anger right through his body, such as he had not felt since his humiliation by Jennifer. It provoked the same reaction.

His mind a blank, a pure white sheet which obliterated all reasoning and sense, he sprang up and flung himself at the crowd. From his mouth there spewed a stream of incoherent words, for he was too furious to frame anything intelligible but an outpouring of hisses and meaningless expletives, and he lunged at the blurred figure of the kennel-maid's brother, swinging the fist which had pole-axed Jennifer. The crowd surged around him, shouting and shrieking. His short-sightedness made a shifting shapeless mass of faces and limbs in front of him, one set of which (in contrast to Jennifer's crumpling at his single blow) now retaliated with a series of accurate jabs to his chest and stomach and including a stinging impact on his ear which made his head reel, until he was separated from the mob by more pairs of restraining hands. And there beside him, as Andrew stood heaving and trembling, quite unable now either to speak or think while his rage subsided and was replaced by shame, there was the round white face of the girl, very close to his, working and mouthing and writhing as she spat her invective at him. He understood not one word of it. He simply heard her hissing, guttural noises, noises, not words as far as he was concerned, and he watched the hostility in her eyes and on the sharp edges of her lips. As he watched her and listened, while the rest of the room seemed to fade into a distant irrelevant background of smoke and sweat and jabbering laughter, he was again helpless to control the lovely lovely caving of his stomach at the flickering wetness of her tongue . . . Before he knew what he was doing, still unhinged by the events of the past two minutes, he found himself ducking down and forwards and clamping his open mouth on to hers. For a second his tongue was on her lips, it ran across the smooth slipperiness of her teeth and then it joined her tongue and slid with it for what seemed like a timeless limitless moment . . . She shoved him away. More hands clutched at his elbows. The room was deafening with shrieks of laughter and outrage. The girl leapt from him, her face agog as though she had been struck, and she glanced down her legs with disgust to see that some of the slime from Andrew's knees had been transferred to her jeans. There was ink on her face too, from Andrew's face. Andrew, in the midst of all this chaos of shouting and slime, engulfed by the mayhem of flying fists and that sudden pain when his ear was punched, his head reeling with lust, his mouth inflamed with the taste of the kennel-maid's tongue, managed to catch a glimpse of his reflection in the glass of a painting above the fireplace and was jolted back to reality . . . for his efforts at washing away the ink and the shoe-whitener had succeeded only in mixing the two together into a filthy grey blur. He looked more like a fiend by accident than he had done by design. This sight revived him to action. He pushed the girl to one side and strode back to Phoebe. The dog had been stimulated by the confusion, enough to have got to her feet and practised a few half-hearted barks, but she trembled at Andrew's rapid approach and in the embarrassment of her disgrace. Now she rolled quite deliberately on to her side and on to her back, offering her belly and splayed legs to the man. 'Get up, Phoebe!' he snapped. 'Come on, up you get! We're going . . .' To his annoyance and to the amusement of the onlookers, the dog would not stand up again. She lay there, her tail swinging through the congealing pool of slime, and she bared her teeth in a razor-edged snarl whenever Andrew bent to her. There was more general laughter. Mrs Stone, who must have watched everything helplessly from behind the bar in the knowledge that it was best for her not to intervene on behalf of the young Englishman in case she should inflame national feeling, now raised her voice tremulously over the crowd. 'Just get the dog out! Go on, please get the thing outside! For heaven's sake, take the rug with you, but just get it all outside!'

Andrew suddenly bent again, flipped over the edges of the hearth rug so that the dog and the slime were enfolded like the contents of some exotic pancake, and he lifted the whole bundle from the floor. Phoebe squirmed and snarled, but he gripped her tight in her straitjacket. She could not get free. He marched like this to the door, which he was unable to open with his arms full, where he turned to the girl. She was standing stunned and expressionless, as though drugged by the effect of Andrew's kiss. 'Open this for me, Shân.' She obeyed. Saying nothing more, looking at no one except the girl and the bruises of smudged lipstick on her mouth, he stepped from the room and strode out of the hotel.

There, on the gravelled drive, his heart and head and especially his ear pounding from the last few minutes' uproar, he stood still.

Over and over, he inhaled long draughts of cold air. The dog lay motionless in his arms, buried in the rug. From within the hotel, the noises of the people who had witnessed an extraordinary fracas built up to a layer of rumblings and chatter, punctuated, as Andrew had anticipated, by the inevitable crowing of the cockerel. This time, however, as Andrew walked away down the drive, someone cut short the cockerel. The last sounds he could hear while he crunched through the shadows of the horse-chestnuts were voices raised angrily in argument, male and female, boy and girl in a dispute which silenced the rest of the room.

'Down you go, Phoebe. I'm not carrying you all the way

home.' At the foot of the drive, where he turned along the road through the village and past the shop, Andrew stopped and put the bundle down. The dog was absurd, her head only appearing from the folds of the rug, her eyes wide and white with embarrassment and fear. She was trembling violently. At first she would not move when he opened the rug, but she lay as she had done in the hotel: her stomach exposed as if expecting a caress, her teeth exposed as if expecting an attack, her tail twitching through the drying stickiness of the slime. The smell of the mess came hot and sweet from the rug as Andrew unfolded it. 'Jesus, Phoebe! Get off there. Come on, let's go home . . .' But still she lay back, distorting her muzzle into a mask of wrinkled snarls, issuing the chain-saw threat. 'Bloody hell!' he shouted at her, and the words clanged along the avenue of chestnut trees. One of the frozen horses started stumbling from shadow to shadow, a massive prehistoric creature moving in a dream, a fossil which had come back to life at the sound of the man's shout. 'For Christ's sake!' And he picked up one corner of the rug, yanking it so sharply that the dog was pitched from it on to the gravel. He screwed the rug into a bundle again so that the mess was folded inside. Phoebe limped painfully away from him, her tail wrapped tightly under her legs, her ears drooping. She arched her back as she went, obviously in some discomfort, and the effect was to make her look utterly craven, whipped and wretched. If Jennifer could see you now, Phoebe . . . he caught himself thinking, with your snarls and your stink and your slinking, grovelling . . . But he joined her on the road, and together, side by side, the man matching his pace to that of the sick dog, they began to walk from the village.

Away from the brightness of the hotel's floodlights, they followed the insignificant light from the torch which Andrew had brought with him. They crossed the bridge over the river, they followed the track through the trees which grew at the waterside. The moon was not so bright now. A shoal of grey clouds had swum across the sky. The air was still, and everything in the valley was quiet save for the slapping of the man's wellingtons and the hesitant footsteps of the dog. What had happened in the hotel, the dog's disgrace, the brawl, his tongue on the girl's tongue, his face disfigured with ink, their exit with the dog wrapped in the hearth rug . . . it all seemed impossible, incredible, the disjointed fragments of some ridiculous dream! It was the hallucination of a junkie or the delirium of an idiot! Especially now, in the muted moonlight and the stillness of the muffling clouds, he could hardly credit the events of the evening with any degree of reality. Had he imagined the whole thing? Was the entire episode a dream? If so, not just this evening, a couple of hours of folly, but maybe everything he had found in Wales! Was Wales a hallucination? What was happening to him? Was he dreaming the corpse of the badger in the woodshed, its adamantine grin? Perhaps, in reality, he was lying in a hospital in Sussex, enmeshed in the heat of a fever, delirious with dreams . . . dreams of a forest so black and clinging that he could not escape its clutches, of a crater so thick with mist that only the sounds of ravens and hounds came clanging from its walls, of a flock of lunatic females which pursued him with their bleating voices and staring eyes . . . Was there really such a cottage as his, sweltering in damp, its walls oozing a kind of sweat which rotted everything? Or was it a part of his fever? And finally, the most ludicrous of all the images which had come to haunt him, was there really a gallery of phallic fungi on the mantelpiece, to taunt him with the effortlessness of their erections? Was he dreaming the stinkhorn?

Another whiff of the rug he was carrying convinced him

that he was wide awake and quite sober. It acted like a draught of smelling-salts, to jolt him back to reality. There was the dog in front of him, moving more easily and increasing her pace with the idea that she was returning to the sanctuary of her basket after her hours in the unfamiliar scents and noises of the hotel. She had unfurled her tail from under her belly and was holding it aloft once more. He would have to do something about cleaning the rug and then return it to Mrs Stone, probably with the accompaniment of a box of chocolates or a bunch of flowers. In any case, as he stumbled after the wavering beam of the torch, as he tried to keep up with the dog, he was without his glasses. In the skirmish in the toilets, they had remained where he had put them down to wash his face, between the taps of the basin. The sooner he washed the rug and went humbly back to the hotel, to beg forgiveness of Mrs Stone, the sooner he would have his glasses again. 'Hold on, Phoebe, take your time,' he called out, but she hurried up the hillside, only occasionally turning to see that the man was following. Soon, there was the white shape of the cottage before them, illuminated now and then when the moon succeeded in lancing the cover of the clouds. The cottage cast a ghostly light of its own, somehow luminous in spite of the surrounding shadows. Behind it there reared the pitch-black mantle of the forest and the stark ridge of the mountain, sharply defined against the remaining glow of the sky. Somewhere there, Andrew knew, was the crater, a closed world of wet slabs, mists and bogs and the metallic clacking of jackdaws. With a shiver, he quickened his pace. Slipping, misjudging the path, cursing the absence of his glasses, he continued now that Phoebe had vanished, and when he panted up to the door of the cottage, she was there, looking up at him and waiting to be let in. He flung down the rug first of all, securing it on the grass in front of the building by placing two heavy stones on it, before unlocking the door. Phoebe went directly to her basket and lay down. Andrew stepped out of his boots and sank into an armchair, without turning on the lights, to sit for a while in the darkness.

As he had hoped, the fire was still burning. The hot coals glowed golden. But he did nothing to revive the flames until he had recovered his breath after the pace and the unevenness of the walk home. It was not late, about eleven o'clock.

Home? He had thought of the cottage as home just then because it felt safe and cool, as the hotel toilets had done before he was wrestled back into the bar. The cottage was quiet and private after the tumult of the evening. Phoebe, by now at any rate, hurried back to its haven. She recognised it as her refuge even if only for the familiar smells of her own basket. But for Andrew the cottage was a long way from home. He thought of his little bed-sitting-room in Newhaven, with warmth available at the turn of a switch, with his books and pictures surrounding him and not in the least danger of disintegrating with the damp, with the car parked conveniently in the street outside, just a few paces from his front door, ready to be driven away without the need to bump and jostle along a rutted track . . . That was home, in Newhaven, not far from the office where he was a trusted young articled clerk with a good future as a provincial solicitor, where he had a company car and might one day have a wife like Jennifer . . . That was home for Andrew Pinkney. However, he'd stay in Wales a little longer yet, he thought as he stared into the blurred brightness of the fire, he'd stay because . . . because (and he realised this with a sudden clarity and obviousness he had not achieved before), because, of course, he had something to expiate. Yes, that was it! He sat up straight in the armchair, relieved to have understood himself. For a matter of weeks he had struggled with the worry of his impotence, as though that was his chief concern. But he was staying in Wales now, when he could easily pack up and drive down to Sussex again, because he wanted to atone for the guilt he must feel for striking Jennifer. He was not yet ready to return. In a naïve way, his ideas of guilt and expiation quite undeveloped in spite of his days and weeks and months as an informed spectator in Lewes magistrates' court, he wanted to feel he was being punished, that he was punishing himself, and then, only then, might he go back and present himself to Jennifer. Meanwhile, the business with the stinkhorn, that deliberate attempt to cultivate the erections he had been unable to promote in his grappling with Jennifer, would be one way to foster the feeling of atonement he was looking for. The jars on the mantelpiece would remind him hourly of the reason why he was in Wales, that he had done something awful for which he must repent. He had not been sent to Wales for a mere holiday.

Thinking this, deliberately fixing a clear picture in his mind of Jennifer's crumpling body that fraction of a second after he had hit her, he stood up and switched on the light. He went to the mantelpiece to inspect the jars. One of the stinkhorn eggs had split right across. The soft shell was ruptured, and inside Andrew could see the bulging head of the fungus as it started to thrust its way upwards. Splendid! Splendid! he thought, smiling broadly his friendly old labrador smile, here was something to spectate through the hours of the night, as midnight fast approached on Hallowe'en . . . And then tomorrow, if all was developing in the woodshed as he hoped, as the badger was bursting and ready to split with the seething soft fruit of the maggots, tomorrow or the following day he would progress to the next stage of the experiment: to gather the dull brown pupae from the sawdust of the woodshed floor, where many of them had already been lying for a week or more. Then there'd be handfuls of fine new meat-flies to feed on the evil-smelling slime which oozed from the erect stinkhorn and carry the spores to other jars which he would have prepared in readiness. More flies to defecate the transmitted spores of the stinkhorn, more burgeoning stinkhorn eggs, more phallic fungi to adorn his mantelpiece and perhaps to be taken back to Sussex as a gift of atonement to Jennifer . . .

Perhaps, perhaps, perhaps, thought Andrew. See how it goes. The experiment might not work at all. The stinkhorn might wilt and slither like slugs down the insides of their jars. He was not a serious mycologist. He was just an enthusiast who wanted to explore a field of his own in order to impress a woman he had offended. Perhaps it would not work . . .

He saw to the fire. A quarter to midnight. He tipped on a little more coal from the coal-bucket, immediately eclipsing the heat and light of the dying embers and replacing them with a smooth curtain of blue smoke which puthered into the gullet of the chimney. It would soon burn up and generate some warmth. There were some logs in the basket, pieces of the mountain ash he had wheelbarrowed down the hillside, and he meant to place one or two of them on the fire when the fresh coal was ablaze. He switched on a table lamp and switched off the main light. He found some undemanding music on the radio. Before he sat down again, he studied the paintings on the wall above the mantelpiece. As for the watercolour landscapes, they were washed with banks of driving drizzle, almost completely clouded by the mists of condensation behind the glass so that only a suggestion of colour and definition was visible. Here in the quagmire of Wales, where everything was mouldy and warped by damp, even the bright frosts of Sussex were smothered. Phoebe's portrait was ambiguous: the eyes streamed tears, either of discomfort or embarrassment, yet from her jaws there dripped the white froth of a rabid pariah-dog. In real life, she was whimpering in her sleep, twitching like a spastic through some complicated dream. Andrew sat in the armchair. He too felt somehow restless as the minutes slipped by. A few timid flames were peeping from around the coals. He sat and wondered whether he also was changing, to what extent he was being altered by the suffocating atmosphere of this dank and clammy country. He sat and watched the jars. He got up, turned off the radio and sat down again. Then he imagined he could almost hear the tearing and splitting of a mucous shell, the ripping of soft fibres, the silent screams of a painful birth as the stinkhorn stirred and forced its head from the ruptured egg. He sat and he strained his ears, and he thought he could almost hear it.

The witching hour approached. He took a log of the mountain ash and put it among the bright new flames, with midnight only minutes away. 'Rowan tree or reed, put the witches to speed . . .' He whispered the old charm, just in time to protect him from all the evils which would rise like vapours and fumes from the blackness of the fir forest, to protect him from the rank and noisome things which would slither from the cauldron of the crater, to protect him from the stale spirits which would come wafting down the hillside behind the cottage like a stench from the tomb . . . With a smile and a delicious self-inflicted shudder, Andrew settled back deeper into the armchair. He glanced at his watch just as the mountain ash flared.

It was midnight.

And the next moment, the flames were extinguished. Andrew leapt to his feet as a heavy fall of soot cascaded from the chimney. It buried the fire. Clouds of thick choking smoke belched into the room. Springing from her basket, instantly awakened from the flickerings of her dream, Phoebe burst into peals of hysterical barking. More soot came down with a rattle and a rush, piling into the grate, overflowing on to the hearth and right across the carpet. Helpless to stop the room filling with smoke, helpless to stop the avalanche of stinking black dust, Andrew flapped his arms about his face. He cried out in a smothered, spluttering voice. The dog fled from corner to corner, whirling like a dervish. The fire flared again, it forced its flames through the dead layers of soot. And with the soot and the smoke, something else then fell into the fireplace, something alive and scratching and spitting, some live thing which was black and mad and shrieking, on fire with a rage to get out of the stinking flames. Horrified, man and dog stood suddenly still and watched the thing exhume itself from the grate. It screamed such a scream that only nightmares can conjure, before erupting into the room. Flapping and black and filthy, it beat from floor to ceiling and from wall to wall, adding its cracked and cracking voice to all the dirt which now settled around it.

The mad thing was a cockerel. With the subsidence of the smoke, Andrew and Phoebe acted together. The man strode swiftly to the door and flung it wide open, turning back into the room to switch on the main light: the brightness gave a ghastly blue-grey glare, reflecting and refracting through a million particles of soot which hung and drifted in the air. And the dog moved like a liquid shadow, slid between the furniture so quickly that she seemed to go through it, to snatch the cockerel's head in her jaws. There was a crunch, like the cracking of a walnut. She shook the bird violently from side to side by whipping her own head backwards and forwards. 'Christ, Phoebe!' the man shouted. But in spite of the shattering of its skull, the cockerel continued to scrabble with its strong claws, raking the dog's chest and throat, and the black wings beat a pall of soot as Phoebe tossed her prize like a piece of rag. 'Get out, Phoebe! Go on, out!' She snarled through her mouthful of juices and splintered bone, slipping out of the door ahead of his attempt at a kick. Disappearing through the clouds of smoke which were now drifting from the cottage, she was lost with the tangled corpse of the cockerel in the darkness of midnight.

He too hurried outside, in his stockinged feet. Footsteps, up on the low roof of the cottage? He spun round and peered up at the chimney. Slithering footsteps on the slates? Voices, muffled laughter, the clattering of boots on the guttering as someone scrambled down . . . 'Hey, what the hell are . . .? Who's there, for Christ's sake?' But he was slow and clumsy in the dark and on the unfamiliar ground, baffled by the absence of his glasses, stifled by smoke, disoriented by the soot, his head ringing with the shrieks of the cockerel and the crunch of its skull between the dog's jaws . . . He ran to the back of the building, his socks in the mud. 'What the hell do you think you're doing?' Someone jumped lightly from the roof, a single dark figure which clung momentarily to the drainpipe before wheeling and sprinting away from the cottage. 'Hey! You . . .!' But too fast, too agile for Andrew. He stood there, having stumbled from the light which fell from the front door, heaving with shock and anger in the billowing darkness. It had happened within a minute, one minute after midnight on Hallowe'en. The swift footsteps faded into the hillside, faded into silence. Andrew waited, panting. Naturally, as he nodded his head and grimaced at the stupid monotony of it, he could only listen as the night rang with the falsetto imitation of a cockerel, the falseness of it somehow more disturbing than the authentic shrieks of the real one had been. He shivered. 'Fuck off, you ignorant Welsh peasant!' he bellowed hoarsely. 'F. . .' Deciding not to shout it a second time, he exhaled the sound of the unfinished word like a long, damp fart. Muttering all manner of oaths against the natives of the country to which he had retreated, he squelched around the cottage and back to the front door. There was no sign of Phoebe, no sound of crackling bones. The cottage exhaled a fart of its own, in the form of a slowly shifting mushroom of smoke and soot which was gradually absorbed by the night. He stepped inside, to assess the extent of the mess.

The smoke had cleared. Even in his bemused myopic condition, Andrew could see the room in a kind of bleary focus. Sitting, or rather lying, in the armchair which he had vacated on the stroke of midnight, there was Shân, the kennel-maid. She sprawled her legs apart and dangled her arms loosely from the chair. From between her open thighs a slim green bottle stood up. Her eyes were closed, but hearing Andrew come into the cottage again, she smiled and put out her tongue in a cat-like snarl. She brought up her right hand to the neck of the bottle. Still snarling, with her tongue slipping round and round her lips, in and out of her little pointed teeth, she closed her fist on the bottle's neck and worked it slowly, rhythmically, up and down.

'Trick or treat, Pinkie?' she whispered, eyes closed, her hand massaging the bottle. 'The trick was my brother's idea. The treat will be on me . . .'

She lifted the bottle to her face. It was open, already half empty, and she ran her tongue wetly over the rim before inserting it deeply into her mouth, tipping the bottle up so that the wine overflowed on to her chin and ran down her neck. Having drunk, she continued to lick the neck of the bottle, pushing out her tongue to its full extent. Andrew could hear it slapping and clicking, as well as seeing its pink wetness. The girl opened her eyes and looked at him. She returned the bottle to her thighs. Once more she caressed it, a little faster than before, gripping a little harder, breathing noisily through her mouth.

'Come on, Pinkie,' she panted, 'you've had your fun with a cock tonight . . . It's my turn now . . .'

Wincing at the crass remark, he closed the door behind him. The room and everything in it was coated with a layer of fine soot. It hung in the air, a damp black cloud of condensation. He could see it on the pictures, on the mantelpiece, all over the carpet and on the furniture, it must be clinging to the curtains and all the wet walls of the clammy cottage. He moved across the room and switched off the main light. The girl was very drunk, her face puffy with alcohol. She was watching him, and when he turned off the light she held her breath, halting her friction of the bottle. He tended the fire. By now it was blazing furiously, burning up all the soot which had temporarily extinguished it, sparking and flaring with a renewed vigour. Kneeling on the blackened rug, he reached into the basket for another log of the mountain ash. Only then did he speak. He brandished the log in front of the girl's face, and once more he recited the charm which had failed at midnight. 'Rowan tree or reed, put the witches to speed . . . Are you a witch, Shân? Are you?' She smiled uneasily. Kneeling there, between her knees, he leaned forward and held the wood close to her face. She was still holding her breath. 'Put the witches to speed . . .' he whispered, and he turned back to the fire, placing the log tenderly among the flames. Both he and the girl watched as the log began to run with flickering golden tongues, while the room and all the soot in the air were lit by the shifting lights. Then, something buckling and caving in his stomach, his mouth dry just as the girl's was wet, he faced her again on his knees and took hold of her ankles.

'Now, the witching hour . . . and here we have a little wet witch, who's been falling over down by the river . . . She'll catch her death if she's not careful. Oh dear, oh dear, look at her little white shoes . . .' They were covered with thick wet mud, the laces were caked with it. Nevertheless, he unpicked them, the left foot and then the right, untied them and slipped her shoes off. 'And her little white socks too, soaking wet . . . Oh dear, oh dear, they'll have to come off as well.' The girl giggled nervously and took another swig from the bottle. While he peeled off her socks, he said, 'Don't I get any of that, you mean little witch?' and he drank from the bottle as she held it out to his mouth. Her feet were cold and very white. He took them one after the other and rubbed them hard. 'Falling over in the mud . . . yes, that's what she's been doing. Look at her trousers, covered with it. This witch has been drinking too much of the magic falling-down potion tonight . . .' Indeed, her jeans too were filthy with mud from the riverside track. 'Oh dear, oh dear . . .' but his mouth was dry again, in spite of the wine, 'let's see what we can do.' He knelt up higher, running a hand slowly up each leg, pausing at the knee, continuing, pressing harder, spreading his fingers over the tight material on her thighs, pausing again with his thumbs deep in her crutch, and up to the buckle of her belt. And this time, when he started to frame the next oh dear, he could say nothing. Only a dry croak came from his mouth.

'Lost for words, are we?' the girl hissed. She put down the bottle beside the chair. 'Yes, Pinkie, these jeans are a bit wet. Best get them off before I catch a chill . . .'

Andrew had already undone her belt. She raised her bottom from the chair, there was a gentle sigh as her zip parted, and with a wriggle she was peeling down her jeans, over her long long narrow white thighs, where Andrew took hold and slid them off her legs and from her feet. 'That's better, much better,' she whispered. 'Soon get warm again now . . .' and she sat forward on the edge of the chair with her legs splayed as wide as they could go while she wrestled herself out of her jacket and tugged the baggy blue sweater over her head. Andrew reacted as though he had been stung by a hornet, leaping to his feet. In the same time it took the kennel-maid to take off her jacket and pullover, he was rid of all but his shirt. Everything else was flung to the corners of the room. Hoarse with desire for the skinny unfinished child of a girl, he heard himself groaning, 'Come on, you pissed-up little Welsh witch-bitch! Get off that chair!' and he was pulling her by the wrist, down on to the rug in front of the fire. She squealed like a rabbit in the jaws of a fox, a half-yelp, half-giggle, and then they were grappling and tangling on the floor. In a moment, they were both grey with soot. Before Andrew tore it away, ripping it from the girl's bony shoulders, her blouse was blackened and streaked, then her bra was filthy with smuts in a few seconds until he wrenched it off, and as she writhed on the rug her knickers were blackened too. Andrew yanked the shirt from his back. Her knickers he peeled roughly down her legs. Laughing, shouting, they slapped their hands into the moist soot of the hearth rug and daubed each other with it. Andrew, his head blank with passion, roared like a camel and kneaded the girl with fistfuls of black dust. She shrieked, wriggling on her belly across the carpet to reach the bottle of wine, and returning, her body entirely caked with soot, her face and hair coated with it, she began to pour the wine on to Andrew. He yelped, he boomed, he snatched the bottle from her and splashed her and then the hearth with it. Now there was a paste instead of the dust, a black sludge of soot and wine which they scooped up, with it oozing like oil between their fingers, and they painted each other's body until man and girl were black and wet and glistening from head to toe. Still they squealed and roared, body to body, mouth to mouth, now on their knees, now standing and wheeling around the room, now with Andrew forced down and pinioned by the spread-eagled, soot-smeared limbs of the girl and feeling the long smoothness of her belly all wet against his, now with the girl snarling like a stoat on her back, her legs linked tightly round him, holding him in a sinewy grip . . . blacker and wetter they became, hotter and more tousled, until the girl lay outstretched on the rug, utterly pliant, her eyes wild with drink and the vigour of the game, her legs and arms sprawled wide apart.

Andrew bent to her, his mouth open and running from her mouth to her throat to her stomach and back again, wanting her with a lust which eclipsed everything else from his mind . . . 'Come on, Pinkie,' she snarled at him. 'Give the little witch-bitch what she wants . . .' He applied himself to her compliant body.

But not quite everything else was obliterated from his mind. Suddenly, so vividly that it seemed to be coming from just the other side of the room, he could hear laughter. Jennifer? The name flashed through his head. He twisted around to see, unable to stop himself from turning to look over his shoulder. There was nothing. Back to the girl again. 'Pinkie, oh come on, Pinkie . . . oh come on . . . yes . . .' and there, in front of him, like something from a nightmare, was the grotesquely blackened face of the kennel-maid. Even her teeth and her tongue were grey with soot, and she was moaning, her mouth wide open, 'Oh, Pinkie, please, please, Pinkie . . . oh you fucking bastard, Pinkie, come on . . .' He worked himself with her. But then he heard the laughter once more, clear and braying, Jennifer's laughter pealing round and round inside the echoing chambers of his head . . . Jennifer? Jennifer? His head was filled with it, he could not blot it out, the laughter rang louder, mocking, contemptuous . . . And he felt himself succumbing to it. The girl was panting, her face horribly distorted. She sweltered with sweat and soot and sweet white wine. 'Pinkie, come on, Pinkie ... you bastard, why can't you ...?' His body sagged on to hers, like a deflating Zeppelin. And then, with a shove of her hands on his shoulders, throwing him off her, she burst out, 'Christ, Pinkie! What's up, for fuck's sake?' She sat up and pulled the parts of her body back together again. 'Or, to be more precise, what isn't up ...?' He rolled away from her and stared at the ceiling, its sooty cobwebs. Fading now, as though it were receding down a long corridor, fainter and fainter until it was absorbed into a kind of ringing silence, Jennifer's laughter echoed through his mind ... Jennifer, Jennifer, Jennifer ... fading and fading into nothing but the emptiness of a memory, leaving his head quite blank again. Having come to him and then vanished a few seconds later, it abandoned him on the filth of a hearth rug, with only a smutty naked child to console him.

Fortunately for the kennel-maid, she did not feel inclined to laugh. Andrew lay there waiting, expecting her giggles. His stomach was heavy with the dread of what he might do if she laughed. She did not. With a great sigh of exhaustion, disappointment and drunkenness, she collapsed slowly backwards and lay flat out again on the rug. There was silence, man and girl lying side by side, naked, lit by the fire, their bodies black with soot. Silence for one minute. The girl's breathing became noisier, more regular. And when Andrew sat up to look at her, hoisting himself wearily on to one elbow, he was amazed to see that she was sound asleep.

'Little witch,' he whispered. 'Poor little witch-bitch ...' Dispassionately, he observed her body. Yes, she was a child. Her breasts were no more than buds, the nipples tiny and pink through the surrounding dirt. Her shoulders and hips and the contours of her pelvis were bony. 'Little girl, fast asleep ...' Once more, as he had done in the hotel, he felt the stinging of tears in his eyes, a rush of anger at the foolishness of it all: his soft big body caked with filth, his cock, heavy and limp like a soft fat maggot, the room in catastrophic disorder . . . What a disaster, he thought, the whole thing, from hitting Jennifer right through to the events of this manic evening! 'Stay asleep, you little witch,' he said. 'Best place for you, out of all this fucking mess!' Then, stung by the inappropriateness of his chosen adjective, angry and abject, he let the tears run down his face, feeling them crawl through the ink, the whitewash, the sweat, the soot. You're truly pathetic, Andrew Pinkney, he mouthed in silence . . . yes, you're big and strong, a capable and intelligent man with a good future and the use of a company car, but here you are sobbing over the body of a sleeping child . . . Shake yourself! Do something about it!

This is what he did. Not bothering to cover his own body, his own flabby nakedness quite irrelevant to him, he got up and went to the kitchen, where he switched on the kettle. In a couple of minutes he had a basin of hot water, soap and a sponge, and the softest towel he could muster from the mouldering contents of his bedroom cupboard. He knelt reverently beside the girl. Leaning across her, he gouged a little more life out of the coals, prodding the logs of the rowan to give another display of flames. In the firelight, it looked as though some disgusting torture had been practised on the girl and was about to be resumed, for her body, skeletal and black, appeared to have been burned, branded and charred by the naked man who once again loomed over her. But now she had slipped gratefully into the oblivion of unconsciousness. Andrew could tell from her breathing and the utterly wasted expression on her face that she was quite stupefied with drink. She would not wake up, he would not wake her as he worked with the water and sponge. Rubbing away the tears from his face, he began to wash the girl as best he could. He wanted to. Then at least she would wake up clean, however else she felt brutalised and misused. Starting from her feet, he wiped off the soot, smudging it and rinsing it away, tenderly coaxing it from between her toes. He poured a basinful of black water down the kitchen sink and came back with more clean water. Three times, four times he did this, sponging her legs white again. He dabbed the dirt from her thighs, soaped and stroked her nest of soft black hair, fearing, when she moaned and let her legs shift further apart, that she would wake up. He held his breath. But still she remained asleep, dreaming perhaps of some future lover who would be kind to her. More water, more soap. Soon she was clean, at least he had removed most of the soot from her body by turning her gently and even washing her back and her buttocks before letting her down on to another towel, and the final basin of water was for her face. How like a child she then was, not only cleansed of soot but of the make-up she had applied! He removed her lipstick, the smudges of eye-liner, and still she slept, breathing evenly through her mouth. He pushed back the hair from her face, and there she lay, as clean as he could have managed, no more a witch, but simply a half-formed adolescent. He raised her head and put a cushion there, he took one long last look at her white, angular body, and he covered her with two blankets, tucking them up to her chin. The fire flared suddenly, the mountain ash exhaling a final flourish of flames. ' . . . put the witches to speed . . .' he said to the embers of the rowan. 'No more witches tonight.' When he had poured away the last basinful of dirty water, he gathered the kennel-maid's clothes together and folded them on to the armcnair. They were filthy, but he could do nothing about that. She was asleep, quite clean, and in the morning would be sober.

Andrew wrapped himself in another blanket. Too tired to

sleep just then, he built up the fire and sat down by it, cross-legged on the rug. He still wanted to be close to the girl. Somehow, he wondered, washing her tenderly while she slept, cleaning every inch of her body and patting her dry was more satisfying than making love would have been. He knew more about her body this way. The washing was a far more intimate thing than mere sex. Because she had been asleep, that was why. Because, in silence, in the hush of such a deep sleep that every muscle in her body was limp and loose, he had been allowed to mould her with his hands, slowly, gently, with respect. And then to wrap her in a warm blanket, to see that the fire was burning satisfactorily. Tending to her had given him a feeling of relief that no orgasm could ever have done. The skirmish with Jennifer, all that grunting and frantic undressing for the sake of their gratification on the sofa! His lunatic grappling in the sludge of soot and wine with this little kennel-maid! What a farce, compared with the simple actions of fetching water and ministering to the sleeping girl on the firelit rug . . .

Andrew might almost have managed to convince himself, as he pursued this line of thought and studied the features of the girl. He might almost have succeeded in diminishing in his own mind the significance of another humiliating failure. But his eyes wandered from the girl's face. His stare moved upwards, from the hearth, past the fire, up to the mantelpiece. And there in front of him was the starkest reminder of what he had failed to achieve.

The second stinkhorn was erect. It had burst from the egg since midnight, thrust its head from the ruptured shell, and was now standing up in the jar, some five or six inches tall. It was a perfect phallus. The column, an inch thick, was white, unblemished by any stain or split, and the bulging head was covered by an oily slime, black and green, not unlike the slime of soot which Andrew and the girl had smeared on their bodies. And, seeing it there on the mantelpiece, not detached from him as the stinkhorn had seemed to be in the shadows of the forest, but before him in the sitting-room of the cottage like an ornament or a fashionable conversation piece, he felt it was inescapable. He could not take his eyes from it. It reared up and mesmerised him, as powerfully as if it were a cobra and he were a mouse.

In its effortlessness, its arrogance, its brazen lewdness, the stinkhorn sneered at him and said, 'Look at me, Andrew Pinkney, and compare your flaccid maggot of a cock with mine!' It said, 'You caught my stink in the softness of Sussex, but you weren't interested then, were you? Now you've come to the drizzling black forests of Wales and entombed me on your mantelpiece, like a party-trick for a party which never happened! Will you stand up and be a man, Andrew Pinkney, or will you mope like a fat white maggot, soft and limp and full of pus? Will you ever be like me, the stinkhorn? I doubt it! You know, the Germans call me "*Hirschbrunst*", which means "the rutting of stags", for they imagine I grow from the spilled seed of an urgent copulation . . . Yes, Pinkie, "rutting"! Will you ever rut like a stag? I doubt it! Look at yourself, your flaccidity, your sagging, your wilting, your craven drooping! And then some people call me "the woodwitch". A lot of good that did you, didn't it, Pinkie? To have me on your mantelpiece, a woodwitch erect and pulsing and dripping with seed, and to have a little Welsh witch-bitch come panting to your fireside, on heat, her mouth open and her legs open, just begging for the kind of rutting I'm famous for . . . and what happened? You play a dirty game on the hearth rug and then you leave the bitch still panting for something you couldn't give her! She's asleep! Yes, look at her, asleep! She's asleep, Pinkie, because she's more likely to find her rutting in a dream than with your maggot between her legs! No, Andrew Pinkney, you'll never be like me, the stinkhorn, the woodwitch, the spurted seed of a stag, *Phallus impudicus*, however long you manage to keep me prisoner. You can try, you can cultivate as many dead things as you like in your woodshed, you can hang whatever corpses you want on those meat-hooks and cull a million dung-flies from them, and you can imprison me in this jar. But I'll always haunt you . . . always! You might even take me with you back to Sussex and flaunt me to that other bitch you left panting . . . She didn't get her rutting either, did she? Unless she's getting it now, while you're in Wales! No, Andrew Pinkney, you can keep me prisoner and spectate my itches, but you'll never be like me! Never, never, never . . .'

In this way, the stinkhorn spoke to him. He pulled the blanket tightly around his shoulders, for he felt a sudden chill in spite of the rowan which burned fiercely on the fire, and he was hypnotised by the phallus he had trapped in the jar. He continued to sit and watch. It was impossible to appreciate the passing of time as he gazed at the thing's luminous white column and its oozing head. From the holes he had pierced in the jar's cap there rose the stinkhorn's unmistakable perfume, the stench of decomposing flesh; it drifted to his nostrils and quite eclipsed the resinous scents of the burning wood. Hours must have gone by. Only when he saw that the phallus was leaning a little, imperceptibly at first and then he was sure of it, when its head began to sag until it rested against the side of the jar, only then did he break its spell over him. The stinkhorn, reared so quickly in the heat and dampness of the room, was wilting just as fast. Andrew moved painfully from the position he had maintained for so long. Yes, it was over, the fungus was discoloured and moist, slithering slowly down the glass and leaving a trail of slime like a snail's. The girl had not moved.

She was sound asleep, breathing regularly. He went to the sofa, too dirty to go to bed and too tired to wash himself, where he lay down and buried himself deep inside the blanket. In seconds, he too was asleep.

He dreamed once more that he was pursued through the forest by a flock of bleating manic sheep. There was always the crashing of undergrowth, the breaking of brittle branches as he stumbled to stay ahead of them. The awful panic of being chased by something more powerful and less rational than oneself gripped him, he could almost feel the hot and fetid breath of the animals which closed behind him. Everything was blurred. And this time, the sheep which led the pursuit, the one with the black face and the gaping white sockets where the eyes should have been, was a horrifying caricature of the kennel-maid and of Jennifer: that is, when it stamped and lunged at him from the shadows of the trees, there was something about its face that he had seen in the soot-blackened and sweat-smeared features of the girl, combined with the earnest seriousness of the blue-stocking which was Jennifer. When he awoke, he was weary from being asleep. The dream, the pursuit of the mad sheep-woman, had drained him. He felt as though he had really been racing over rocks and through bracken, for his limbs ached when he shifted under the dampness of the single blanket. It was light. He peered from the sofa. He sat up painfully.

The girl had gone. The blankets and the towel where she had been lying had been slung on to the armchair where he had folded her dirty clothes. She must have got up and dressed while her bestial equivalent was harrying Andrew through his dream. Phoebe was in her basket. The girl must have found her waiting outside when she left, she must have let the dog in. Phoebe unwound herself from the basket and slunk slowly across the room, seeing that Andrew was awake, to push her face into his outstretched hand, as she had always used to do. He caught the smell of her warm fur, mingled with the damp and the sweet scent of the slime which had dried among the tangled hair of her tail. She sat by the sofa and submitted to his fondling, torpid from sleep and from her night outside with the splintering bones and the scattered feathers of the cockerel. The room was smudged all over with soot, a fine layer of it which coated everything. On the hearth, the congealed mess of the wine and soot paste was matted into a pattern of handprints and fingermarks, the daubed signatures of himself and the kennel-maid who had painted each other's bodies in a frenzy of lust.

Sitting up, he pulled back the blanket and inspected his body. He was entirely blackened. There was something quite primitive in his dispassionate appraisal of his body and of the room . . . a primitive man who saw around him the evidence of a night's ancient ritual, the oldest and most important ritual of all, that of the mating of male and female, the union of the two beasts for the transmission of seed. He might just as well have been a caveman in his cave, for all the trappings were there around him: he was naked and black, in the way that cavemen are depicted in school history books; he was emerging from under his blanket with a head full of dreams of the hunt, in the way that cavemen would dream; his abode was a place of sooted walls of rock which ran with moisture and where everything had been touched by the smoke of the previous night's fire; there were strange daubings, the imprints of a man's hand and a woman's hand near where the fire had been, as though a record had been left to commemorate their coupling, as though it were important to leave a mark as evidence of the act; and here was the caveman's dog, coming to his side after a night spent crunching bones and spitting feathers . . .

Yes, Andrew Pinkney, he thought . . . so it's come to this. Only a few weeks ago you were an articled clerk in Sussex, with all the trappings associated with that status and that place. And now you're a caveman on a Welsh mountain, where smoke and soot and sweat and blood are the essential ingredients of your lifestyle. But, Andrew Pinkney, there was one thing missing from last night's ritual, wasn't there? After all the heathen rites and the hoo-ha, after the dancing in the firelight, after the painting of the flesh, after the sacrifice of a cockerel in the flames and in the teeth of another beast . . . after all of that, there wasn't any transmission of seed, was there? You didn't manage the most important part of the entire rigmarole, did you? You missed the point of the whole complicated performance! All that ritualised foreplay, which men and women have been practising since they were living in caves on this same hillside some ten thousand years ago, the celebrations of fertility, the worship of the phallus . . . and what happens? Nothing. Nothing happens. The man and the woman go to sleep. That's all that happens.

He stood up from the sofa. Pulling back the curtains, he saw another morning of grey drizzle, with the fields and the mountains all but obliterated by a dense drenching mist. He wrapped the blanket closely round his shoulders and shuffled to the hearth. The second stinkhorn, which had taunted him through the night with its luminous erection, had collapsed into a jelly and now resembled nothing more than a gobbet of phlegm which an old man had spat on to a pavement. In the remaining two jars, the eggs were unaltered. Their hours of lewdness were still to come. And Andrew determined to be ready for them. He would not simply spectate the next time. He would not be hypnotised into a stupor of envy and shame. He would promote the transmission of spores. He would sire a new generation of stinkhorn, set the flies buzzing into the jars, to gorge on the dripping seeds of the phallus . . . The slogan ran through his head: save the stinkhorn, save the stinkhorn, save the stinkhorn . . .

And the sibilance of it was echoed in the sighing of the drizzle, it was whispered in the blowing of the mists which wrapped themselves more closely around the cottage.

V

There was work to be done that morning, the first of November.

Andrew switched on the immersion heater. In one hour's time, there would be enough hot water for a bath. He opened the front door. Phoebe went outside into the slow rain, sniffing long and deep into the grass and searching out the remains of the cockerel she had killed and eaten that night. She disappeared behind the cottage. Having dressed in the dirtiest clothes he could find, covering the foolishness of his filthy body, Andrew set about cleaning the room. He shook out the rugs, he boiled water in the kettle, he filled basin after basin and washed down the walls, he knelt by the hearth and wiped away the encrusted soot. When he took down the pictures and cleaned them, he revealed squares of whiter wall which still had been scored by rivulets of condensation and the silt of soot they had carried. Every corner was infiltrated by the black cloud. The few books were grey, they coughed a sooty cough when he riffled their pages. The curtains were sweaty with damp soot, as though an exhausted miner had used them to wipe down his aching body. Andrew shook them vigorously, he shook out the blankets which he and the girl had used, again and again he wiped up the settling dust with more and more clean water, and when he thought there was nothing else he could do apart from actually hosing the walls and the ceiling and floor, he ran the vacuum cleaner over and over the carpet, over the rugs, over the furniture, until he switched it off and stepped outside for the peace and coolness he suddenly wanted. He needed air, clean, sharp, fresh air.

Standing in front of the cottage, a hot man streaked with blackened sweat, he inhaled deeply and felt the drizzle settle like a cold kiss on his forehead. His glasses . . . he was missing his glasses. And there was something else yet to be cleaned. Rumpled on the grass, there was the rug which Phoebe had soiled in the hotel. Swearing through his gritted teeth, he attacked it with another basin of soapy water, melting away the congealed scabs of slime, dissolving the knots of matted material and finally dousing the rug with a concentrated solution of disinfectant. He did all this in the driving mists. He knelt on the grass and scoured the rug while the rain clung around him, a suffocating silver cobweb of drenching drizzle. Why was there no air, even here, outside the cottage? Why couldn't he simply breathe a breath of fresh air, without swallowing a mouthful of water? Was there any air in Wales, for Christ's sake? Or was it a straight choice of soot and dust inside, mist and drizzle outside? He cursed the country he had come to, where there were mountains and forests and waterfalls which were acclaimed worldwide in the tourist brochures but which, for the most part, were entirely obscured by smothering cloud. As far as he could tell (and the cottage was supposed to enjoy one of the best vantage points in the county), Wales was nothing more than one dense billowing cloud of wet mist which shifted in a wet wind, changing shape in the aimless gusts of drizzle, but always a cloud. Save for the square bulk of the cottage behind him, there was nothing else solid to be seen. There was no mountain, no crater, no forest. There was no air. He felt as though his head and his lungs were being drowned under a mass of damp cotton wool.

He left the rug lying on the grass. Inside the cottage his impression of being suffocated was intensified in the bathroom. Having turned off the immersion heater and run the bath, he stepped out of his dirty clothes. The bathroom was the same cloud of wet mist he had left outside, except that it was warm. The air swarmed with droplets, he saw them swirling when he exhaled, he saw them flutter when he breathed in. It was a thick bank of steam which engulfed him, which wrapped its folds around him, which forced its vapours into his nostrils and filled his whole head with a white fog. He felt the weight of the moisture on his lungs. Within seconds of sinking into the water, it was grey with soot. He fell back, plunged his head into the hot grey water, lay there, immersed, to listen to the rumblings and the cries and the whistling of his own ears. He sat up and blew like a manatee, soaping himself time and again until his flabby flesh was shining white once more, he clambered to his knees and soaped every crevice of his body to be clean of the sweat and the wine and the soot in which he had revelled with the witch who had come to him on Hallowe'en. He felt better, much better, with every smear he rubbed from his skin. The caveman was being stripped and scoured of his primitive daubings! he thought. In this way, he was returning to the twentieth century! But when he surged out of the bath, standing up like a god from the black water, all glistening with soap, he inspected himself in the mirror and found that some vestiges of the night's debauch remained . . . he still had most of the goatee beard and its sinister moustache, there were streaks of ink around his eyes, and a trickle of red ran from the corner of his mouth. He scrubbed his face with a nail-brush until the skin was sore, managing to fade the stark lines of black, but still there remained a smudge of grey, like a bruise or a birthmark around his chin and his eyes. Short of continuing until he drew blood with the bristles of the brush, there was nothing more he could do. For another day or two, he would carry the stigma of his Hallowe'en disguise, the mark of the vampire he had tried so clumsily to imitate.

Air! He had to get some air, or else he would smother! Dressing quickly in the living-room, he saw that it was as steamed and clammy as ever, perhaps there was even more condensation on the walls and on the pictures after his efforts with the soap and hot water. He gave no more than a glance to the jars on the mantelpiece. For the time being, his priority was to flee the cottage on its invisible hillside as fast as possible, to find somewhere to breathe for a few hours. The more he thought about it, the heavier the weight of the mist seemed to press him down and hamper his movements. He was being crushed by the pressure of the cloud. There was only one place to flee to, where he was hopeful of finding some air which was not too thick and wet to breathe . . . The sea-shore! He had been there before and promised himself another visit, to the estuary near Caernarfon. Now that he and the cottage were clean again, he would quit the hills for the afternoon.

When he shouted her name, Phoebe ran around to the front door. She had a few black feathers in her teeth. Andrew pulled them from her and she trotted away, spitting some morsel of sinew or gristle from her mouth. Watching her, he saw the caked fur of her tail and this confirmed his decision to go to the coast, where the dog would get a good salt soaking by chasing sticks in and out of the sea. He remembered too how he had found the remains of a bird already in the chimney, when he had first lit the fire some weeks before. Was that a cockerel as well? Was his employer aware of the spelling error he had emblazoned on the cottage, and had he already had the cockerel trick played on him during the summer? Was it the idiot Huw, the kennel-maid's brother, who had put that other bird down the chimney? Most likely, if he had tried it one night in the summer when the solicitor and his family had been there, the bird had just jammed in the blocked chimney and the occupants of the misnamed cottage had remained oblivious of the practical joke. The idiot's trick must have gone unnoticed. At least this time the joker had had the satisfaction of seeing Andrew emerge from the cottage, coughing and spluttering, had seen the dog spring out with the wreckage of the cockerel in her jaws, and had enjoyed the triumph of his crowing. Would he ever know what his little sister had done as an encore to his surprise? 'Come on, Phoebe, let's get out of here for a while.' Andrew followed the dog down the track to where he had left his car, a little lower down the hillside. Without his glasses he would have to drive slowly and carefully, but he had to go somewhere to breathe even if it meant a myopic journey along unfamiliar roads. He would return to the hotel only when he had finally removed all the ink from his face, in a day or two, when the rug was dry; meanwhile, he had packed it around the water tank in the cottage. Only then would he take the rug back and reclaim his glasses, and apologise to Mrs Stone.

As he splashed with the car across the flooded bridge at the foot of the hillside, when he saw the river overflowing the bridge in one smooth silken wave, he decided exactly where he would go to clear his head that afternoon. He would follow the river to its estuary. It seemed a neat idea that, just as he was determined to ease the pressure of water which was building up around him from the engulfing wetness of his surroundings, he should see exactly where all that water disappeared, exactly where the swamp that was Wales emptied eventually into the sea. He would take pleasure in watching the water drain out. It would feel to him as though he were opening some sort of safety valve in his head and releasing the weight of the water which had built up. Once he reached the road and was facing towards Caernarfon, he paused and pulled out the map which his employer had lent him for his stay in the cottage. It was the first time he had bothered to look at it, so seldom had he been out in the car. 'Let's see then, Phoebe. Where are we?' The dog sprang on to his lap in answer to his question, concerned only that they were on an expedition which might culminate in a walk or a swim. Perhaps she too was relieved to escape the clammy folds of the mountain's mist. Pushing her away while he consulted the map, grimacing at her smell, he read that they had just forded the river Gwyrfai near the village of Salem. He ran a finger along the snaking line until it came to the sea. Foryd Bay . . . that was the estuary of the bulging river, that was where the unbearable weight of the water slid to sea. That was where these mountains and this valley shed their load of water.

*

It was midday when they arrived at their destination. The sky cleared as Andrew drove from the hills. In the distance, across the Menai Straits, the island of Anglesey stretched flat and green and handsome . . . To Andrew it was a refreshing view of a piece of England which had somehow become attached to the slimy grey slabs of Wales. He swung the car through the lanes to the south of Caernarfon. There were high hedges and lusher, more even fields now that they came closer to the coast. More and more like England, he thought, as the weight of the mountains and the blackness of the forest seemed to lift from him . . . less and less like Wales. Ahead of him, a glimpse of the sea was as brief and as exhilarating as the flash of a trout's belly in a green pool. He felt his spirits lifting with every mile. The air was cold and clear, it blustered through the open windows of the car with the tang of salt in it, it blew away the festoons of fusty cobwebs which had hung in Andrew's head. Phoebe yelped like a fox, standing on the passenger seat and furiously flagging her tail. Closer and closer to the coast they travelled. The lanes became narrower. They passed a few fields of caravans, and even they seemed neat and white and clean, gloriously suburban, splendidly English! How civilised, he thought, that all these people had come from cities like Chester and Shrewsbury and even from Cheltenham with their fresh little caravans and their well-maintained saloon cars, just for a fortnight before returning to their suburban existence! The sky was such a pale blue as to be practically white, a clear and luminous sky like a new fall of snow. The mountains were behind him, he could make out their clinging fog with a glance in his mirror, but ahead there was only the last flat fields of the coastal farms, a few more twists in the high-banked lanes, a glimpse of crisp black and white cows in a green meadow, and suddenly the expanse of the sea spread silver and smooth to an invisible horizon . . . Marvellous, marvellous, marvellous! . . . the word rang over and over in Andrew's head. Phoebe whirled and leapt beside him, her voice cracked with pleasure. At the first opportunity, now that the road turned and ran parallel to the beach, he stopped the car. Phoebe was out before he could unfasten his seat belt. She bolted from the car, black and furious and alive with the scent of salt and seaweed, haring across the shingle to the water's edge. He struggled from the car, into a coat and wellingtons, locked up and looked around for his first appraisal of the coast.

The tide was going out. Acres of glistening wet sand stretched to the sea. In spite of Phoebe's noisy arrival, flocks of waders speckled the shoreline, scores of curlew and redshank and dunlin and knot; they rose and shifted in a series of flickering clouds, moving from flat to flat and settling again. There were oystercatchers, determined that neither their voices nor their feeding grounds should be yielded to the dog, for they piped as furiously as she yelped, returning to the sands in a black and white whirl of confetti as soon as she had scampered on and left her delicate footprints where the birds' beaks had been probing. Turnstones lived up to their name with commendable seriousness, prising over the pebbles of the foreshore, shaking out strands of weed for the countless sand-hoppers and sea-spiders which burrowed there. There were a few ringed plovers, moving with the pipits and almost as inconspicuous, there were dozens of starlings which had matched their colour to the predominant browns of the boulders and weed, and there were gangs of carrion crows working the waterline for a morsel among the flotsam and jetsam. The crows rose time and time again with a mussel in their beaks, to drop it on to the rocks and smash it open, and then they floated down like rags to jemmy the cracked shell. They were burglars, beachcombers, scavenging ruffians, and Andrew loved to watch them. He followed the dog. He went crunching across the shingle and scuffed his boots into the line of scum which the sea had deposited, mostly plastic bottles and the sodden remains of wooden crates tumbled together with weed. Millions of insects wriggled in the rotting vegetation. No other people were there on the beach, no other dogs. Under the white sky which shone the sea silver and made the sands as bright as glass, the man and his dog walked and breathed as they had not breathed for weeks. Phoebe dashed wildly in and out of the sea. Andrew inhaled until he felt his lungs ache with their scouring of salt. Marvellous! He was renewed, invigorated. A weight was lifted from him. His face went pink, flushed with a fresh pumping of blood which nearly suffused even the smudges of grey ink, and his eyes smarted short-sightedly as he gazed into the glare of the air and sea-water. Marvellous!

Sure enough, they came to the estuary of that river, whose name he had forgotten. It was a disappointment. Nothing much more than a trickle ran from a brackish drain, feeling its way through a maze of marsh grass which crackled and popped as the mud dried out, and then the river was consumed by the sea. Was that it? Where was all that water which drained from the crater and coursed down the sides of the valley? Where was the water which glistened on every slab, which dripped from every branch, which squelched under every boot, which found its way through the walls and the roof of the cottage? Here, all that water was swallowed into a marsh of muddy creeks and spiny grass . . . And, as though to remind him of what he had left behind in the hills, there was a smell of staleness which rose from the estuary. Something sweet and rotten had been washed down the valley and brought up here. What was it? He glanced back to the beach which he and the dog had come crunching over, where there were curlew, elegant and wise and exquisitely mirrored in the polished sand . . . He looked at the phantasmal flights of knot which flickered and faded and flickered in fidgeting flocks . . . He watched the oystercatchers shuffle themselves like a conjuror's card-trick . . . All of these things under a white sky, in air which was clean and sharp, where the mists of the stale mountains could not reach . . . and still his mouth was touched with a taste of something rotten. Even here, in his nostrils there clung a whiff of something past its best. That line he had traced with his finger, so neat and innocent on the map, connected him with the stinks he had tried to leave behind. He had not escaped them after all. There was no pleasure to be had in seeing the river absorbed into the greater mass of the sea, because the river carried its own taint to the very end.

Something was dead in the river. The man and the dog could smell it.

The expression on Phoebe's face changed as drastically as it had changed on the painting in the cottage. Her yelps and grins, the bobbing of her plumed tail, all the exuberance she had let loose by dashing in and out of the sea, altered now that she was close to the mouth of the river. She curled her tail tightly between her legs. She skulked at Andrew's heels, and when he reached down to touch her head she bridled from him and started up her buzzing high-pitched snarl, contorting her face into a mask of teeth and snickering lips. Some smell, some stench had reached her. It reminded her of the thing which the man had hung in the woodshed, that grinning thing which swung and stank on the meat-hook. Something else was dead close by. It was not just the river and the refuse it bore with it to spew into the sea . . . Some dead thing was nearby, oozing its vapours of putrefaction as an advertisement for death. The dog hunched her back. Again she spun from the man's proffered hand, she bared her teeth at it as though the hand were the source of the smell. Andrew sniffed the air. The rankness of the slow river and its standing pools of brackish water was in his nostrils. He inhaled, turning his face this way and that, trying to pinpoint the direction from which that stronger, riper scent was blowing, until he saw five or six crows beat upwards from the depths of a creek, from where they had been hidden by mudbanks and marsh grass. They cartwheeled away like cinders in the wind, calling hoarsely as they flapped from the river. The dog accelerated her snarls into a series of ill-tempered barks. She pointed her face where the crows had been. Andrew set off, marking the spot which the crows had left, striding towards it.

And then even he, a mere man, ill-equipped for following scents, was struck hard by the power of the stink of dead meat which rose from the marsh. Reluctantly, obsequiously, the dog went with him, her belly almost brushing the ground in her efforts to efface herself, to erase herself from the impact of what she knew they would find. Suddenly, the edge of the creek gave way beneath the man's boots. He slithered down the bank of a deep channel, tearing with his hands at the tough grass to slow his fall. Sliding on his backside, turning and twisting, he tumbled helplessly into the mud, where he landed with his feet in the water some six feet below the bewildered dog. She looked down at him from the top of the collapsed bank.

And there was the dead thing.

It was a swan. In death it was as splendid as it had been in life. Some creatures might cower and fawn in the attitude of being dead, as though by dying they ceased to make a contribution to the state they had left . . . But this swan was still as grand and as theatrical as it had ever been when it beat along the estuary. It lay spread-eagled in the grey mud, breast upwards, both vast white wings stretched out like sheets, sheets which might have been rumpled and stained by lovers. The column of its neck was straight. Its beak was open, as if it were singing that song which dying swans are reputed to sing. There were no eyes, now that the crows had paid their call and taken them away. The bird was huge and white, somehow bigger and more spectacular than any swan which Andrew had seen before. It made an art of being dead. Around its webbed black feet and around its legs there were yards of nylon twine which an irresponsible angler must have discarded up the river, to become entangled and to pinion the swan's feet together. Andrew lay next to the dead bird. The smell of it was so strong as to eclipse the smells of the river and the mud. Its belly pulsed with the movement of maggots, there were flies crawling speculatively from the swan's open beak and buzzing around its empty eye sockets. Above him, Phoebe was silent, stunned by the stink and by the spectacle of death which the bird so proudly presented. She stared down. She started to snarl at the droning of flies.

'Splendid . . .' whispered Andrew, manoeuvring himself on to his feet. 'Well done, Phoebe! You've done it again! We can use this, can't we . . .?'

From that moment, the idea of clearing his head with a bracing walk on the seashore was forgotten. He had come to the beach to blow away the smells of damp, to cleanse himself of rotting things. But now all he could think of was the stinkhorn, those innocuous jars on the mantelpiece which had within them the power either to give him strength or to humiliate him. The stinkhorn flooded his head once more. A vision of their glowing phallus flashed before his eyes, it fused for one dazzling second with the column of the swan's straight neck as though the swan and the stinkhorn were inextricably linked . . . and of course they were, for Andrew Pinkney, for the festering of the swan and all the busy workings of its corpse would help him to foster a new generation of stinkhorn. Swan and badger . . . he ran the words together in his mind, let them rub together like pebbles in a stream . . . Badger and swan . . . Alive, they were utterly independent of one another. Dead, they joined forces and found a single shared purpose.

It was perhaps a good thing that the beach was deserted that afternoon, for any passing rambler, ornithologist, jogger or fisherman would have witnessed a bizarre sight. The dog herself could not bear it. She fled along the shore, raising a cloud of clamouring curlew as she made for what she imagined would be the familiar security of the car. Andrew saw her go. He ignored her. There was work to be done and it would be easier without Phoebe pestering him. He took hold of the swan by the neck, just below its head, tested the strength of it in case it had already decomposed so much that the head would just come off in his hand, and he hefted the dead bird out of the creek. In spite of its size, it was very light. Like the badger, it must have died of starvation, unable to forage successfully with its feet bound together. He then dragged it behind him along the smooth sand. An observer might have thought that the bird was still alive: its wings flapped open and closed now that they were exposed to the sea wind, its body bounced sometimes up and down over the undulating flats. Along they went, man and bird. The man leaned against the breeze, his wellington boots slapping rhythmically and noisily on his calves. His long blond hair blew about his ears. His cheeks were flushed with the walking and the crispness of the November air, although the skin around his eyes and mouth was smudged with grey. There was a strange, obsessive light burning in his face. Engrossed in this operation, he was no longer missing his glasses. He walked on and listened to the sliding, slipping, slithering of the bird as it swept across the sand. The swan submitted. It lay back and trailed the wreckage of its wings beside it, it dangled its flat black flippers and their ravellings of twine. Man and bird left an unusual signature on the beach . . . before the tide returned and erased the evidence, there was a succession of heavy booted footprints, over which the sand had been lightly brushed by some dragging, skidding object . . . A sleuth might have concluded from the trail that a poor wretch, weighed down by his boots, had been pursued relentlessly by a light-footed whirlwind of a fiend, a creature from the sea perhaps, which dogged the man's heels wherever he tried to turn . . .

But Andrew Pinkney pressed on.

As he approached the car, Phoebe grew hysterical. She saw the apparition coming along the beach, closer and closer, the man who was rapidly becoming a stranger to her so that she hardly recognised him as her master who had brought her to Wales, and the big white stinking thing he was towing towards her. She ran round and round the car, her barks becoming more high-pitched with every circuit, her tongue lolling and slavering, her eyes rolling. When he arrived and lifted the tail-gate with one hand, still holding the throat of the swan with the other, she could not contain her horror at the sight of what he was doing. She sprang forward. Leaping, she raked the hand which had opened up the back of the car, she closed her jaws hard on it. Then she fell to the ground as lightly as a cat and dashed away again. Andrew shouted a single unlovely word. Blood was welling fast from the bitten hand. Swearing loudly at the dog, which wisely stayed out of range of his boots, he swung the body of the swan into the car and leaned in to fold the wings across the bird's breast, holding his breath against the stench which was intensified by the enclosed space. From under the wings, where the skin had been broken by the crows, handfuls of plump yellow maggots scattered from the corpse and writhed blindly on the plastic upholstery. The hard dry cylinders of pupae tumbled too. A swarm of black flies broke from the swan's mouth, there was a rush of wings through the tunnel of its neck as a mass of blackened tunnellers were released from their shift down the mine. He reeled back, nauseated by the sight of the swan's yawn of flies. Eyeless, it stared at him. For a few seconds he was as mesmerised by the droning of the flies, the spillage of maggots and the empty sockets which the crows had pilfered, as he had been by the stinkhorn the previous night. Only by stepping back again and cracking his head on the tail-gate of the car did he rouse himself, to the persistent barks of the dog. He slammed the door shut.

'Right, Phoebe . . . Come on, you little bastard!' And he went for her, brandishing the lead which he had had in his pocket.

Again, it was fortunate for Andrew that no one saw the ensuing scene. He baited the dog with his dangling hand, which by now was dripping blood from its fingertips, he squatted down and offered her the hand once more. Phoebe was past the stage of responding normally to his commands. She was breathing so heavily, her yelps were so fractured that he could hear the rasp of her breath in her throat and the rattle of her lungs. He crouched, swinging the bloody hand before her face. 'Come on, Phoebe, come and get it . . .' She also crouched, punctuating her snarls with long, rattling breaths, until she could bear the tension no more and she did what the man wanted her to do. Bellying towards him, quick and low as a snake, she darted her teeth at his wet fingers. He felt the pain of her bite. He saw, uncannily clearly as though it were the frozen frame of a film, the look of an untamed, untameable beast in her eyes, and his other hand flew round to seize her by the scruff of her neck. Straightening up like an uncoiled spring, he tore the one hand from the dog's mouth and twisted the grip of the other in her long coat. 'Right, you bitch!' he yelled. 'Time you had a lesson . . .!' The dog squirmed in mid-air as he held her away from him, she emitted a long scream, as a child does in the throes of a nightmare. Andrew flung open the back of the car once more. He shook the dog before the folded white corpse. She writhed more violently still, averting her face from the swan and increasing the pitch and passion of her cries. She scrabbled with her feet, she wrinkled her muzzle into a snout more like a pike's or a polecat's, but she was helpless in the man's grip. 'That's where you're going, my girl! Take a good look at it!' So saying, he bundled her forward so that she landed with a squeal of disgust on the body of the swan, and he slammed down the car door. 'Bitch! Fucking bitch!' he bawled at her through the window.

Unlocking the driver's door, he got in. Without another glance at the bleeding wounds on his hand, he started the car, turned it around in the lane and began to drive away from the coast.

The view of the drizzle-drenched mountains was no longer a shrinking square in his rear-view mirror. The open expanses of the coast were forgotten now, behind him. Ahead, filling the entire windscreen, looking grey and black until they lost themselves in the hanging cloud, the mountains blanked out the puny attempt Andrew had made to clear his head. He drove on. The car was a capsule of frenzied sound and hideous smell. Phoebe, imprisoned in the back with the dead swan, never once relented of her crying. She grieved like a widow, quite unable to stop her howls, she could not escape from the closeness of the dead thing. Andrew wound down his window, but still he was engulfed by the stinks and vapours which issued from every orifice of the corpse. Nevertheless, he was calmer, more contented now than he had been when he awoke that morning to survey the chaos of the cottage and when he remembered the events of the previous evening. Once more he had a purpose to his stay in Wales! It was not simply a holiday to be aimlessly filled by walking the dog or by reading novels before he resumed a life in suburban

Sussex . . . No, he had something to expiate, and he had found a way to help himself do it! Why fight against the mountains and their cloak of rain? Why run from the mists which enveloped the hillsides? Why shrink from that blanket of the black forest? They were all there to be used in the furtherance of his experiment, whose quintessence was an atmosphere of clammy damp! On the mantelpiece of the cottage, waiting for his return, were the eggs of the stinkhorn; behind him, alive with maggots and the tunnelling of flies, was the other half of the equation he was trying to work out. Put the two together, leave them time to couple in their own mysterious way . . . and there would be something to show for his visit to Wales. This country was a bog. He would be glad to quit it. But while he was in it, he could use it!

He drove faster, eager to get back. His short-sightedness no longer seemed to be a handicap as he accelerated wildly through the narrow lanes. His feet were clumsy on the pedals, since he had not changed out of his wellington boots, he trod heavily and brutally on the accelerator. Only a vision of the stinkhorn hovered before him. Its white erection gleamed in his mind's eye and made the details of road and traffic just an irksome irrelevance. In the same way as he had seen the stinkhorn fuse with the swan's neck, now the image flickered with any column or pole he passed . . . It guided him home, like a candle seen dimly through mist. He no longer heard Phoebe's sobbing cries, the stench of the corpse no longer nauseated him, he was hardly aware of turning from the road and negotiating the flooded bridge across the river, he did not feel the jolting of the car as he drove up the track, he scarcely noticed how the mountains closed around him. All of this was a blur in the background. The real issue, the real point in focus, the matter in the foreground of his vision was the stinkhorn, that devotional candle he was yet to light. In this way he drove up to the cottage, finding it as ever smothered with a white wet fog.

Phoebe fled from the car the moment he opened up the back. He had never seen her move faster, even when she had been in mad pursuit of the sheep. She streaked to the front door and quaked there, wanting only to regain the sanity and the well-known scents of her basket. Andrew left her to quake. 'Fuck off, Phoebe!' he snarled at her. 'Fuck off, Phoebe!' he said again and laughed, savouring the symmetry and the rhythm of it. Her welfare was now less important than his business with the swan. Holding his breath, he leaned into the car and took the bird again by the throat, this time using the hand which Phoebe had bitten. As he lifted the swan and laid it down on the grass, a few droplets of his blood fell on the bird's breast, splashes of red on the pure white feathers. He returned to the car, swept from it the pupae which had scattered from inside the corpse's hollow frame and then he closed the door. The sound of the swan's dragging over the grass was softer than its progress across the sand . . . now it whispered as the man drew it up the slope towards the woodshed, the feathers hissed on the wet hillside. And as they came closer to the little outhouse, two powerful pungencies collided head to head and made that place a reeking morgue. Andrew unlocked and opened the door. Maggots dripped from the badger's nostrils, they writhed from its anus. Flies blundered from its eyes and spun dizzily from its mouth, gorged to a stupor on the sweetness of the putrid flesh. There were scores of pupae in the sawdust on the ground. The stink buzzed from the woodshed as the rotten, pulsing thing swung silently on its hook. Still the badger grinned, satisfied with its work. Gagging on the smell, Andrew approached with the swan, towing it with him to the doorway. It was easier to lift than the badger had been, much lighter and more manageable.

He ducked into the building, his face brushing for a second on the badger's flank, and he raised the swan's head to the next hook. The hook pierced the bird's throat in the cleft beneath its beak. Gently, afraid that the flesh might tear with the weight of the corpse, he let the swan hang . . . It creaked and stretched as it took the strain. The neck pulled as taut as a cello string, the body bulged as all kinds of fluids and sacs and tubes adjusted to the new position, there was a groan from inside the belly as something broke or a clutch of maggots seethed from one bruise to another. The enravelled feet dangled like a pair of fruit bats from a tropical tree. And slowly, with a cracking of stiffened joints, those massive wings subsided . . . they collapsed and relaxed at the swan's sides, a fitting shroud for a noble corpse.

'You are beautiful . . .' the man whispered. 'You beautiful beautiful creature . . .'

He forgot the stink of the badger and the swan. He was lost in admiration. The two bodies hung side by side, sometimes touching as they swung on their hooks. Head down, the badger leered at Andrew. Its jacket of barbed wire cut into the punctured sac of its belly. No more blood dripped from its snout on to the logs of the mountain ash, although there were red rosettes on the white wood. The swan stretched up its head and let down its wings. The only blood on its feathers was from the man's hand, a gash of blood as though its throat had been cut.

Smiling, pleased with what he had done, Andrew Pinkney stepped out and walked to the cottage. He let the dog in. He took off his boots and went directly to the bathroom, where he spent a long time washing his hands.

VI

WHEN HE awoke the following morning, Andrew Pinkney felt nervous.

His stomach was tense in the same way it had always been tense on the first day of a new school term, on the first day of a new job, before an evening out with Jennifer. It was because the business with the stinkhorn was being forced to a head. He had walked with the dog through the forest again, through the woodland too, right up to the crater and back, to see if there were any more stinkhorn left and to see if he could dig up any more of their eggs. There were none. They were finished. The only eggs which remained ready to rupture this year were the two in the jars on his mantelpiece, perhaps the only two in the county, the only two in Wales, the only two in the British Isles. That was what made him nervous. He lay in bed and thought of the responsibility he had taken on. What did he know about the stinkhorn? Nothing, except what he had read in Caernarfon library, a few facts gleaned from a few books, with the occasional dry crust of information he had picked up from Jennifer. And yet he was now entrusted with the sole-surviving eggs and the self-imposed task of trying to promote their hatching, their growth into full-blown fungi and then their re-generation. A flashing reminder of the upright white column of the last stinkhorn jolted him out of bed. A vision of it seemed to shimmer in front of him. He remembered the swan which now teamed with the badger to help him fulfil the task, the swan and the badger which now teemed with maggots. It was time for the harvest!

He washed and dressed quickly, hardly bothering to look at his face in the mirror. Phoebe was slow to stir from her basket. Perhaps the stink of the swan was still on him, for she recoiled when he urged her to move. 'Get out, Phoebe, go on out!' and he tipped her abruptly from her nest of blankets, on to the floor. Limping to the open door, she went out. Underneath the privet bush, she hunched and squatted and squeezed two long dry turds on to the wet grass. Andrew was relieved to see this instead of the slime with which she had been smitten, and he was glad to see that the day was drier and clearer than it had been for a week. The air was quite still. The mists hung over the mountains, white and folded, as though a team of decorators had covered them with dust sheets while they painted the sky with an undercoat of uniform grey. At least it was not raining. Andrew set about preparing for his task.

Rummaging through the kitchen cupboards, he found two saucepans and took them to the outhouse. His nervousness protected him from the stench of the two corpses. Because he was active, because he was busy and he knew exactly what he had to do, he breathed evenly the fetid fumes from the badger and the swan without feeling nauseated.

'You first, badger,' he said to the mask which smiled grotesquely upside-down. 'You've been very patient, waiting here in the woodshed, quietly getting on with your work. Nothing spectacular, just a businesslike decommissioning. So it's your turn first.' He held a saucepan under the creature's dangling snout. 'Right, badger, what've you got for me? What've you got to show for all your work?'

With his other hand he reached up and started to shake the meat-hook to swing the badger round and round, from side to side, to bounce it gently without straining the corset of rotten barbed wire which held it in mid-air. The first few maggots plopped from its nostrils into the saucepan. They landed with a curiously attractive musical sound, not unlike the thoughtful improvisation of a minimalist composer. More and more fell in a shower when he punched the animal's flank, then he put the saucepan on the logs so that he could use both hands to squeeze and massage the hanging sack. As he did so, as he listened closely to the gurglings of fluid he could coax by pummelling and to the flutings of internal farts he could produce if he pressed hard enough in the right places, he was thrilled to see the maggots tumble from the twin exhausts of the badger's nostrils together with dozens of developed pupae. In a couple of minutes the saucepan was an inch deep with the writhing larvae. Concerned that, by shifting the badger in its wire, he might tear the softening hide and cause the corpse to rip away from the hook, he stopped the massage.

'Good boy, badger. You've been busy, haven't you? That's plenty from you for the time being.' He turned to the swan. 'Now, you're new here, aren't you? I don't want to rush you when I know everything's a bit unfamiliar on your first morning, but you can't just hang around doing nothing. Let's see what you can do, shall we?'

He bent down and picked up the saucepan. Holding it out, he took one of the heavy wings, lifting it up and away from the bird's side. There was a soft ripping sound, like the tearing of silk. Under the wing, where the skin was purple and raw and had attracted the beaks of the crows, there was a hole the size of Andrew's hand from which he could almost hear the movement of maggots; it came to him as silently and subtly as the sigh of a breeze, on the very edge of his hearing. The flesh heaved with the maggots' working. 'Oh yes, oh yes, you're doing well, for only your first day here. I think you've got the idea all right. Let's see now . . .' All he did was to row the joint of the wing slowly up and down so that the skin did not break too much, and the maggots rained from the swan's side. Those that missed the saucepan dropped dully on the stack of logs. He lifted the other wing. The harvest was a bountiful one, and he, the harvester, reaped it with excitement. He held the saucepan under the swan's tail, swung the bird tenderly on the hook lest its throat should rip, while the fruits of the harvest fell ripe and plump from its anus. The crows had been there too, tearing with their beaks. All kinds of bubblings and whistles broke from the bird's belly as Andrew shook it, things were caving in, things were collapsing inside there, with a sigh and a squelch. The saucepan was three inches deep, there was more fruit than he could ever use. Still he was thrilled by the juxtaposition of the two corpses . . . They were so different, so incompatible! They had had nothing whatsoever in common while they were alive, but now they were working together side by side, white feathers caressing grey bristle, and yielding such a bumper crop! More importantly, using the second saucepan, Andrew knelt on the floor of the woodshed and gathered from the sawdust as many of the more mature pupae as he could find, pupae in a more advanced stage of development. They were dry and hard and brown, like long grains of rice, and they would soon be flies. With the two saucepans, he returned to the cottage.

Phoebe observed from her basket. There was something very housewifely about the way that Andrew went about the next part of the operation. He arranged two empty jam jars on the draining board of the kitchen sink, before running out to the woodshed once more and coming back with his hands cupped around as much sawdust as he could hold. He sprinkled a bed of this, about half an inch deep, into each jar. Then, ignoring the maggots in one saucepan, he used a spoon from the cutlery drawer to pick out the pupae from the other pan and sprinkle them into the two jars. They dripped on to the draining board, on to the kitchen floor, blind stupid things taut with pus, dropping into the sink. They popped under Andrew's feet and left a juicy blob where they had burst, like a smear of snot wiped from a child's nose. But he continued happily, until both jars were more than half full; tearing a square of adhesive cellophane from a roll, he stretched it tightly over each jar like the skin of a drum and pierced each skin just once with a knife to allow a little air inside. He put the two jars of pupae beside the hot water tank, in the warmth of the cupboard in the living-room. In this way, he played the conscientious housewife, tidying the kitchen afterwards, washing the spoon he had used, also covering the immature maggots in the other saucepan and putting them by the water tank . . . Except that Andrew Pinkney was not bottling a winter's supply of green tomato pickle, he was not making jam. He was bottling pupae which would soon change into big, buzzing flies, growing bigger and noisier and stronger. And then, when the stinkhorn was ready, he would release the flies to feed on the fungi's dripping heads . . .

The next thing was to prepare the containers to which he hoped to introduce the flies after they were gorged on the slimy spore mass. The flies would both carry spores on their bodies after contact with the stinkhorn and also pass the spores, unharmed, from their digestive systems when they defecated. So Andrew must make ready a number of suitable receptables for this crucial stage. It was easy, as far as his amateurish notion of the procedure was concerned. He still had the plastic bag he had used when first carrying the stinkhorn eggs from the forest to the cottage, and it still contained plenty of the soil and leaf mould he had dug from around the eggs. He found two more jars, which he cleaned thoroughly with soap and boiling water, having some half-baked idea that real scientists would insist on the conditions being sterile; in the bottom of each, he put a wad of moistened tissue paper and he added on top of this a few inches of the soil from the forest. That was it. Each jar had a screw-on lid which he pierced with a knife. How long did it take for the mature pupae to change into flies? They had already been lying in the earth and sawdust of the woodshed floor for over a week, so they were in the last stages of development. What could he do if the next stinkhorn were to thrust up its head before the flies were ready? Go stumbling about the woodshed, banging his head on the rafters, blundering into the two decaying corpses, and try to harvest a clutch of flies which were mature and ready for the mission? No, he'd wait. Perhaps tomorrow, or the next day at the latest, everything would be in place: item one, on the mantelpiece an erect and oozing stinkhorn, one of the last in Britain; item two, a jam jar bursting with eager meat-flies, lusting to be unleashed on the putrefaction of the stinkhorn; item three, a warm and damp receptacle of forest earth to which the intoxicated flies could be transferred and where a new generation of stinkhorn would be . . . what was the word? Spawned? Jennifer would have known. And fourthly, if all went to plan and, more by accident than design, Andrew's game resulted in the growth of another egg or two, he might then wrap up his sojourn in Wales and speed down to Sussex with a surprise for Jennifer! What a relief that would be! To get out of the drizzle and the mists and the baying of the hounds, to return to the sanity and freshness of Sussex! But not yet . . . He'd try not even to think about it, now that things had gone so far.

There was a lull. What more could he do?

He wandered into the bathroom and inspected his face, having ignored it first thing in the morning in his enthusiasm to be busy with the stinkhorn. He filled the basin, although the water was cold, and he attacked his chin and the skin around his eyes to try and remove some more of the ink. It was fading fast, and more vigorous rubbing dissolved it more. There remained nothing more disfiguring than what looked like the darkening of bristle, a four o'clock shadow, which appealed to Andrew; his face needed shaving only seldom to remove the fine golden down from his pink cheeks. Now, looking and feeling more rugged than usual, pleased with the effect of the smudging as he turned his head from side to side and examined himself in the mirror, he decided there was no reason to be coy about his appearance. He'd go to the hotel and return the rug, he'd reclaim his spectacles too. In the condensation which formed from his breath on the mirror, his eyes were blurred. There was only a hazy image of a red, featureless face, big and soft and bland, like an old carp staring through the slime-covered glass of an aquarium. His hair was longer and more unruly still, strands of golden weed which masked the fish's face. It was only his glasses which had given definition to his features, and now they were missing, so that he was altered, rubbed out, shifted out of focus in the same way that the watercolour of Phoebe had been changed by the running damp . . . After a few weeks in Wales, he was a different person from the one whom Jennifer had liked and favoured and finally humiliated . . .

He fetched the rug from the cupboard, where he had wrapped it around the tank of the immersion heater. It was dry and clean, smelling of disinfectant. Certainly, he thought, it was cleaner than it must have been before, as he remembered the state of the mangy spaniel which had scratched and gnawed itself raw on it. Folding it, he put on his jacket and wellington boots.

'No, Phoebe, this time you're staying here. Maybe it's a bit more tactful if I take this back on my own.'

The dog, seeing him step into his boots, had begun to uncoil herself from her basket, but now she wound her warm body once more into the blankets. He bent over her. After her frolics in the sea, she smelled good again and her coat was glossy. Not a whiff of her sickness rose with the unmistakable staleness of damp.

'Good girl. When I get back I'll give you another blanket. You stay here . . .' He left the cottage and walked down the hillside towards the river.

There was no heron that afternoon. Instead (and he wondered whether they were mutually exclusive on this stretch of the river) there was a cormorant fishing. It was half-submerged in the smooth water, only its head and neck and the very top of its back above the surface. The bird cruised about, black and lethal, its sinuous neck and the up-tilted beak giving the impression of a silent submarine which had lifted its periscope for a while before resuming some murderous business underwater. When the cormorant dived, its entire body cleared the surface for a split-second and then it entered the water as smoothly as a pin through the meniscus of oil. He did not see it reappear, nor did he know what fish it might be hunting so many miles upriver in early November. As always on these occasions, he found himself thinking of Jennifer, who would without doubt have been able to inform him of the cormorant's tastes in freshwater fish, as well as knowing whether the heron and the cormorant were compatible as far as sharing a beat was concerned. He walked on. From the blackened remains of the bracken a pair of pipits faltered into the air, and their feeble voices reminded him of the sound of a rusty pair of scissors opening and closing . . . And the rest of the walk was passed in a blank, he noticed nothing more as he racked his brain about the truth or the origin of that image, the rusty scissors, as he puzzled whether it was something he had once read in a book, whether it was something that Jennifer had said to him, or whether it had just occurred to him quite spontaneously. A pair of pipits . . . a pair of rusty scissors . . .? He was still undecided, unable to accept that he might have conjured the idea himself, when he wandered distractedly up to the hotel and found himself standing on the gravelled drive outside the front door, with the rug folded under his arm.

Someone was playing the piano again, not a few random scales and strummings as he had heard once before, but stepping gracefully through the sparse phrases of a nocturne by Erik Satie. It gave Andrew a thrill of enormous pleasure, both to recognise the piece and to hear its stylistic elegance ring from the building into the still air of that afternoon. In all the wilderness he had encountered since coming to the cottage, not only in the sense of the wet inhospitable countryside but in respect of its inhabitants too, who smelled of sweat and whose idea of a joke was to drop a live cockerel down the chimney and into a lighted fire, there was only Mrs Stone who had any of the qualities of grace and reserve which he prized in his friends in the south of England. To be fair, he admitted, he had not met many local people. But as soon as he had first seen her, behind the hotel bar, he recognised in Mrs Stone's weary smiles that she held herself just a little apart from the people she served with drinks, that she played the aloof and haughty heron to the dark, voracious, oily cormorants whose beat she had come to share. Heron and cormorant managed to live side by side, theirs was an uneasy, untrusting relationship . . . and here, in the gloomiest valley of the wettest mountains in Wales, Mrs Stone had chosen to roost. Tall and grey, elegant and spare, she stepped coolly among the cormorants. Andrew Pinkney listened to her music, the Satie which was as spare and refined as she was, and he imagined her long fingers on the keyboard. He had stumbled on an oasis here in the dark valley, where such music cut straight through the smother of the mists. It was so human, and civilised . . . it sliced the afternoon into ribbons, it humbled the barbaric ugliness of the wet slabs which rose sheer behind the hotel. He waited and listened until the piece was finished, then he rang the doorbell.

Mrs Stone came to the door. For a second she looked puzzled, as if she could not recognise the young man who stood there with his bundle. Before he could speak, she said, 'Oh, it's you. I couldn't place you for a moment. You look different . . .'

'Hello, Mrs Stone,' he began. 'I've brought back that rug I took away with me the other night. You know, on Hallowe'en?' Nonplussed that she said nothing in answer to this but was looking quizzically at him to continue, he went on, 'I'm very sorry about what happened. Not just the dog, of course. She couldn't help that, I suppose. She was sick. I really shouldn't have brought her with me.' He cleared his throat. 'No, I mean all that unruliness afterwards. Lost my temper a bit, I couldn't stop myself . . .' Still she said nothing, offered nothing to ease his awkwardness. 'So here I am, Mrs Stone, to apologise for all the trouble and to bring back the rug which got messed up.' Holding it out to her, seeing her step back with distaste from the folded rug, he quickly added, 'Oh don't worry, it's perfectly clean now. I've given it a really good cleaning and doused it with disinfectant. Perfectly dry too . . .'

She listened to this with her fingers clasped together in front of her, a tight, lipless smile on her face. 'Right,' she said, unclasping her hands, 'well, I'll take it then.' She accepted it from him and lifted it to her face, to sniff it. 'Certainly smells all right anyway. It's probably a lot cleaner than it was before, with my mangy old spaniel on it.' At last she brought a little warmth to her smile. 'How's your dog now? Recovered?'

Andrew relaxed, seeing that his apology was accepted. He remembered not to shift from foot to foot, to keep his hands out of his pockets, as he had been told quite forcefully by the irritable old headmaster who sat on the bench in Lewes magistrates' court, and he recounted to Mrs Stone his theory that the dog must have bitten into a toad he had found near the cottage and must have swallowed some of its poison. Mrs Stone nodded and smiled, holding the rug as if it were a baby. As soon as he paused, she put in quickly, 'Oh, I've just worked out why you're looking different today! Glasses! You're not wearing your glasses. Makes your face look quite different somehow . . .'

'Well, that's another reason I've come down, as a matter of fact,' he said. 'To pick up my specs. You know, when those lads dragged me out of the toilets, when Phoebe was . . . when she was ill, I left them there, on the wash basin. I was in the middle of trying to get all that ink off my face when they came in and manhandled me out. So I left my specs behind.' He managed a foolish laugh. 'I've still got some of the ink on my face now, as you can see! Have you got my glasses, Mrs Stone?'

It turned out that she had not. No one had handed them to her, on Hallowe'en or the following night. She had personally cleaned the toilets, both ladies' and gentlemen's, as she was obliged to do most of the time off-season, and there were no glasses left on the wash basin. Andrew was puzzled. 'Well, that's very strange. I wonder where they've got to. I can just about manage without them for the moment, while I'm still on holiday up here, although things are a bit blurred, you know . . . But I'll really need them when I drive all the way back to Sussex. Six hours, that's what it took me on the way up. I need them for work too. Wonder where they've got to . . .'

To his great surprise, as he stood there and scratched his blond curls in puzzlement, as the woman waited politely for him to add something or to retire down the drive, the piano playing resumed. The clear, simple notes of another Satie piece (this time Andrew's favourite, 'Le Piège de Méduse') came lilting from the open door. Astonished, he frowned and glanced up at Mrs Stone, who was smiling absent-mindedly, a distant look in her pale eyes. 'What lovely music!' he said gently, so as not to disturb the limpid sound. 'Who's playing?'

'Yes, it is nice, isn't it?' the woman replied. 'It's young Shân. You know, from the kennels. She's a nice little pianist. She quite often comes over to use the piano. Such a waste otherwise, because I can't play a note myself. Lovely to hear the old piano being . . .'

Andrew pushed roughly past her, into the hotel. He ignored the woman's look of indignation and strode through the door, following the sound of the music. He trod down a darkened corridor, hearing behind him Mrs Stone's fluted 'Excuse me?', he turned the handle of a heavy panelled door from behind which the music was coming, he burst into the room. The music stopped. There was the girl, sitting at a grand piano, jerking round to stare in amazement at Andrew. For a second the man and the girl gazed in silence at one another, while Mrs Stone breathed heavily over the man's shoulder. Andrew was petrified with disbelief. He saw the little girl dwarfed by the bulk of the piano, tiny and frail in the high-ceilinged room, he had heard such delicate music from her fingers . . . She looked as saucy and as brittle as a sparrow. Her hair shone, her face was flushing pink with surprise. But Andrew experienced a nightmarish flashback, to her grunting black mask and the limbs of her boyish body splayed beneath him, to the sensation of her hot wet skin slipping and sliding on his . . . 'Oh . . .' was all he managed to say, and then he articulated the single word 'Shân . . .?' to express somehow his bafflement, his embarrassment and the upsurging of renewed desire in that one syllable. Then, before she could say anything, he covered his confusion by asking in a strangled voice, 'My glasses? You didn't know where my glasses were, did you?'

'Of course she doesn't!' the exasperated tones of Mrs Stone burst out. 'What would she be doing in the men's toilets? That's ridiculous!'

But the girl spoke up, her voice as clear and as measured as the music she had been playing. 'Oh yes, Mrs Stone, in fact I do know where Andrew's glasses are.' The man and the woman listened to the kennel-maid. 'My brother's got them, Andrew. He picked them up from the toilets after you'd left with the dog. We were going to drop them off at your cottage on the way back home, but somehow we . . .' And her voice trailed off to nothing. 'We were going to stop by, but . . .'

She looked back to her sheet music and pretended to study it, her face and throat hot with her memory of Hallowe'en, and Andrew again felt that melting sensation in his stomach as he remembered how he had washed her little body, how she had slept so deeply while he turned her and sponged her and dried her before enfolding her in blankets in front of a flaming fire. Without looking at him, she added quietly, 'Come up to the kennels tomorrow, Pinkie, in the afternoon. You can get your glasses back then.'

Having said this, she turned to him and smiled, showing her white pointed teeth, running the tip of her tongue across her lips. For just that second, long enough for Andrew to feel a chill like an icicle piercing his chest, she was the little witch-bitch once more . . . For just one second . . . Then she spun round to the piano, resuming the piece in the middle of a phrase as though she had never stopped, as though Andrew had never come into the room. The music picked up, rounded and true. In a daze, he negotiated the figure of Mrs Stone, who was still holding the rug to her narrow chest, he passed down the corridor to the silver light which beckoned outside and left the hotel without speaking another word.

He walked down the drive and across the river. The sky was already beginning to darken by the time he was unlocking the front door of the cottage to release Phoebe. All the way, he heard the hypnotic threads of the kennel-maid's music weaving through his mind, weaving a curious pattern which linked him with the girl and the Welshness she embodied, and which linked with his life in Sussex too, where he was accustomed to hearing such music. It reminded him that, different though he had found things in Wales during the past few weeks, he remained of course only hours away from all the routine trappings he was used to in the south: the people and the places, his bed-sitting-room, his involvement with Jennifer, his daily tasks in the office. The music traced him back there as directly and as simply as the river had connected him back to this bog of a valley when he had tried to escape to the coast. The little witch was wielding another of her spells, just as she had mesmerised him in the firelight and defeated the antidote he had attempted to apply in the form of the rowan. That night, she overcame his counter-charm, sucked him down to her level, blackened him and smeared him with her occult daubings. Now, her spell was in the music she wrought from the piano. It said to Andrew, more plainly than words could have said: 'This is the kind of charm you're accustomed to! Return to it, and leave us to our ravens and our mists and our packs of hounds. Leave us to our mud and our smells of sweat. Go back to the music you know, which is ordered and cool, which has discords which are easy to resolve, which is limpid, calm and cerebral. It makes sense to you, Andrew Pinkney. Return south and pick up the piece where you left off, as though you had never been here. This is the kind of charm you're used to, this music. Not the stinkhorn! You'll never understand the stinkhorn! Don't tinker with the stinkhorn! Go back, while you can still recognise yourself . . .' That was what the witch was saying this time.

Yes, he could go home perfectly easily, this very evening if he chose to. It would take him less than an hour to pack his things into the car, to leave the cottage at least as tidy as he'd found it, and then he could drive cautiously south (without his spectacles) and be turning the key to his bed-sitter in Newhaven in six hours' time. Why not? After a night's sleep in his familiar bed, he'd wake up in Sussex as though everything that had happened in Wales had been a bizarre dream! There was no badger and no swan and no maggots; there was no clammy cottage engulfed by cloud; he'd never heard the melancholy baying of those hounds and the echoes of the crater; he'd never really seen that black choking thing drop from the chimney and leap out of the flames; the caveman and the witch-bitch had not danced in the firelight, their bodies anointed with wet soot . . . and most importantly of all, he had never worshipped the stinkhorn! He would awake to the sounds of a piano being played in the next room, cool delicate music, the same music he'd been listening to when he had drifted off to sleep the previous night, before his long and complicated dream. What a dream! How he'd been changed in it! But now he was restored to himself, to his cool clean sheets and the cool calm music . . .

He watched Phoebe bolt from the cottage. She squatted by the privet bush and trickled her golden stream. The evening was getting dark. There was no moon, it was buried somewhere deep inside the blue-black clouds. No stars. Not even the scalpel-light of Venus cut through. No sounds. Not even the hounds. All there was in the world, in the entire universe, was the man and his dog, enveloped by the night. Stepping into the cottage, he stood silent and still in the darkness. Then, he might almost have decided to start packing, as again he heard, running through his head, the simple strains of the music which the kennel-maid had played. But he did not.

He set about lighting the fire, rolling up a few sheets of newspaper into the grate and then going into the kitchen with the hatchet. In no time he had taken down a shelf from inside a cupboard and, in the living-room again, he split it into splinters with which to kindle a fire.

'Living off the land we call this, Phoebe,' he said, as the dog left her basket in anticipation of some heat. 'We backwoodsmen get our fuel from the forests and we kindle our fires by dismantling the kitchen cupboards. Steeped in country lore, that's me . . .'

He slipped out to the woodshed while the nest of paper and splinters was flaring. In the torchlight, the outhouse resembled a grotesque wayside shrine in which travellers had hung offerings to their god. The smell was a blow from a heavy fist. Side by side, badger and swan swung slowly on their hooks, their frames stuffed with maggots. He leaned between them, brushing his hand on the dissimilar textures of feather and fur, and soon he was laden with logs. He chose the contorted limbs of ivy he had cut from around a silver birch one afternoon, which he reckoned would have dried out enough to burn well. Reversing from the woodshed, struggling with the torch and the logs, he set the swan and the badger swinging in a macabre dance, two totally disparate partners swaying to the tune of their own humming putrefaction. He left them to the privacy of darkness.

The fire burned up briskly. The knots and entangled sinews of the ivy, which looked so ugly among the flames, like the wrinkles of a giant toad or some other prehistoric creature, gave out a lovely perfume as they burned. It reminded Andrew of the smell of chestnuts roasting. The room became warm, full of the incense of ivy. And, in the light of a single lamp, he thought for a second time of writing a letter to Jennifer . . . not to mention any of the strange threads of events which surrounded his obsession with the stinkhorn, but simply to recount a few innocent impressions of the cottage and the countryside. It was the sight and the scent of the ivy in the fire which gave him the idea, that here was something quaint and bucolic which might appeal to her down in the suburbs of Sussex. He wanted to write to her about his afternoons with the bow-saw and wheelbarrow, how he cut the choking serpents of the ivy from a slender birch, how the ivy then filled his room with perfume, how it gave him pleasure both to cut the wood and then to smell its burning. What else could he tell her? There was the cormorant, of course, his afternoon on the sea-shore where the sands were busy with waders; there was Phoebe's temporary sickness which maybe the toad had caused; there was that music, the Satie which he knew she liked for its elegant quirkiness . . . No. No. While he sat by the fire and even went so far as to reach for some paper and a pen, he realised there was nothing to tell her which was not completely and inextricably bound up with the stinkhorn. It was impossible to disentangle any of those things from the business of the stinkhorn. What would he tell her when he returned to Sussex? Everything? Or nothing? He could think of no middle way. Here in Wales, in the cottage which ran with damp and disfigured the watercolours of Sussex and of Phoebe, where he felt he was being sucked into the wet mountainside, where the people and the sheep and the birds were caught in the meshes of a spell he would never understand, there was nothing which had not been touched by the magic of the woodwitch. Nothing! And after all, that was why he had come in the first place, to absolve the crime he had committed as a result of his impotence, to face here in Wales the judgement of the stinkhorn. There was no escaping it. There was no separating it from the country it held under its charm.

He screwed up the paper and tossed it on to the fire. The ivy spat a flame at it, and soon it was gone. On impulse, he threw the pen there too. It squirmed into a mess of sizzling plastic. Then it too was gone.

*

It was nearly midday when Andrew awoke the following morning. Instead of rising refreshed from a long dreamless sleep, he lay torpid under a tangle of malodorous blankets, feeling that he was surfacing from an anaesthetic after an operation on some distant part of his body. He ached in every joint, the sheets were damp with sweat and the moisture in the air, and his head felt as though it had been stuffed with cotton-wool by a hamfisted taxidermist. Groaning as he glanced short-sightedly at his watch, he struggled from the bed and sat there, head in hands, staring down between his thighs at the clammy whiteness of his feet. They were unappealing things, cold and moist and yellowing, and from them rose that whiff of corruption which the whole cottage exuded, the smell of an airless place which the sun never touched, the inside of a crypt where there were dead things busily decomposing. Just as he was studying his feet (and likening them to the gawping sightless creatures he had culled from the corpses in the woodshed and garnered into jam jars), he heard an unfamiliar sound which made him sit up and listen quizzically to it. A drumming sound . . . The persistent thrum of some kind of machine, like a small power-drill or an electric razor . . . Phoebe was asleep in her basket, she barely twitched when Andrew padded past her and into the living-room to find out what the sound really was.

It was the flies in the jam jars.

In both jars, a cloud of them was buzzing stupidly from the bed of sawdust, blundering against the walls of glass and then rising giddily to the cellophane which was stretched tight over the mouth of the jars. As the flies drummed their powerful, brand-new wings on this transparent ceiling, the hum went up and the water-tank cupboard droned as busily as a city sweat-shop with its ranks of sewing machines.

This is good! thought Andrew. Very very good! . . . that at least one part of his experiment was working. And he pictured with pleasure those dangling corpses of the badger and the swan, working night and day to make sure that the supply of maggots would continue, dripping the ripe fruit of pupae to develop in the sawdust of the woodshed floor, so he could rear many more litters of lusty meat-flies. He found himself oddly satisfied that one side of his equation of flies and stinkhorn was primed and ready to work; it seemed so easy to rear the blundering flies that he felt a surge of eagerness to rear more and more of them, even though there would never be a need for so many in the experiment he planned to carry out on the two remaining stinkhorn eggs. Why did he shudder with pleasure at the idea of those dead things in the woodshed, knowing that their harvest of maggots would be massively in excess of what he actually needed? For the sake of the two stinkhorns, the last two in Britain? How many hundreds of flies could he feed on the spores of the stinkhorn? And how many millions of spores would be transmitted by them? No, he could never use more than a fraction of the flies he might cull from the woodshed . . . Nevertheless, it gave him satisfaction to cull them. He equated this with the pleasure he took from collecting timber from the woodland, sawing the logs, stacking the walls of the outhouse, continuing to stockpile the fuel in the certain knowledge that he'd never use more than a fraction of it in his short stay in the cottage. Yes, that was it. In the same way as he'd carry on cutting and gathering timber, he thrilled to see his meat-flies thriving in their jars and was eager to foster more and more and more . . .

He pondered vaguely along these lines, as he stood in the living-room and scratched at his groin through his pyjama trousers, as he pulled open the curtains to admit the light of another metallic-grey day. A leaden sky weighted down the hills and the fields, the pressure of it squeezed yet more water from the mountains and drenched everything. November in Wales, he thought . . . when the country is erased by a grey cloud, sheeted with grey drizzle! When little stirs and is alive, apart from the sheep which are soiled with mud and entangled in their own excrement! When the ravens and the jackdaws are nothing but the distant cries of creatures buried in the mist! He found himself thinking, with a weary sigh, that December and January and February and March would probably be exactly the same, perhaps with the creaking of ice to give a harsher, more brittle ring to the slabs of the slippery rock. Phoebe looked up at the light from the window. She did what Andrew felt like doing: she put down her head again, shut her eyes, sighed, and fell asleep once more.

In the jars on the mantelpiece, nothing new had happened. There were the remains of two defunct fungi, blobs of slime which curled up and dried on a bed of moist earth, and there were two eggs which blinked sightlessly from the soil. Andrew was ready now for the next erection, whichever one of the eggs should burgeon first. In the water-tank cupboard, as though they were straining with eagerness at the taut cellophane which imprisoned them, the flies drummed their wings and brawled drunkenly together. The noise rose and fell, like the murmuring of an expectant crowd in the dim intimacy of a theatre. Andrew smiled with satisfaction, to see the eggs patient and blind on the mantelpiece, to hear the flies hysterical in the cupboard. He studied Jennifer's watercolours. They ran with damp, their bright and frosty colours washed out by the trickling moisture behind the glass, so that her compositions of Sussex sunshine were transformed into dismal impressions of a Welsh November. In all the pictures now, it was raining: banks of drizzle billowed over the Sussex downs; angry grey clouds smothered the Sussex coast; blankets of sea-mist rolled in from the English Channel and obliterated the white cliffs; trawlers and dinghies skulked at their moorings under a sullen sky . . . The Cuckmere estuary was no longer a shining silver snake with its head in the sea and its coils in the green meadows. It was an earthworm, wrinkled and bruised. Phoebe had stopped snarling. Her picture had lost the definition of teeth and eyes which made her look so aggressive. That phase was past. Now her face was all but dissolved, as though she had been burned in a ghastly fire.

And, in one corner of the glass of her frame, there was a little green slug, about an inch long. It had crept that night across the wall and slithered on to the picture. Andrew followed the trail of its slime backwards and downwards, to a patch of the carpet which was particularly wet. Lifting the carpet, he uncovered a dozen or twenty slugs, green ones like the one on the picture, coiled closely together, entangled and dormant. Were they asleep? Do slugs sleep? Was this something that even Jennifer, the omniscient Jennifer, might not know? Would his mentor, his guru, have to admit her ignorance at last? He gently laid the carpet down, a moist blanket of darkness to cover the family of sleeping slugs, and he returned to the one adventurous slug which had preferred to explore the glistening, slippery walls of the living-room while its brothers and sisters slept. It hesitated on its corner of the picture, perhaps bemused by the sheer featurelessness of the glass after the irregularities of the wall. It waved its antennae. Were its eyes on the ends of those inquisitive fingers? Andrew had no idea. Could it deduce any impression of the terrain ahead by brandishing them like that, could it make out beneath the glass a contorted image of the dog that Phoebe had once been? All the time that Andrew was dressing, while he doused his own altered face in the bathroom, as he flinched from its intolerable expressionlessness in the mirror, while he boiled water in the kitchen and sipped some coffee, the little green slug remained still. It would not yet venture on to the smooth surface of the picture. There was something it was not quite sure of, something in the texture of the glass or in the image beneath it which might make it wish it had not been tempted to quit the nest under the damp carpet for a night of gentle exploration . . .

How alike they were, the slug on the picture and the wasted blobs of the stinkhorn in their jars! In their colouring and their shapes and their glistening skins, the exhausted fungi were very similar to the slug, as they wilted against the glass and fainted to the earth. It seemed suddenly to Andrew that one of those fungi had now risen from the dead and was reincarnated in the form of a little green garden slug, about to cross the glass of a picture frame, to peer wonderingly down at the blurred impression of Phoebe's face . . .

'For Christ's sake, Pinkney!'

He determined to shake off the torpor which the atmosphere seemed to enforce on him. Just because the rest of the country was going into hibernation and the covers were being drawn across a slumbering landscape, it did not mean that he would also remain dormant. Admittedly, he and Phoebe were changed by a month in Wales . . . they looked different, they acted differently and thought differently away from the tidy suburbs and the trim countryside of Sussex, but he was not going to surrender to the feeling of apathy which the weather cast over everything.

'Come on, Phoebe!' he called sharply. 'Get out of that basket, you idle creature!'

Before she had time to do more than raise her head from the blanket, he tipped over the basket completely and sent the dog sprawling on to the floor. Even then she was reluctant to stir, but she unwound herself painfully and arched her back like a cat. Somehow, as in her portrait, her features were blurred, either by too much sleep or by the last shreds of a dream which continued to cling there. Her face was a slate wiped clean by sleeping, a palimpsest on which nothing new had yet been inscribed. It was a face which was waiting for this new day to mould something new out of it.

'We're going out, Phoebe. Come on, girl, let's try and find some air in this place.'

He put on his boots and his jacket, and picked up the bow-saw. It seemed the obvious thing to take with him on a walk, as natural for him to reach for the saw as it was to pocket Phoebe's lead. But, as soon as they stepped from the cottage and were enveloped by the shock of a much colder day than they had imagined it to be, Andrew changed his mind about cutting wood and straight away decided on another destination for their walk. Because the clear cold air, with almost that grip of a frost which pinched around Andrew's nose and brought a tear to his myopic eyes, carried from the crater the belling of the hounds. He turned without hesitation to replace the bow-saw inside the front door, and locked the door behind him. 'Don't need that today, Phoebe. Come on, this way . . .' And with a wave of his arm to indicate to the dancing dog the direction they were taking, he trudged up the track behind the cottage, towards the woodland, towards the dead black fir forest, towards the crater. Phoebe, woken to exhilaration by the prospect of a run, sped on ahead of him. Hearing so clearly the musical voices of the hounds, he remembered what the girl had suggested as she turned from the piano, that he should climb up to the kennels and reclaim his glasses. That was what he determined to do.

There were no sheep as the man and the dog pressed on into the woodland of silver birch. For some reason they had all drifted down the hillside and towards the river, as he had seen at midday from his living-room window. So he felt easy about letting Phoebe sprint on and disappear from time to time among the trees. Most of the leaves were down, forming a dense carpet of wet black vegetation. The bare trees now exposed those shallow caves high up on the cliffside, the cells to which the name of the cottage should have referred if it had not been misspelt. 'Caves in the cliffs' or 'the cave in the cliffs' . . . that was how the lady in the post office had translated the name as she dispelled his original idea of 'the cockerel in the cliffs'. And here, among the wintry woodland of oak, birch and mountain ash, all the little caves were visible, including the deepest one in which he had sat and meditated and which he had thought of as his 'hermit's cell'. Seen from below, it was indeed quite high and remote, having a steep cliff of jagged boulders beneath it, affording a splendid view across the valley and down to the river, if only the mist lifted to reveal something of the countryside. But now, Andrew strode onwards through the open woodland of deciduous trees, with just a thought that, sometime before he left the cottage and drove south again, he might scramble up to his hermit's cell for another few moments' quiet retreat.

The dog had already sprinted on. He looked upwards, panting from the pace of the climb which was dictated by her, and there she was, slim and black and alert, at the gate which led into the shadows of the plantation. When he arrived there, he was badly out of breath. Leaning on the gate, he waited until the thudding of the blood in his head was still. Meanwhile he noted once more that they were about to enter quite a different world from the one of the slender birch and the gnarled knotty branches of oak . . . for, ahead of them, where the track grew narrower and darker, there were only the blackened ranks of the fir forest where little light could penetrate. The trees grew in tight formation, like the battalions of a silent and sinister army. There were shadows and deeper shadows and then the deepest darkness. And before he was ready to clamber over the gate, he was aware of the closeness of the hounds' barking. He thought he heard shouting too, one or more human voices mingled with the baying of their hounds. Phoebe looked up into his flushed face and she flagged her tail before unexpectedly wheeling away from the gate and trotting back in the direction she had come, as though wanting to continue her frolics among the birch rather than go into the forest. 'No, Phoebe, this way. Come here, come on!' But it took Andrew an exasperating few minutes to persuade the dog to come to him and then to clip her lead on to her collar, for it seemed that that would be the only way he could make her jump over the gate. Yes, the hounds were close by, in the quagmire of the crater perhaps, or even somewhere in the forest. Their chorus floated through the cold afternoon air. And the afternoon grew darker, as man and dog dropped over the gate and breathlessly entered the plantation.

Together they climbed the path, higher and deeper into the forest. Phoebe slunk alongside the slap-slap-slapping of the wellington boots, all her ebullience gone as she quivered at the sound of the hounds. Andrew too felt the gloom infect him. Above, the narrow strip of sky was gun-metal blue, clamped down on the hillside like a steel trap, screwed on to the mountain like the lid of a coffin. There was silence which only the panting breath of the man and the dog interrupted, and then suddenly, explosively, the pealing of the hounds welled up and faded down among the black trees. One moment the hounds seemed to be to their left, for a great shout of baying rose into the grey sky and there were human cries which seemed to orchestrate the dogs' voices. But then, to Andrew's right, from somewhere close by in the closed ranks of the forest, the chorus reached a more dramatic crescendo before it was absorbed into the dense cover. The effect which this shifting of sounds achieved was to disorientate the man, to disable his sense of direction, so that all he knew was that he must continue to climb, that so long as he was striving upwards he must be moving in the direction of the kennels, that he must try to ignore the ebb and flow, the surge and counter-surge which the outbursts of shouting inflicted on the balance of his senses. And all the time it was getting darker, both from the bristling branches of the plantation and from the lowering lid of the sky. Colder too . . . The air snapped at his face as he scrambled up the rough track and dragged the reluctant dog with him.

Two new noises then erupted simultaneously.

One of them was sudden and brutal. It came and went in a matter of seconds. The other was a pervasive layer of sound which seemed to have been switched on by the brutal suddenness of the first. A single gunshot rang out from somewhere just ahead of Andrew and Phoebe, less than fifty yards ahead, and that was the brutal noise which stunned the man and the dog into immobility while the forest rocked with the explosion. At exactly the same moment, that steely sky unleashed a hail storm, rattling the trees with a torrent of icy pellets.

Andrew dragged the dog from the path. Together they huddled close to the shelter of the plantation. Looking up through the dense cover of branches, he saw the sky turn black and muddy like a wash of charcoal, as though the gunshot had wounded it and pierced it to release the fall of ice. The forest grew very dark. The trees groaned under the sudden bombardment. There was no sound of the hounds, but, as he strained to hear through the rattle of the hail, Andrew thought he caught the tramping of human footsteps higher up the track, from where the shot had come, and a cry which was answered by another, gruffer shout. The hounds had been in the forest, wherever they had gone now, and there were people shooting and shouting. The hunt was all around them, somewhere in the heavy cover, moving up to the crater . . . Now the place was a blanket of shadow. It rang with the drumming of ice.

He pulled the hood of his jacket over his head. 'Let's go, Phoebe! No, this way!' and he tugged her on to the track and continued upwards. Head down, he felt the volley of hail striking his hood and his shoulders, he saw the ice firing into the grass at his feet, he heard it clatter into the trees. The dog wrapped her tail between her legs, her ears were flattened for protection tightly against the sides of her head. She growled meanly and hugged the slapping boots. In this way, determined to retrieve his glasses even if it meant stumbling into the very centre of the hunt, his mind set on the proximity of the kennel-maid and her brother, he struggled higher into the darkness of the forest.

He stopped dead, as did Phoebe, when a tiny white creature shot out of the trees to his right and confronted him with its mask of teeth. It was a terrier, very sturdy and bow-legged, completely white apart from its black ears, which now barred the way, emitting a high-pitched growl.

'Jesus . . . Who are you?' Andrew said, surprised to meet the fierce little beast so deep into the plantation. 'Where have you come from?'

In answer to this, and reacting to Phoebe's equally persistent growl, the terrier backed away from Andrew's boots and wheeled to the edge of the track. There, in the longer grass, while the hail continued to fire its salvoes from a blackening sky, it made its stand and would no more retreat from the oncoming man.

'What's that you've got there? Let's have a look . . .'

Ignoring the terrier's threats, Andrew moved closer. Phoebe bristled and made herself look almost twice her usual size by standing erect, raising her hackles into an impressive black mane. She increased the revolutions of her chain-saw snarl. She revealed a mouthful of teeth. Her lips quivered, black and tight and flashing a fleck of foam. And Andrew saw that she was not so much threatening the terrier, as the prize which the tiny dog was guarding.

Slung into the long grass, there was a dead fox. It was quite small, smaller than Phoebe, with a lovely, very red, very warmly coloured pelt. It was the only warm thing in the forest, where everything else was black or grey with the overwhelming gloom, or silver-white with the shards of ice. Lying there, the fox was like a flame, dead now and slowly cooling, but reluctant to be quenched by the lifelessness of its monochrome surroundings. Andrew ignored the terrier, which danced away, yapping, as he knelt to the fox. He held Phoebe from the dead animal. He stroked the fox's coat and found it as warm as Phoebe's would have been, as hot as the life which had been extinguished only seconds before. The fur was thick and almost orange on the animal's flanks and back, fading into the palest ochre under its belly. A vixen, he saw, turning her gently over, and as he did so, a jet of hot golden urine ran from her and into the cold grass. She had gleaming black ears and the loveliest, finest black feet he had seen, feet which a Siamese cat would have been proud of. A bright wet button-nose, eyes of amber, very long sharp teeth and a pink tongue awash with blood, blood which welled from her jaws and dripped hotly on to Andrew's hands . . . He inspected her paws and pads, again and again he ran his fingers through her coat, just as though she were a fireside dog, and expected her almost to turn her delicate head and lick him or nip him. She did neither, having a wound the size of a saucer behind one shoulder where the single concentration of shot had struck. She was mourning the loss of her brush . . . it had gone, the fine orange flame of her brush, to leave a raw stump and a blossom of blood.

Andrew stood up straight. The terrier moved in again to

reclaim the prize for itself. It snickered into the vixen's mask and nipped her black ear-tips, it dodged the imagined threat of her frozen snarl and flew to her back, ripping out tufts of russet fur, scattering them across the path. 'No, Phoebe, not you! You leave her alone!' He pulled the dog away from the fox. The hail eased. The clatter of it on his hood became a patter. The trees shrugged off the grains of ice as nonchalantly as a bride shrugs off the grains of rice. Only the track remained whitened, a trail of silver which wound onwards and upwards through the black forest.

It was twilight. And into it, lower down the path, briefly illuminating the black and white scene with a brilliant orange spark, another fox appeared. Bigger and darker than its dead mate, it flew out of the trees on one side of the track and halted for a second, branding the half-light with the flame of its redness. It dismissed the tableau of the man and his black dog, of the hysterical little white dog and the mutilated vixen . . . it melted silently into the trees on the other side of the track. As it disappeared, only seconds behind it and now filling the silence with their baying cries, six hounds burst from the cover. They were big dogs with heavy coats, with long powerful legs and wide shoulders, and they came crashing out of the undergrowth. The effect of this blundering appearance so hard on the phantasmal silence of the fox was explosive. Andrew felt his heart pounding. The blood rose instantly to his face.

And Phoebe did what she had only done once before. She writhed somehow from her collar, twisting and slithering in a blind panic at the intrusion of the hounds. She fled wildly up the trail.

'Phoebe! Phoebe!'

Andrew's voice cracked as he bellowed the word, again and again. But he was powerless to stop her. She vanished like a shadow, just as the fox had flickered like a flame. To his horror, he saw that the hounds had veered from the flight of the fox as it faded into the thickness of the trees and were dashing with their fluid, easy, loose-limbed strides in the direction which Phoebe had taken. They sped past him, cream and brown and black and tan, their shaggy coats thick with mud, their tongues flying and flecking the hail-strewn grass with foam. The last hound hesitated beside Andrew, distracted by the scent of the vixen. Paralysed with terror of what was happening, he gaped as the beast thrust its broad head forward and licked at the vixen's blood with which his hand was stained. It spun away in pursuit of its companions, in pursuit of the little, dark, fox-like dog which had arrested their attention and had become the focus of their lust for blood. A second later, he was alone with the slender orange body of the vixen, for the terrier too had gone tearing up the trail. His mind went blank at the idea of what might soon be happening higher in the forest. His head was pounding with blood, his short-sightedness was compounded by the claustrophobic gloom which the sky continued to inflict on the mountainside. He started to scramble after the dogs. He slipped on the hailstones. He slithered with his clumsy boots on the wet rocks and the mud. Cursing the darkness, encumbered by his jacket and its suffocating hood, he clambered on. When he found some pocket of breath remaining within him, he panted that single, hopeless word, 'Phoebe, Phoebe, Phoebe . . .' so that its syllables became a part of his laboured breathing. The lead and the collar dangled uselessly from his wrist. Ahead of him he saw the thinning of the trees which meant he was nearing the edge of the plantation, and above the line of trees the slabs of the crater rose sheer, glistening and black into the pall of cloud which enshrouded them. The belling of the hounds swelled up. He stumbled to his knees on the sodden ground, hardly able to breathe. Every part of his chest strained to find more air, his thighs cried out for him to stop his blind assault of the mountain . . .

There, while he lay in the mud and saw nothing but stars before his eyes, while he tasted the welling of vomit in his throat, he heard the hounds go suddenly silent. They were silenced by the explosions of two more gunshots.

He lay still. He listened to the echoes of the shots which clanged from wall to wall of the crater. Then there was utter silence. Not a hound whimpered. No raven panted in the mist. Not a jackdaw chuckled on the slippery slabs. The hail had stopped.

Painfully, his hands cold with the mud and the ice and the drying blood of the vixen, Andrew struggled to his feet and went up the path. The cloud was right down. His wet blond head felt the chilly cobwebs clinging. He forced back the hood of his jacket, breathing deeply to quieten his giddiness. Twilight had hardened into the darkness of a November afternoon.

He reached the edge of the forest and stepped over the remains of a barbed-wire fence which separated the trees from the marshes of the crater. The first thing he saw was the dim shapes of the hounds, their pale tails erect and twitching. They drifted silently in the long grass, shifting away in twos and threes, dispersing but always returning to the same spot, to drop their heads and sniff, to shake their heads and worry something which did not move except when they moved it. Time and again, as Andrew waited at the fence and watched, the hounds limbered easily to that place, where something in the grass drew them back. And then they would turn the thing over, pull it this way or that, fold it or stretch it or wring it. Once, they lifted the thing up, clear out of the grass, so that, even in the gloom, Andrew could see it was something black and very wet and twisted like a piece of rag.

His boots squelched through the quagmire. As he drew closer to the hounds, they turned to him, wagging their tails and grinning with pleasure. They nuzzled his hands, expecting his approval, eager for his congratulations. One of them brought a gift, to show this man that it had done the job for which it was usually rewarded. In its jaws it carried a long black flag of fur, wet and very muddy, which it nuzzled into Andrew's hand. But the hound did not expect the reward it received from the man who took the gift so gently from its mouth.

With a roar of rage, Andrew lashed out with one boot and caught the hound heavily in the ribs. The animal squealed and sprang away, whimpering like a child. As the man whirled from dog to dog with his boots, they fled from the thing to which they had gathered so fondly, they drifted dumbly over the marsh and faded like spectres in the mists. Andrew trod forward. He was holding the flag of fur in one hand, dangling the lead and the collar from the other.

The thing was Phoebe. It hardly resembled the creature he had known and loved. Now that it had no tail, for he was holding that in his hand, the dog looked very small and slight. And, being tossed and turned and trodden into the icy mud of the marsh, its form was blurred by the water into nothing much more than a fragment of torn black fur. Its face had been crushed. There were teeth and ribbons of its tongue where he had never seen them before. One of its eyes dripped a string of mucous pearls, the other stared wonderingly into the grass. Where the gunshots had ripped, its entrails tumbled like strange, ripe fruit. Quite altered, quite different, the Phoebe he knew from this broken thing. He knelt to it, just as he had knelt to the dead vixen, but this time he could barely bring himself to touch the dead animal. His hand recoiled from it. 'Phoebe? Is it really you?' He knelt in the water of the crater and bowed his head, suddenly overwhelmed by the realisation of what had happened. Over and over, he then caressed the bedraggled pelt of the dog, he bent his head to kiss it but could find no part of its head which had not been disfigured by the teeth of the hounds or remoulded by the mud. He felt tears flooding his eyes, he saw the hot tears drop from his face and fall on the dog's mangled throat. He heard footsteps coming closer, the sucking of mud on boots. But he did not look up, only listening to the approach of the boots through the bog of the crater.

The footsteps stopped, very close to Andrew and the dead thing. There was silence, then the sharp metallic sound of a shotgun being broken open. Two spent cartridges fell into the mud beside the body of the dog. Andrew remained still, head down, intent on the neat clean tubes which had landed there, shocked by the contrast between their compact simplicity and the ragged formlessness of the dead animal. With his fingers, he flicked the tears away from his eyes. Slowly, silently, he raised his head. Two sets of boots . . . The twin barrels of one shotgun, black and lethal in the drenching darkness of the mountain . . . His eyes followed the line of the gun, from its dumb muzzles to the breech from which the cartridges had been ejected and which now exhaled a plume of acrid smoke. It was the kennel-maid holding the gun. Beside her, her brother stood grinning inanely, his vacant expression compounded by the thick black lines of Andrew's glasses which rested crookedly on his nose. The girl smiled faintly and the tip of her tongue glistened between her little pointed teeth. There was a sheen of sweat on her face. She couched the gun comfortably in the crook of her arm, inhaling the smoke from it with a narrowing of her eyes and the flaring of her nostrils. Her brother held the bright red brush of the vixen in one hand, with the little white terrier clutched under his arm.

Andrew straightened up, the terrier began to growl. Brother and sister exchanged a few rapid words in Welsh. They stopped smiling. Somehow, without the grin, the boy was more grotesquely comic behind the lenses of Andrew's glasses. He spoke, very quietly, before Andrew had formed any idea of how he was going to express his outrage.

'You know what? You should keep your dog on a lead, that's what . . . Told you once before, didn't I? Didn't you hear us hunting? Eh? You must've heard the hounds from down at . . . what's it called, your place? Cockerel Cottage?'

He turned to his sister and chuckled, but she was drained of expression, the sweat shining on her pale face. She said nothing, only watching Andrew's eyes and waiting tensely for some reaction from them. The boy went on.

'And didn't you hear us shooting? Eh? We got a fox in the forest, you know, a pretty little brant-vixen. Look . . .' and he thrust the brush of the fox close to Andrew's face, 'look, here's a bit of it I cut off! You must've heard us! You got to be daft letting your little dog go running off without a lead. Eh, Shân?'

Once more he turned to the girl, the grin as crooked and as ill-fitting as the black spectacles. She whispered, 'Daft, yeah. You must've heard us . . .' and her voice trailed off. She licked her lips and swallowed, her mouth too dry for more than a few unoriginal words.

'It's like this, see,' the boy was saying. 'What we always do is send the hounds through the cover,' indicating the forest with a wave of the vixen's brush, 'and we just wait nice and patient here in the . . .' He rattled a couple of words in Welsh which clearly meant the bowl of marsh and steep slabs that Andrew had always thought of as simply the crater. 'Got pretty dark this afternoon, didn't it, specially with the . . .' The boy groped for the English word.

Andrew heard himself say it for him. 'Hail.' The girl jumped at the sound, not expecting to hear him prompt her brother. 'Hail, yeah, that's it,' the boy continued, 'and the hail breaks up the scent too, makes the hounds lift their heads for a minute . . . So it gets pretty dark, doesn't it, and we wait here, her with the gun 'cos she's better with it than me. Sure enough, the hounds break cover, bit confused by the hail, and go tearing after your little . . . Well, it all happens in a second, doesn't it? In the dark and the hail and all that, my darling sister lets fly at the first thing that comes out, the first foxy little thing to come streaking through all this long grass. Same size, same sort of shape and tail flying like that . . . Sort of all happens in a second.' By now, embarrassed by the sound of his own voice, hampered by his clumsiness in expressing himself by having to translate in his head before speaking, uncomfortable in the face of the Englishman's continued silence, the boy began to fidget. He twirled the brush in his fingers and clutched the terrier more closely to his side. 'Well? Don't just stand there . . . Was an accident, see? If you kept the thing on a lead and kept out of the way, it wouldn't have . . .'

Andrew's hand shot suddenly forward, so fast and unexpectedly that both the boy and the girl flinched from the shock. It flew at the boy's face. But there it stopped, in mid-air. It plucked the glasses clean away. The boy was so surprised, clearly expecting a blow, that he stumbled backwards, recoiling from Andrew's fist. He tottered for a moment and sat down heavily in the marsh. The terrier wriggled from his grasp, sprang from tuft to tuft of the tough grass and in a second was gone into the thickening blackness of the winter evening. The girl spat some vicious expression at her brother. Andrew put on his glasses and now saw clearly for the first time since Hallowe'en. Before the boy could extricate himself from the pool of mud in which he was sitting, Andrew stepped forward and stood over him.

'Yes,' he said, no more loudly than the boy had spoken. 'An accident.' He leaned closely to the boy's face, speaking through gritted teeth. 'In any case, you'd better have this. Add it to your collection . . .!' And he brought round his hand to lash the boy as hard as he could, first on one cheek and then on the other, with the mud- and blood-soaked whip of Phoebe's tail. The boy pulled away, cursing, rolling more deeply on to his back and his side in the icy water, but too late to avoid the blows. Welts of blood and mud stood up on his face. While he struggled to his feet, Andrew tossed the length of tattered fur at him. Turning to the girl, he snapped at her, his mouth very close to hers, 'Take him home, you poor little witch-bitch, before I knock some of his teeth out! I thought you told me *he* was supposed to be the trigger-happy member of the family . . .' He felt his anger start to ooze, as though he had been grazed and wounded and had had to wait a while for the blood to well through the raked-over flesh. Now, having surfaced, the anger was ready to run hot and fast, to fly anywhere. The girl saw this. She must have seen the renewed definition of Andrew's eyes, that he was about to erupt and expend his rage as quickly and as violently as possible, for she hissed something at her brother and moved athletically out of range of the Englishman's reach.

'Go on, you fucking cave-peasants!' Andrew began to shout. 'Yes, go on, fuck off up into the mountains!'

He lunged at them, roaring, and something in his blondness, the whiteness of his features which suddenly swelled purple with fury, something in the shagginess of his wet blond mane made the brother and sister turn from him and stumble away, splashing through the marshes, half-running, half-staggering over the clumps of spiny grass. He watched them fade into the gloom, two small dark figures dissolving as their hounds had done in the lowering clouds of the crater. He listened to their fading footsteps. He heard his own breath rasp in his throat, the heaving of his chest . . . And then there was no sound, only the running of water down the slabs, a layer of sound which was so inescapable that it registered as a kind of silence . . .

When they had gone, when the hounds had vanished and the terrier as well, he was alone in the crater. He turned to the corpse of the dog. A kind of romantic scenario flashed across his mind, of himself kneeling to stroke and kiss the head of his beloved pet and weep a few more bitter tears. It should have been the appropriate thing to do. But he could not. The twisted thing which lay trampled in the mud, with its teeth and eyes rearranged, with its bowels steaming and pink, with a coil of liquid excrement oozing hot and yellow from the rent where its tail had once been, was nothing like Phoebe. How could he kiss it? How could he continue to love it? 'Is it you, Phoebe? Christ . . .' He tore off the lead which had been hanging from his wrist and slung it from him, into the darkness. Very quickly, with his teeth clenched against the wave of nausea rising in his throat, he stooped to the thing and seized it where he guessed the scruff of its neck should be, straightening up with the body dangling from his hand like the remains of an old umbrella. It came out of the mud with a sigh of suction. He held it away from his chest, his head averted, and he swallowed very hard to keep down the taste of vomit. The corpse was black and slick, water poured from it and left it skeletal, its limbs jutting in the awkward angles to which they had been broken. Coils of shit spattered into the grass, splashes of brilliant viscous colour in the sombre shadows. Gagging at the stink of the rising steam, Andrew tramped in the direction of the forest, his arm outstretched to keep the thing away from him. With difficulty, he negotiated the barbed wire and then he was moving fast through the plantation, down the track. There were only his own clumsy footprints in what was left of the fall of hail, coming towards him, the evidence in the silver carpet of ice of how he had slipped and stumbled in pursuit of the chase. It was very dark. But the trail was easy to follow, white like a strip of bandage and winding steeply down through the black trees. He came to the body of the vixen and paused for a moment. She was dead, but she was still very pretty, blemished only by the wound of the single shot which had killed her and by the desecration of her brush. Momentarily he wanted to stoop and pick her up with his other, empty hand. No, he thought . . . she'd have to stay in the forest and be dismantled by the ravens. He moved on, following the pale light of the path, aware that the night had shut down the mountain and the valley and the forest once more. Even in the woodland of the birch there was very little light, for although the hailstorm had passed and left a veil of ice on the fallen leaves, still the sky was muffled by a layer of thick black cloud. He picked his way among the oak and the rowan, making out the angular shape of the cottage below him. The wellington boots slapped, his breath made plumes of smoke in front of his face, the black dead thing dangled and dripped a complicated festoon of slime from its belly. And the man stepped to the front door of the cottage.

He put down the thing he was carrying. Unlocking the door, he was in and out in a matter of seconds, bringing the torch from the living-room. He shone it on the corpse and caught the leer of its broken mask in the circle of light. Taking a deep breath, he picked it up again and followed the torchlight to the woodshed.

Somehow the stench was a comfort. And so was the droning of the flies. When he stepped inside, he felt secure in the close, warmer darkness which the beam from the torch made golden. He relaxed. The hum of industry! The feeling that things were working! The atmosphere of bustle and business and commitment! The badger turned slowly on its hook and stared at Andrew. It smiled. It sighed and released a clutch of dry pupae from its nostrils. The swan shivered its vast wings, caressing the bristles of the badger with its silvery breast. A cluster of flies tumbled noisily from under its tail, like drunks being manhandled from a pub. The bird and the beast hung on their hooks. Andrew ran the torch-light up and down the badger and the swan, comfortable in the little woodshed . . . there were the logs he had so lovingly cut, stacked neatly by the walls, sweet-smelling, drying to be ready for the flames.

He felt easy in the outhouse, in the shrine he had prepared to the god he worshipped. It was the shrine which he dedicated to the stinkhorn.

He put down the torch on the logs so that its beam shone up towards the rafters. The feel of the place had calmed him after the exertion of the chase and his rapid descent through the woodland, there was something soothing in the presence of the two dead things and their work-force of flies. And here was another dead thing. Using both hands now, having lost his disgust for it, he swung the dog in front of his face and looked for the right spot on its mutilated body. Its head hung down, like the badger's. He lifted it easily higher, to the next vacant hook. The tip of the hook pressed for a second into the matted fur of the dead thing's belly, found a place where already the skin had been broken by shot and by the teeth of the hounds, and it slid smoothly and deeply in. Andrew held his breath. Very gingerly, not sure how secure it would be on its ruptured belly, he let go and stood back. The dog rearranged itself now that it was inverted: it hung on its hook, the tangle of viscera falling over its chest, the diminishing flow of slime seeping down.

'Splendid . . .' he whispered, picking up the torch. 'Yes, you'll do . . .'

He retreated to the door of the woodshed so that he could have the overall view of the scene: the interior of a dilapidated stone outhouse, its clutter of tins, paint and paraffin, the walls stacked with an assortment of logs, birch and rowan and oak and even some twisted limbs of ivy; and, illuminated by the single golden beam of light, his three dead things in different stages of decomposition. The dog was just a beginner, with a lot of catching up to do. Badger and swan and dog, on their three hooks, with the torch- running tenderly up and down their dangling bodies . . . All of this so that the presence of the stinkhorn might be perpetuated.

The torchlight led him back to the cottage. Turning on the lights, he glanced briefly at the basket and its rumpled blankets in the corner of the room, but, before any twinge of sentiment could be triggered by the sight of it lying empty, he was distracted by the drumming of the flies in the cupboard. The two jars were stuffed with buzzing black insects. More and more of the pupae had developed rapidly in the heat and the tumult, so that the jars vibrated with a riot of clambering bodies, the beating of hundreds of pairs of wings. Repelled, Andrew turned from the scene, his heart pumping again wildly as it had done in the forest. A vision of the stinkhorn swam into his mind and burned there, eclipsing everything else into a dim blur.

He spun round. A cold panic gripped him as he surveyed the mantelpiece.

The penultimate stinkhorn had risen to a full erection. But now, already, it was wilting. Its head slipped down the inside of the jar. In the warm dampness of the cottage, while he and Phoebe had been clambering upwards through the forest, while he and the dead thing had been slithering down again, while he had been making his third offering to the shrine, his god was up. It must have stretched itself aloft within the prison of its jar, fine and white and brazen, with no mesmerised onlooker to worship it. Quite alone, unspectated, the stinkhorn had risen to its one and only occasion. Not a soul on earth had seen it. Andrew groaned. Both hands flew to his head, smeared with blood and mud and excrement, where they gripped into his hair with a passion of frustration. He bolted back to the cupboard and grabbed one of the jars in which the flies were writhing. 'Here, take these!' he was panting, 'please, please! These are for you!' and he attempted to make his sacrificial offering to the exhausted phallus. He slammed down the jar of flies, frantically unscrewed the lid of the stinkhorn's jar, put it back on the mantelpiece and took up the flies again. In his hurry, in his clumsiness, as he tore off the cellophane skin, he dropped the jar on to the hearth . . . It smashed into hundreds of pieces. 'Christ, oh Christ!' he screamed, as scores of flies broke on to the carpet and grappled hysterically to get themselves airborne. He trod away in horror, but the flies rose in a single, droning black cloud and beat around his head. He shouted, he flagged his arms and windmilled them, but this only sucked the swarm more densely to his face. They banged their heavy bodies into his mouth, against his glasses, they drummed at him as vigorously as they had drummed to be released from their prison, while, on the rug, popping under his feet as he danced to disentangle himself from the flies, the spillage of pupae lay on their bed of sawdust. Unable to think clearly, Andrew thought only of the stinkhorn, the image of its recent erection burning in his head. He reached forward to the mantelpiece and seized the jar whose lid he had unscrewed, and, lurching across the room, his mind ringing with curses and all kinds of bizarre blasphemies against the god he had worshipped, he tore the door open . . . He flung the jar as far as he could into the darkness of the hillside. The cloud of flies followed him out of the cottage. Just as he heard the shattering of the jar against a rock, as though they had heard it too and were desperate to search out the relics of the thing for which they had been reared in confinement, the flies blew away from his head and vanished as one mass into the night. Andrew was panting like a walrus, still trembling from the panic which overwhelmed him. He ran his hands through and through his hair to shake out any laggardly insects, he stared away from the light of the cottage . . . There, he found the blackest expanse of the opposite hillside and focused hard on it. For the time being, the spectre of the stinkhorn was gone.

When he was almost calm again, he went inside. With a brush and dustpan he swept up the mess of sawdust, he made sure all the shards of glass were picked up too and went around to the back of the cottage to deposit them in a heap of ashes. In those few moments in darkness, he made up his mind about what he was going to do next, so that there was no drama or passion in it. He wanted everything to be quite clear, quite uncomplicated, so that nothing would distract him. After all, the jars which contained the obsolete stinkhorns, still on the mantelpiece, were no use. Why had he kept them there? They were finished! They were gobbets of dead mucus! He collected them, the two jars in which the phalli had risen and fallen, never to rise again, and, one after the other, he hurled them with all his might where he had hurled the first. He listened with satisfaction to the splintering of glass. He smiled to hear the sheep stampede.

This done, he stepped into the cottage and closed the door. 'No more clutter now,' he said. 'There's just you and me, and nothing else.' He addressed this to the single jar remaining on the mantelpiece. Of the four which had been there, one was left. In it, the last stinkhorn egg in Britain lay warm and ripe in its bed of moist earth. 'Just you and me and a few flies.' He sat down in the armchair. 'I'm going to watch you. I'm not going to let you get away.' He wondered whether to wash himself, for he was very dirty. No, he'd remain smeared with mud and blood. He wondered about lighting the fire, to comfort his vigil. No, no fire tonight. No distractions. He wanted nothing, no dancing golden flames, no aromatic sizzling to spoil his concentration. Turning the lights down, he reached for a blanket. That was all he needed. There was no need for a fire.

He noticed then the portrait of Phoebe. The little green slug had not only crossed the expanse of glass, but it had been back and forth half a dozen times. In doing so, the slug had finished the job of defacing the picture which the damp had so thoroughly begun. The trails of slime glistened on the glass. There was nothing much left of the dog's face, for its eyes and its teeth had been rearranged into a blur of black and grey. So, he thought . . . the stinkhorn had escaped the tomb of glass in which he'd tried to imprison it. The silver slime of the slug was the stinkhorn's signature, on Phoebe's death-warrant.

Andrew rose from the armchair and went into the kitchen. Picking up the salt cellar, he returned to the mantelpiece. 'There,' he said, 'this is for Phoebe,' and he poured the salt on to the slug. Instantly it writhed from the glass. It landed on the hearth, where he administered more salt. The slug contorted and shrank into a ball of green pulp, like snot. 'Go on, you bastard . . . Scream . . . Can I hear you screaming?' When the slug lay still, Andrew put down the salt cellar. He removed the disfigured painting of Phoebe from the wall and placed it, face downward, in the dog's basket. Having done this, having resisted a surge of sorrow which threatened to overcome him when he smelled the familiar scent of the dead creature's blanket, he took down the rest of Jennifer's pictures and leaned them against the wall in a corner of the room. Good. Good.

No distractions. No bleary impressions of Sussex. No memories of Jennifer. No Phoebe. No picture of Phoebe. No relics of the obsolete fungi. No fire.

He settled down to the vigil. Outside, as ever, the mountain and the forest and the woodland were smothered by the night. The cottage huddled under the black blanket. And inside, waiting and watching, there was Andrew Pinkney, never flinching his eyes from the one unblinking eye of the last egg. Long into the night, he awaited the hatching and the arrogant erection of his one remaining stinkhorn.

VII

THE HOURS of the night limped by, cold and painful.

Huddled in his armchair, Andrew watched the jar and its imprisoned egg as determinedly as a falconer would watch his falcon. That was how a man might tame a wilful, haughty bird of prey, bend its will to his, by keeping it awake until it finally accepted defeat and slept on his fist. For Andrew, the task was to remain alert enough to catch the first stirrings of the egg, whenever that might be, in the bleakest and most silent depths of the night or at dawn the next day, or later still, or later still, or . . . Hours or possibly days could pass, and he must be vigilant or be beaten by the stinkhorn.

His head became heavy and it nodded. And then he would lurch himself awake, rub his eyes and stare once more at the mantelpiece. Nothing had changed. Only, wherever he looked, at the ceiling or the bare walls and their blossoms of mould, he saw the ghost of the woodwitch, hovering like a pale, unearthly candle before his vision. It was branded on him. It was everywhere, following him. He could not shake it off with any amount of rubbing or blinking. When he closed his eyes, the stinkhorn burned more brightly still against a background of darkness, a white, ethereal column which had come to haunt him. The need for sleep became greater as the night wore on and he felt colder. When he dozed, his head falling on to his chest, then the spectre of the stinkhorn was eclipsed by a persistent dream which flickered in and out of focus like an ancient newsreel . . . He was in the forest. He was being pursued through the black, clinging trees. As he ran and stumbled and fled, his face was lashed by the branches, everything was dark, there was no path, he blundered blindly among the ranks of the trees and felt their bristles sting him and cut him. Behind him, the sound of his pursuers grew louder, their inexorable splintering footfalls through the undergrowth, louder and louder, closer and closer, until he was sure he could feel the weight and the heat of their breath on the back of his neck . . . He was shouting, he was struggling to breathe, he was suffocating in the smothering grip of the forest, while the footsteps over his shoulder increased in volume and became a rhythmic crashing, faster, noisier, nearer . . . Then, unable to fight his way any further through the trees, he would turn to face the hunters. This was when the nightmare shifted from one blur to another, for at one moment it was the sheep which thrust their blackened, manic masks at him and breathed a blast of fetid breath, and then it was the hounds, lolling their fleshy, blood-flecked tongues, and then they became a pack of braying women, imbeciles the lot of them, big women with hard smiles on their mouths, a pack which was led by Jennifer and by the kennel-maid and by Mrs Stone . . . Just as he was pinioned by the stares which glinted from Jennifer's glasses, or as the kennel-maid's tongue loomed pink and wet, when he felt the heron-woman's gimlet beak come close, he would leap to wakefulness, find himself swathed deeply in his blanket, its damp folds wrapped about his face. He sat up, trembling, sweating. In horror of the dream, and panic-stricken that he might have slept through the stinkhorn's performance, he jumped to his feet to inspect the jar . . .

Nothing had changed.

He paced the room, with the blanket around his shoulders. He recited aloud some clauses of the 1968 Theft Act (for he knew no poetry or dramatic speeches), he sang a few verses of the hymns with which he had been indoctrinated at school, but always the lure of sleep led him back to the armchair. The imprint of the stinkhorn glowed in front of him. The night stretched ahead and seemed to have no end; like the forest which was the killing-ground of his dreams, it gathered around him and would not let him go. More fitful sleep, and again the nightmare of the pursuit among the trees . . . More dreadful inspections of the egg in the jar . . . More hours alone in the silence with only his tuneless voice for company . . . And the unshakable presence of the stinkhorn.

At last it was dawn. There was a frost. The hillsides were turned to steel. As the first light of morning silvered the room and Andrew realised with relief that he had not so far been side-stepped by sleep into missing the bursting of the egg, he went outside to stir himself. It was very cold. The landscape was a place of bone in which he too felt fleshless and bloodless. Everything was hard, beaten by the frost into sheets of dully glinting metal. His footsteps rang hollow on the frozen grass. He took the key to the woodshed, went there and back twice for some coal and an armful of logs, confident now that he could have the fire lit without jeopardising his ability to watch the jar. He ducked among the three dead things, whose smell was somehow quenched by the cold, setting them swinging on their hooks, re-arranging a few pots of paint and a bottle of turpentine in order to reach some of the first logs he had cut some weeks before, those that would be driest. Locking the woodshed, he returned quickly to the cottage. Now he found that the room was really cold, that the fingers of the frost had reached in and touched everything while he went busily back and forth for fuel. He seldom took his eyes from the mantelpiece for more than a minute at a time, lighting the balls of newspaper which ignited the kindling wood which struck the yellow flames from the coal. And then a log or two. It was rowan this time. But it had no power over the woodwitch. He had discovered that some nights before.

The room warmed up and Andrew continued to man the stinkhorn. Quickly the windows became blurred with condensation, he saw the moisture like a sheen of sweat on the walls, he watched the patches of green mould and imagined he saw them spreading into odd and various shapes, of birds and animals and clouds and islands. But, whatever fancy his imagination took, he could never erase the pale phantom which shimmered before him. Over the course of the morning, he made cups and cups of coffee, black, because he had not been down to the village for milk. He was comforted by the drone of the flies in their jars, that they grew stronger and were ready to carry out their part of the experiment. It helped him to remain watchful, although he was very tired, to see that the flies were not inclined to sleep; he instilled in himself the notion that it would be unfair, pulling rank, for him to snatch the blessed relief of sleep, while the flies, so vital to the operation, drummed restlessly at the glass walls of their jars. Sitting beside the fire, he watched the rowan flare and felt the warmth of it on his legs. He thought that soon he could go home to Sussex, depending on when the stinkhorn chose to hatch. Possibly even tomorrow, he'd throw his few remaining things into the car and drive south, bearing gently his single precious trophy, a jar to which the spores of the stinkhorn had been transmitted by the flies. Yes, one more day in the stew of the cottage, Cockerel Cottage, whose misnomer had resulted in a number of extraordinary happenings . . . Another day to endure in the shadow of that mountain, under the shroud of the forest, and perhaps he could go home! Get some air! See some sky! Breathe, without feeling the damp clinging to his lungs!

Despite the rising temperature and the increasing clamminess of the atmosphere, nothing altered on the mantelpiece. Stimulated by the volume of the flies, wanting something to do, anything to keep him alert and vigilant, Andrew decided he could risk being out of the cottage for a few minutes on end. Another harvest from the woodshed, that was what he'd do. If he were going to leave soon, what a shame not to reap as much of the crop as possible! Invigorated by this idea to stir himself, he searched the kitchen until he found exactly what he needed at the back of a cupboard: a set of plastic containers, unfortunately without their appropriate lids, boxes of different sizes for storing various foodstuffs in a refrigerator. He took them with him across the thawing turf, to the door of the woodshed, recoiling from the renewed stench which blew from the swinging corpses. And for half an hour, with regular returns to the cottage to be sure he was missing nothing, he plucked from the badger and the swan every maggot he could find. The dog had nothing to offer him. He worked hard, as all harvesters must. The cooler air and the activity refreshed him after his night of wakefulness and the morning's torpor in front of the fire. Box after box he filled with maggots. The strange fruit tumbled from the badger's jaws, from its nostrils and its eyes. He pummelled the belly of the beast, he milked a procession of maggots from the animal's anus. They oozed from the discolouring wounds which the barbed wire had inflicted. The badger groaned under his massage, it gave up with a sigh all the busy blind miners which had been tunnelling the chambers of its obsolete body. He turned to the swan. Under each wing there was a rent where the harvest was easily plundered. By shaking the bird's emaciated neck, he induced a spurting of maggots to rain into his containers and overflow among the logs. He unhooked the swan and swung it upside-down, its head stiffened in the position which the hook had dictated, while an orderly single file of maggots fell out. So he went on, returning the swan to its hook, giving a final hug to the badger's deflated belly, pulping the bird's breast, until he was satisfied that all was safely gathered in. There was no more. All the containers were writhing with the plump yellow larvae. The maggots were very ripe. Finally, he scooped handfuls of pupae from the sawdust on the floor of the woodshed, delighted to find that already there were brand-new flies sculling their wings among them, and he filled one container with a mess of pupae, sawdust and a rowdy assembly of the freshly hatched insects. Gently, careful to avoid any spillage, he carried the entire crop back to the cottage. With a reassuring glance at the mantelpiece, where nothing yet was different, he passed through the front room and into the kitchen, where he busied himself with sheets of cellophane to keep the harvest safe. He put the container of pupae and new flies near the warmth of the water tank. It was the afternoon. The woodshed was locked once more. Andrew returned to his armchair by the fireside, happy to have been busy, feeling better for the activity, satisfied to know that the kitchen was occupied by hundreds and hundreds of maggots and that there were plenty of mature pupae in the water-tank cupboard. How many of them would develop into flies before he vacated the cottage? Would he still be there to witness their fruition? The muttering of flies continued. He wondered whether the sound might stir those thousands of pulsing things to quicken into flies so that he'd have a great black cloud of them to release . . . He built up the fire with more coal, placed a tangle of ivy there. The scent of it filled the room. Sitting comfortably in his armchair with the blanket across his lap, he inhaled the perfume and closed his eyes.

The warmth of the fire . . . The droning of the flies . . . The smell of roasting chestnuts . . . A November afternoon becoming dark and pressing closely to the windows of the cottage . . .

This time, when he slipped into the abyss of sleep, he did not dream.

The ivy saved him.

One moment he was lost in a splendid oblivion, warm and relaxed and untroubled, and then he was wide awake again. He sprang up to rescue his feet from the hot coals and smouldering ivy which slipped from the fire, skidding across the hearth and on to the carpet. Having burned through one coil of its twisted limbs, the ivy had leaned and unbalanced, to tumble from the fireplace. He quickly reached for the tongs and returned the wood to the flames. Its perfume rose from the singed rug. As his eyes followed the spiralling plume of smoke, they were arrested at the mantelpiece. Only then, salvaged from the depths of sleep, did he remember the object of his vigil.

The final stinkhorn was erect.

Alone, unchallenged, it seemed to Andrew Pinkney to be the finest specimen of them all. The jar was only just big enough to contain it. The fungus had stretched up its thick, white column; its hooded head, honeycombed with the stipples of oozing oil-green and viscous black, was some six inches out of the earth. The masterpiece of the stinkhorn stood up: the forest's unashamed caricature of the human phallus, at which the ancient peoples of the mountains had marvelled for century after century . . . the object of their wonder and witchcraft, a totem, a thing to be prized and loathed and feared, a pale mocking shape which taunted them with its unwholesome smells, which lured them to its clammy clearings, which reeked with the buzzing of flies, which became the stuff of their folklore, their superstitions, even their primitive worship. The stinkhorn was woven into man's dreams, ever since there were men on these hillsides. It hovered, dim and white and putrid, in their nightmares. It was a symbol of their manhood. Its very transience was essential to the magic, that it came and went so quickly, as a witch of the woods would flicker faintly and then vanish among the dark shadows. And here, on the mantelpiece, was the best of that coven of witches, the most handsome, the most potent, and the last of the year which had reared it.

Stung into action by the realisation that he had only been alerted by an accident of the fire, Andrew bolted to the cupboard. He seized a jar which was so dense with flies that it had all but fallen silent, with the insects packed closely together and hardly able to move. He dashed back to the hearth and put down the jar of flies on the mantelpiece. Then, breathing deeply, trying to steady himself, determined that no clumsiness should spoil his final chance, he picked up the stinkhorn. It swayed dangerously. 'Christ, oh Christ! Be careful!' he heard himself grunting, his teeth clenched, for now he saw how fragile the thing really was and how top-heavy in the shallow soil. No wonder it was over so fast, this fine erection, no wonder it was so easily unmanned . . . It was made of nothing but frail tissue . . . there was no blood in it, no gristle. It was all a show! It made a spectacular, arrogant entry, it stood up straight and tall, but there was nothing to it! Any blundering shrew which brushed against it in the forest would destroy it in an instant . . . It made a grand showing for an hour or so, only to be quickly demolished by flies. Like all ghosts, there was no substance to it.

He unscrewed the jar. The pungency of dead meat hit him, just as it did in the woodshed. As gently as he could, he knelt and placed the open jar on the hearth. He stretched up and took the jar of flies. Kneeling there in the firelight, with the two jars before him, he was the priest at some mystic sacrifice, bowing to the offerings which he laid on the altar. The jars gleamed with dancing flames. They shone with golden sparks. In one of them, one half of an equation which Andrew had been trying to juggle for weeks, a host of flies glinted blue and green and glistening black. In the other, the other half of the equation, the stinkhorn was a white candle, its flame oozing. Andrew slowly peeled back the cellophane skin which imprisoned the flies. They were stupid from the crush. Before they could untangle themselves and spin upwards from the jar, he tipped it gradually over the head of the fungus. He held his breath. The room was silent, save for the whisper of the flames. The first few insects dropped from one jar into the other. More followed, grappling together like schoolboys. With his finger, Andrew persuaded more and more to tumble around the stinkhorn, until the soil from which the egg had thrust the phallus was deep with flies. He swiftly screwed the lid on to that jar, he covered the other jar with cellophane. Still kneeling there, his golden head alight with the flicker of the fire, he trembled to see how his equation balanced.

Slowly, clumsily, as though they were awakening from a long sleep, the flies around the base of the stinkhorn separated one from another. They tested their brand-new wings. First one, then a few more, started to scale the sheer walls of glass. Higher and higher they climbed, half-flying, half-crawling. Yes, there was something which drew them on, something which told them to quit that bed of warm moist earth and strive towards the top of the jar. When the first fly spun away from the glass, dizzily crossed that airspace which was so trivial for the fly and so important to Andrew, when it landed and stuck on the stinkhorn's head, Andrew rose from his knees with a great shout of excitement. A second fly followed. A third, a fourth, a fifth, and each time he bellowed. Until the head of the stinkhorn was completely hidden by a cluster of flies, gorging themselves on the slimy seed.

His elation was short-lived. It collapsed like a punctured lung. The shouts stuck in his throat.

At the peak of his exhilaration, Andrew was overcome by a feeling of awful loneliness. For a few weeks he had lived alone, with Phoebe his only company, and never felt lonely. Now he was bursting with something to tell somebody, to show somebody, he needed someone with whom to share his excitement. There was no one.

The darkness and the sheer weight of that mountain which loomed behind the cottage seemed to bear him down, to crush him into nothing but a speck. The night folded around him, to squeeze the life from his body. He felt as though he were shrivelling to nothing, as the slug had shrivelled, as the stinkhorn would inevitably shrivel. Phoebe was gone. There was Andrew Pinkney, and nobody else on the whole of that hillside, not another human soul with whom to share his sense of achievement, no one to hold close and feel warm against the dampness and chill of that benighted place . . . He stood at the hearth, numb. So intense was the realisation of his loneliness, that all he could think to do was to pick up the key to the woodshed and to run out there with his torch. He fumbled with the padlock. Throwing open the door, he stared despairingly about him and flashed the light from the floor to the rafters. No one else, just the man, alone and very lonely, so lonely that he had no alternative but to share his moment of joy with the three dead beasts in the woodshed . . . a dead badger, upside-down on a meat-hook, grinning; a dead swan, its throat pierced by a meat-hook; the broken remains of a dead dog, with a meat-hook through its belly. Jesus . . . this was all the company he could find in the shadow of the mountain that night . . .! He put down the torch and covered his face with his hands. In the beam of light which illuminated the interior of the shrine, watched by the three silent, stinking, dead things, he sobbed until his chest ached, until his big soft face was streaming with tears.

When he could cry no more, he wiped his eyes and came out of the woodshed. There was no solace to be found there. Locking the door, he returned to the cottage, where the flies stuck stupidly to the remains of their feast. Tomorrow he could go home, he thought with a massive sigh of relief. Dirty, tired, feeling quite hollow, as though every last part of the pith had been cut out of his body, he curled up on the sofa with his blanket and sank into the quicksands of sleep.

The shadow of the stinkhorn flickered faintly in his head . . .

*

That feeling a small boy has when he awakes in the spartan featurelessness of a boarding-school dormitory, when he comes to consciousness and remembers that this is the last morning of term, that within hours he'll return to all that is familiar and warm at home . . .! Something very like that indescribably lovely sensation filled Andrew's heart when he next opened his eyes and stared around the room. Home! Yes, this day he'd go home, to the civilisation and sense and routine of Sussex, his guilt expiated by the events of his weeks in Wales! With the same eagerness he had felt as that boarding-school boy, unable to stay in bed a moment longer, he unwound himself from the blanket and stood up. As though in celebration of the occasion, the morning sent a bouquet of warm sunlight on to the hillside opposite the cottage, picking out an emerald meadow studded with a flock of clean, white sheep. Splendid! he thought. So there really was a spark of brightness in that dismal valley, if only on the day he'd chosen for his departure. It cheered him quite disproportionately to the actual warmth of the morning, for he suddenly felt that his breast could burst with happiness. He grimaced guiltily at the sight of Phoebe's empty basket, wiped her from his mind. Glowing like a schoolboy in anticipation of his release, he began his preparations to leave.

He switched on the immersion heater, which gave him an hour before there would be water for a bath. Hurriedly dressing, he went to the car, which had been so little used over the past month, and drove it as close to the cottage as he could. The track was very slippery, so the wheels spun and churned in the mud, but he managed to move the vehicle nearer so that packing it with his few belongings would be easier. Already he felt himself returning to normality, before he had even left the place. The shreds of cool sunshine and the activity of organising his departure made the cobwebs drop away from him. He thrilled at the weight of his glasses, comfortable and heavy on the bridge of his nose. Simply getting in and out of the car, the smell of the upholstery, reminded him of the tidy life which beckoned him back. In the cottage, he folded his clothes and packed them into his suitcase, looking forward very much to washing everything thoroughly when he arrived home, anticipating the scent of freshly laundered shirts and the crispness of the smart suits he wore in the office. On impulse, he went to the bathroom with a pair of scissors, where, in front of the mirror, he snipped away the heavy locks of golden hair which had encumbered his brow. The curls fell from around his ears until the sink was sprinkled with cuttings. Better and better! he thought. He wanted to cast off the shabbiness, the scruffiness, the mould which clung to him, and be renewed to the twentieth century. How could he have lived like this? How could he have behaved as he had done? He wanted to shrug off the spell which the country had cast on him.

Keeping out a set of clean clothes, he carried his case to the car. He paused to wonder what he should do with Phoebe's basket and with the spoiled pictures. For the time being, his priority was to clear the cottage so that he could give it a good clean before he left, so he brought the basket and the pictures out and laid them on the short grass by the woodshed. He tried to ignore the smell which filtered to him from the shed; all that was a part of the aberration of his stay in Wales, something soon to be erased from his memory. He shut out the stink from his nostrils. He carried the plastic containers from the cottage, for how could he clean the place and leave it presentable for his employer's next visit when every space was cluttered with maggots? In fact, many of the pupae, so ripe when he had harvested them, were already changed to flies which hurled themselves loudly on the cellophane skins. He shuddered, feeling the boxes vibrating in his hands with the turmoil of the big black flies. He left them all near the woodshed, near Phoebe's basket and the washed-out watercolours. For the rest of the morning, postponing his bath until he was satisfied, he attacked each room of the cottage in turn with sponge, hot water, disinfectant, duster and vacuum cleaner. He spent a long time on his hands and knees, scrubbing the floors of the kitchen and bathroom, he emptied the ashes from the grate. Certainly the place would be better for his visit. He was determined to leave it cleaner than he had found it.

He bathed, luxuriating in the deep, soapy water. Time and time again he knelt up in the bath and scrubbed himself, to scour away any last scum of the damp dark atmosphere which might cling to him . . . any mud he had brought from the crater, any blood from whatsoever wounded beast, any sweat of a nightmarish chase, any tears of bitter loneliness or bereavement, any traces of soot or the sludge of soot and wine, any faint lines of ink on his face, any saliva from a tiny pink tongue . . . He wanted it all off, to see it all go down the plug hole, down that unpronounceable river and away to sea. He must get clean! And soon, glowing pinkly from the heat and the scrubbing, he dressed in his clean clothes.

All of this took him into the early afternoon.

There was, of course, one item he would take with him to Sussex as a memento of his stay in Wales, as a trophy.

He went to the front door, to examine the remains of the stinkhorn in the daylight. While he had been sleeping, the final phallus had fallen, as the others had fallen, to nothing more than a coil of wet wasted matter. But the flies which had fed on its head were buzzing vigorously about the jar.

'You lot are coming with me,' he told them. 'Let's get you organised for the trip.' From the kitchen, where he had kept it separate from the other containers he had removed to the woodshed, he collected one of the receptacles of earth he had earlier prepared for this stage of the experiment. There was no point in keeping the defunct stinkhorn any longer. It was finished. The show was over. The ghost had evaporated into thin air. The flies were more important, carrying millions of spores on their bodies and in their digestive systems. Outside, in the chill light of afternoon, he transferred as many of the gorged insects as he could from the jar with its derelict fungus to the other. He screwed the lid on tightly. In that matter-of-fact way he reduced the entire experiment, all its dragging and digging and bottling and harvesting and waiting, to its quintessence. Hurling away the wilted corpse of the last woodwitch, he listened delightedly to the smashing of glass on the rocks. No more stinkhorn? Was that the end of the woodwitch? Would it continue to haunt him? In his hands he now held the trophy to be taken from that place, all that was left of the experiment. Not much to look at, he thought wryly . . . Was this the reason he'd come all this way to Wales and spent such a traumatic month in Cockerel Cottage? For this? An old jam jar buzzing with dozens of meat-flies? Was that the result of his banishment? Would anything come of it?

Slipping the jar into the pocket of his jacket, he went back inside the cottage to check that he had cleared all his things. He tried each room, looking in drawers and under beds, touching for the last time those blooms of green mould on the walls. Wet whitewash remained on the tips of his fingers, a powder of sweat and plaster-dust lingered in corners and in cupboards, despite his efforts to improve the place. He thought he was ready to go. He'd left nothing in the cottage, everything was clean and tidy, the car was packed, he was bathed and he was dressed more smartly than at any time since he'd left Sussex. Thank goodness he had his glasses! he thought as he stood in the kitchen, thinking about his long journey, the route he would take and the time he should be home. It was two o'clock. In his pocket, the jam jar hummed with flies.

He felt a spasm of guilt and annoyance about the

woodshed, its grisly contents, and the obsolete possessions which he had put on the grass outside its door. Damn . . . couldn't he just leave them all behind? Couldn't he simply put the dog's basket and those pictures in the woodshed, as a contribution to the fuel store for the next visitor to break them up and use them to kindle the fire? And the dead things? Now that he was clean and smart, having already slipped into the frame of mind that he was finished with all that and was leaving it all behind, Andrew was irritated to be drawn back into a consideration of the badger, the swan, that dog which had been Phoebe. Just leave them there? Yes, he thought briskly . . . it would be Easter before his boss came to Wales, in more than five months' time, and long before then the corpses would have withered to nothing but a few dry bones, dropping from their hooks to be scattered by rats among the stacks of logs. The next person to go in there would first of all have a very pleasant surprise to see so much wood, cut and dry, ready for the fire, and later might fleetingly wonder at the whitened bones . . . There'd be nothing more to suggest the gruesome things which had once swung so usefully from those quaint old hooks on the rafters. Good, he thought, going through to the living-room . . . that was the problem solved. Now it was time to lock the cottage, to push those things into the woodshed and lock it up, and he'd be off. A tidy end to his stay in Cockerel Cottage . . .

Meanwhile, the flies buzzed more loudly in his pocket.

At that moment, he was surprised to see the movement of a big white animal, which was not a sheep, on the hillside in front of the cottage. And another, then a third, three pale creatures limbering easily through the broken bracken and coming closer with each loping stride . . . The three hounds moved like ghosts, fluid and athletic and dim against the beaten landscape.

Andrew's heart lurched. Immediately, his mouth went dry. Oh Christ! Not now! Please, not now! he prayed . . . not now, when I'm just about to leave and never come back! The girl appeared from round the bulge of the hill, calling to the hounds in Welsh. Her figure was engulfed by the big jacket, the baggy trousers, she seemed weighted down by those great boots. The curls of her short black hair, under a man's hat, formed a kind of ragged halo around her white face.

'Oh Christ . . .' There was nothing he wanted to say to her, nothing he wanted to hear her say. His mind raced with notions of avoiding the girl. She was striding nearer to the car, glancing inside it and then looking up to the cottage. He could not see where the hounds had gone. Christ! If they were nosing around the woodshed, attracted by the smells! What if she started to poke about the pictures and the dog's basket, wondering what all those maggots and flies were doing in . . .! The last thing he wanted now, with the car ready to go, with the cottage tidy, was to start explaining anything to the kennel-maid or to listen to any schoolgirl apologies for what had happened to Phoebe . . . He just wanted to leave.

Praying that she would not glance at the cottage again and see him, he slipped out of the front door and pulled it silently shut. There . . . it was locked. He'd left it for the last time. He darted around the side of the building, wishing that he was wearing his wellington boots instead of the smarter shoes he had put on, and headed quickly towards the woodland. His hermit's cell! Yes, it would be ideal now as a hiding place from which he could watch the girl until she went off with her hounds. He sprang from tuft to tuft of the tough grasses, to avoid as much as possible stepping into the marsh. When he looked around, panting for breath, he saw that one of the hounds had come lolling after him, very friendly and soft, with its tongue dangling from a smiling mouth, moving easily over the boggy ground. Cursing the persistent dog, he turned and strode on, relieved to reach the first of the silver birches and pause among their twisted trunks. Above him now, the ground rose very steeply: tumbles of long wet grass and fallen leaves, bulging outcrops and boulders from which the trees had grown in all kinds of gnarled and knotted shapes; the oak split from between the strata of the rock, the rowan ran its roots along the lines of any crevice which afforded a grip, the birches were weary and grey with a covering of lichen. He started to climb. His shoes slipped as he scrambled higher. There was the hound, hesitating at the foot of the hillside to watch the man climbing. It coiled itself effortlessly before launching the first series of leaps, from crag to crag, between the trees, coming higher much faster than the man had managed to do, so that he renewed his efforts to reach his cave before the dog did. Out of breath, with the beginnings of a stitch nagging at his side, he worked himself up the face of the wooded cliff. His glasses almost dislodged themselves from his nose, he paused, sweating, to push them firmly into place. When he arrived at the ledge where the caves were, he fell heavily on to the grass, quite careless of his clean trousers, forgetful for those minutes of the climb that he had been only moments away from leaving the cottage, concerned solely with the exertions of his legs and chest in order to avoid the kennel-maid. Lying there, he twisted round to survey the open ground below.

The first hound had almost reached him. Some fifty feet beneath his vantage point, two other dogs were quartering the marsh, fast approaching the bottom of the birch wood. The girl looked very small, seen from high above, like a little child. He heard her shouts and whistles come filtering to him through the bare branches. Just as the hound scrambled on to his ledge, Andrew stood up and backed into the deepest cell. He hissed at the animal, 'Piss off, you ugly brute! Go on, get out of it!' But it nuzzled forward affectionately, perhaps remembering the man from the previous day, possibly recalling in the dimness of its heavy head how it had pressed into his hands that tattered black trophy of the hunt. 'Bastard dog, piss off!' The animal swerved easily from the arc of his foot, the kick went very wide, but the movement sent a clutter of leaves and acorns from the ledge, fluttering and bouncing down the steep cliff. The girl looked up. The man shrank into the recesses of the cave. Catching sight of the errant hound, she shouted a series of commands and exhortations in Welsh, from which Andrew could only gather that the animal's name was Moonlight. Confused, it glanced from the man to the girl below and back to the man, waving its erect tail. 'Look, bloody Moonlight, you daft creature!' he hissed again. 'She's calling you . . . can't you bloody hear her? Piss off, for Christ's sake!' He heard the whisper of footsteps in the leaves, the heavier tread of the girl's boots, and realised that she and the other hounds were climbing too, to investigate the reason for Moonlight's interest in the spot. Exhaling explosively, running his hands through his hair, he resigned himself to waiting for the girl, aware that he would never shake off the attentions of the hound . . . He recovered his breath, straightened his clothing. 'Come on, Moonlight, you monster, come here . . .' and the dog strolled to him, with a broad grin and giving a long-drawn-out yawn of satisfaction at the touch of the man's hands on its velvet ears. This was the unexpected scene which first greeted the two hounds as they sprang up to the ledge, a scene which set all three animals barking deliriously, so that the girl, scrambling as fast as she could to find out what her hounds had cornered, was flushed pink when she pulled herself to the height of the cave and peered in.

The girl sprawled on to the grass. The hounds drifted

away from Andrew as if he had never been there, to bestow all their noisy affection on their mistress. She panted some order to them, she brushed them off with an irritable gesture of one arm, too breathless to speak. Andrew had nothing to say. The hounds fell into the grass as well, silent once more. So, for a minute, the man and the kennel-maid and the animals rested on that narrow ledge in front of the shallow cave which he had thought of as his hermit's cell, high up on the steeply wooded hillside.

Gradually the girl recovered control of her breathing. 'Good,' she said at last. 'Found you.' She stood up and shrugged her clothes into shape after the efforts of the climb. 'I wanted to see you, after what happened yesterday.' She flickered a smile, uncomfortable before Andrew's silence and his unwelcoming face. 'Tried the cottage,' she said, waving a hand in its direction, 'but you weren't in . . .'

There was a short silence, the girl waiting for some response. He blurted out, 'Wasn't I? Well, here I am, just taking a last little walk before I go.' He was annoyed with himself for being unable to match her candid expression. Looking down at his muddy shoes, he said, 'I'm about to set off for Sussex. The car's all packed and ready.'

There was a longer silence, while Andrew thrust his hands into his pockets. He felt the jam jar vibrating with the bumbling of the flies.

'Oh, you're going,' the girl said. 'Anyway, I wanted to tell you we were . . . that's me and my brother . . . wanted to say we were sorry about your little dog, and all that . . .' Andrew did not look up at her. 'Bit of a mess, the whole thing.' She went on defiantly, to fill the silence. 'An accident though, like Huw said, what with the hail and the dark and so on . . . nobody's fault really.' Seeing that she would have no acknowledgement of her apology, she concluded it briefly. 'Well, that's what I wanted to say, that's all. Glad I caught you before you left, would've felt bad otherwise . . .'

Andrew sensed his anger rising as he heard her voice go trailing on. But it was a dull kind of anger, something numb which had no energy to demonstrate itself in an outpouring of rage. He could not speak. The girl moved close to him. He saw that she was clean and pink now, quite different from the sooty witch with whom he had grappled on the hearth rug, she was somehow quite different from the little witch who had been dwarfed by the grand piano. Different . . . except that she smiled that sudden twinkle of a smile and the tip of her tongue appeared from between her tiny white pointed teeth. 'Come on, Pinkie,' she said very softly, her face close to his, 'aren't I forgiven?' She ran her tongue around her lips, she lifted one grubby paw and touched his neck. 'Pinkie? Don't go home without forgiving me. That wouldn't be very nice, would it?' She shuffled even nearer, until her body in its cladding of baggy clothes was pressed to him. Still he said nothing, looking dully down into her eyes, but he felt in his pocket a sudden surging of energy from the jar of flies. They rioted against the walls of their prison. And sensing their power, feeling it course through his body, he lowered his head to the girl's. 'That's it, Pinkie,' she breathed, her mouth very wet, and then his mouth was on hers, his tongue and teeth with hers, while every piece of his body and mind was concentrated solely on the heat of the kennel-maid and while everything else was reduced to a blur of nothingness . . . Only he felt still the buzzing electricity of the flies in his pocket, charging him like a dynamo, sending a surge of energy through his belly, activating such a stirring in him that the girl sensed it and crushed herself into him, so that she burrowed one hand expertly into his trousers and clenched it hard on his hardened cock . . . 'Pinkie . . .' she panted, disengaging her face breathlessly from his, 'that's a good boy, Pinkie,' with her hand closed tighter still. 'This must mean you've forgiven me, mustn't it?' And she started a slow rhythmic motion, gripping and relaxing, clenching and unclenching, while the man stared dumbly down at her, while she flickered her tongue across his lips as delicately as the touch of a moth, while she breathed into his mouth. There was silence in the woodland, such a silence that the next time the flies set up their riotous protest in Andrew's pocket, the girl heard it, the drumming together of wings, the brawling of maddened bodies inside the jar. Her rhythmic massage hesitated. The flickering tongue was still. 'Pinkie? What's that? What've you got there?' And her hand, as though it knew the connection, as though it instinctively knew that the source of the man's power was so close by . . . the hand withdrew from the suddenly sagging cock and flew straight to Andrew's pocket. She knew. 'What's this?'

The girl stepped away from Andrew, slipping the jar out of his pocket. As she brought it up to her face to examine it, the jar misted for a second from the heat of her hand, from the heat of the man's cock, but the mist vanished just as suddenly as the energy was gone from the man. The power drained from Andrew. She stared into the jar, her face very close to the glass. 'What do you want with these, Pinkie? What the hell've you been up to?' He saw her serious expression split into the stoat-grin once more, as she backed away. The hounds were lolling in the long grass, Andrew transfixed at the mouth of the shallow cave, the girl grinning into the jar. 'You great big schoolboy, Pinkie!' she giggled. 'Playing with flies, like a kid in a playground! What are you going to do with them? Pull their wings off, eh?' And she began to laugh more loudly.

Rousing himself from her kisses, from the taste of her tongue and the clenching-unclenching of her hot little hand, he took a step forward. 'Give me the jar, Shân,' he said hoarsely, attempting to smile. 'It's just a little game I've been playing, that's all. Here, give it to me.'

'A game?' She shook her head, her face serious again. 'No, I don't think so, Pinkie. No, it's not a game, is it? You don't want to go tinkering with things you don't understand, do you? Not now that you're on your way back home . . .' Once more she started to laugh, a bright tinkle of laughter which reminded Andrew immediately of the bright music she had somehow winkled from the vast black coffin of a piano. 'You go home, Pinkie, and leave this kind of thing behind. Like this . . .' And, laughing more and more loudly, stepping further back from the advance of the man, she began to unscrew the top of the jar. The flies fought more furiously than ever, sensing their release. The girl laughed, the sound ringing hard through the cover of silver birch, while her pink tongue glistened with bubbles of saliva and darted over the sharp points of her teeth.

A wave of panic swept through Andrew. His fear was compounded by the expression of glee on the girl's face, that she was the witch appointed as the stinkhorn's agent to secure the release of his precious flies, to end their imprisonment and prevent their removal from their land of mists and mountains . . . 'No, give them to me!' he snapped, stepping forward, the anger rising within him. 'I'm taking them with me!' But she laughed, she flashed the points of her teeth at him, and she continued to unscrew the lid of the jar.

He was too clumsy to stop her. As her laughter rang in his head, hard and metallic and mocking, as the first of the flies spun from the jar and buzzed away, he lunged at her to snatch the jar from her hands. She writhed like an otter to avoid him. His anger blanked out everything except her laughter, which seemed to jangle as hard and as discordantly as the bells of a godless chapel, her laughter which pealed through the woods and through his head . . . another, more powerful spell cast by the woodwitch. Until he roared his rage at her, until he lifted his fist and crashed it with all his strength into her face.

The laughter continued in the woodland, its echoes fading to silence. But the girl was gone.

Numb, still intoxicated by the stinkhorn's charm, he watched the kennel-maid spin from him. She arched away, away from the ledge, her body suddenly weightless, turning over and falling like the body of a fish in mid-leap. Her laughter stopped the same instant as she struck the first tree. Thereafter, the girl's descent continued in silence, for her limbs were so encumbered by heavy clothes that they made no sound as she cartwheeled from one projecting boulder to another, as she bounced like a rag-doll down the cliff, striking tree after tree, now spinning from a blow on a slab of rock, now rolling in the air before glancing against a lower ledge, falling and falling and always falling, until her body lay still, more than fifty feet below the hermit's cave . . .

For a minute, Andrew remained still as well, staring down through the trees at the girl. She lay on her front, her head turned to one side, sprawled comfortably as though sleeping in the luxury of a big, soft bed. And in that minute, the woodland blithely resumed the movements and sounds of its everyday lives, unconcerned by the spectacle of a briefly plummeting body. A pair of jays cried harshly to one another, before beating black and white and brilliant blue from the branches of oak, vanishing again with a couple of undulating swoops. A magpie chattered, an ugly sound like the clacking of a rusty old lawnmower. High above the trees, a buzzard wheeled and diced with a raven, both masters of flight in their contrasting styles, the former smoothly evading the rolls and pitches of the latter. The hounds, one moment alerted by the shouts, simply flopped once more into the long grass and lolled their fleshy tongues. Andrew looked down at the girl. Unconsciously, his hand went back to that pocket. But there was nothing. The charge of power was over, as ephemeral as the stinkhorn itself. He made his way from the ledge, slipping and slithering from boulder to boulder, while the hounds sprang nonchalantly around him. Quite quickly he was at the foot of the woodland. Picking up the girl's hat and stuffing it into his pocket, he broke from the cover of the silver birch and walked over to the girl.

Unlike the badger and the swan and the dog, this dead thing did not flaunt itself. They had seemed to relish it, the chance to put on a show . . . grinning jaws, like the teeth of a steel trap; a mantle of massive white wings, the corpse's ready-made shroud; bowels which oozed steam, eyes which were rearranged or burst . . . This girl might have been asleep. When he turned her gently over, kneeling to take hold of her shoulders, she lay back with her eyes half-closed, her hair tousled, and her mouth slightly open in a kind of smile, showing the tip of her tongue very wet between dry, bruised lips, as if she had just experienced the most satisfying orgasm. She was unquestionably dead. Something odd in the angle of her neck suggested that it was broken. Otherwise, the only concession she made to death was the flowering of a big round bruise on her right temple, like an exotic bloom slipped tenderly into her hair by a lover. But, as Andrew knelt over her, a sudden gout of blood broke from her nose, from the force of his fist and the trauma of the fall, spurting on to her lips, into her mouth.

Beside her, in the grass, the jam jar was shattered. The girl had not let go her hold on it even as she reeled from the man's punch, even as she bounced from rock to rock. Now it was broken. The last of the flies crawled from among the splinters of glass.

The hounds drifted away. As they had done in the forest, no longer interested in the body of the little vixen, they trotted off, the three of them, without a glance or a sniff in the direction of the dead kennel-maid.

'Little witch . . .' he whispered. 'Poor little witch . . . What are we going to do with you?'

He held one of her hands in his, while she smiled up at him through a mouthful of blood. A procession of incriminating evidence came to mind as he forced himself to think clearly about his next move, as the first flickers of panic twitched at him. What sort of a character reference might save him this time? A man who, only weeks before, had narrowly escaped a prosecution for beating his girlfriend unconscious! And here, in Wales, a man who provoked brawling in the village hotel, his violence witnessed by a dozen people! Had he hit the kennel-maid's brother? He couldn't remember. This little girl had shot Phoebe, the day before, and now he'd punched her from the top of a high cliff . . .! And finally, the crawling of crippled flies from the broken jam jar reminded him starkly of the contents of the woodshed . . . What kind of a man kept a gallery like that? Whose recommendation could save him from that?

The dead girl smiled at him. She held the power of the stinkhorn.

'Come with me, little woodwitch,' he said quietly.

Her neck groaned and her head rolled as he picked her up, so that she seemed to be twisting to peer over her shoulder. She was very light, no weight at all for a man the size of Andrew Pinkney. For a second, her face was very close to his, with a tiny wet bubble of blood on the tip of her tongue, that blurred, dreamy expression of a female temporarily sated with sex. He could smell her mouth. Swinging her easily across his shoulder, he heard something crack very softly as her head lolled behind him, he felt the warmth of her thigh against his cheek. With her boots knocking rhythmically together, he picked his way over the marshy ground, towards the cottage. There was no sign of the three hounds. He was alone on that hillside, with the body of the kennel-maid bumping gently and sometimes creaking. The sky was beginning to darken. Another November afternoon leaned more heavily on the mountain.

He put her down on the grass in front of the woodshed door, as tenderly as a father lays his sleeping daughter in her cot. Taking her hat from his pocket, he slipped it into the pocket of her jacket. He felt for his keys and found them, not to open the front door of the cottage, but to unlock the woodshed and step inside. For a moment, he sized up the space he had left, that the stacked logs or the odd tins of fuel would not hinder him, and reaching up to the rafters, he touched the one hook which remained vacant. It was very cold. The tip of it was very sharp.

The woodshed was loud with the swarms of flies. They were busy around the badger's snout and in the ruptured flanks of the swan, some of them were showing a preliminary interest in a sac of fluid which quivered from the belly of the dog. And outside, surrounding the girl, all the containers were drumming with heavy bodies, the taut cellophane was battered by a storm of wings. If he closed his eyes, he could imagine he was inside a power-plant of some kind, where all the air was throbbing with a low, insistent hum. He could feel the vibration of energy. He hesitated like this for a minute, and the pulse of power had never been stronger, through his ears and through every pore of his skin as the atmosphere hummed, through his nostrils as the stench of the woodshed surrounded him. And before him, more brilliantly emblazoned on the darkness of his eyelids than ever before, there shimmered the spectre of the stinkhorn . . . erect as he had failed to be erect, cocksure as he had never been, splendidly tumescent as he knew he could never be. The stinkhorn was everywhere, in his ears as the air hummed, in his nostrils, in the charge which surged through him and filled his belly, imprinted on his vision. When he opened his eyes, it remained there. Its spell was on him.

He stepped outside. The girl smiled. She was in cahoots with the stinkhorn, a member of the same coven. She would make a fine new offering to the shrine . . .

He leaned over her and took hold of her lapels. Her head rolled as he sat her up. When he straightened, she stood with him. Her face lolled very slowly forward. With both hands occupied, he had no other way of stopping her forehead cracking against his, so, instinctively, as though it were the most natural and loving thing to do, he pressed his lips once more on her mouth. The weight of her head gave the unmistakable impression that she was administering the most passionate of kisses, her mouth was still hot, it fell wider open and her tongue was wet and soft on his . . . Andrew's head reeled with desire. He returned her kiss, tasting her blood, moaning her name, his lips devouring her lips, his teeth clicking on her teeth . . . The stinkhorn was bright behind his closed eyes, and he felt the rising warmth in his belly as his own poor imitation coursed with blood. The air drummed with flies.

Blowing, licking his lips, he blinked and swung the girl into the woodshed. With a glance at the rafters, he composed himself with a series of deep breaths before lifting her from him with a sudden straightening of his arms. But the weight of her was beginning to tire him. A squadron of flies, detaching itself from the badger's anus, swarmed about his face and made him stumble on the logs. Some of the flies settled on the smeared blood and saliva around his mouth. Spitting, breathless, he was forced to lower her while he rested; she sat on a stack of wood, like a ventriloquist's dummy. Andrew wafted irritably at the flies, the movement of his hand catching the side of the badger and initiating a shower of maggots from its nostrils. They fell among the sawdust, where, while he regained his breath, he popped them with the toe of one shoe until their yellow pus was a single smudge on the whiteness. He waited while another charge of strength ran through him, then he took a firm grip again on the girl's lapels. One . . . two . . . three . . . he counted, shaking his head to dislodge more flies, and he hefted her upwards.

There was a loud crack as the crown of the kennel-maid's head struck the rafters. But, as he felt the body sag, it snagged and hung there. The tip of the hook had pierced the dead thing in the soft skin under the jaw, and now it swung in mid-air while the man stepped back panting.

'Lovely, lovely little woodwitch . . .' he whispered to the dead thing.

A cloud of flies broke from beneath the wings of the swan, to be joined by another cloud which spun dizzily from the badger's jaws. At first, the droning swarm blew about the gloom of the woodshed in a desultory, aimless manner, clustering now in the dog's congealed fur, banging noisily on the big dry feet of the swan. They strafed the man, drawn to the stickiness of his mouth, maddened by his flailing hands. But ultimately they knew where they were bound. In tight formation, they suddenly sped up to the rafters and landed as one black and inquisitive congregation on the girl's face.

'Of course . . .!' the man exclaimed. 'Of course!'

More of the flies abandoned the three other dead things

for the upturned mouth of the fourth. He watched them gorging on her, on the blood, on the saliva, as he himself had gorged on her, just as the flies had gorged on the oozing head of the stinkhorn. For the power of the stinkhorn was in her, ever since she had confiscated the jar of flies from him, and now the flies were drawn inexorably to feed . . .

'Of course!' he said again, darting out of the woodshed. He snatched up the plastic containers, in which thousands of insects were butting and battering, he dashed once more inside. 'These weren't meant to be wasted!' he cried. 'The harvest was for you! Of course it was! These are all for you! Yes, all of them . . .!'

And, one after the other, he ripped open the tight skins of cellophane. Box after box he tore open. His hands trembled to feel so much power, to feel the weight of the flies shuddering in his grip before he unleashed them, to feel the air in the confined space around him throb with their galvanic energy. Within seconds, as his whole body started to shake and he shouted his exhilaration in a harsh untutored voice, the inside of the woodshed was engulfed by an enormous thunderstorm of flies. They were black, violent, hectic creatures, whose wings combined to make a single roar of anger. He felt them in his hair, in his ears and eyes and mouth, but he stood there, shaking, shouting, in a kind of ecstasy to be in the shrine of the stinkhorn while one great host of the stinkhorn's communicants joined to celebrate their sacrament. . .

Gradually the swarm settled. The flies gathered to gorge on the face of the dead thing. The air in the woodshed fell still. There was a warm, reverent, enveloping silence as the entire congregation fed on the woodwitch.

Andrew Pinkney spent a long time, or so it seemed to him, staring up at the body of the girl. Her neck, distended by the tug of the hook beneath her chin, was very white. He was surprised how little blood appeared where the skin was punctured, just a tiny blob like a jewel which broke and ran a quick trickle into her collar. He could not see her face, for it was covered by a crawling mat of flies. Her arms dangled loosely by her sides, her legs pulled straight by the weight of the big boots. He watched her, while she stopped swinging and was perfectly motionless, while the inside of the shed became dark, for it was evening in the valley and the night pressed hard on the heels of the retreating day.

Alone with the four dead things which hung on their hooks, the man lingered in the shrine. When he felt a wave of weariness fall on him, he sat on a stack of silver birch, reluctant to leave, and he listened to the silence as it was fuelled by the contented whisper of the flies. He was warm and safe in the woodshed. It enfolded him like the womb. Nothing could harm him there. Nobody would laugh at him. Such was the lull in the air of that fetid place that a splendid, slumberous apathy weighed him down . . .

Until, perhaps an hour later, he was aroused by a shrieking explosion from the far side of the valley.

Startled from his torpor, he stood up and staggered outside. He was just in time to see the night sky scored with sparks, red and golden sparks which fizzled and fell back to earth. He rubbed his eyes, wondering what it could have been. There was another detonation across the valley, and there rose above the river a barrage of exploding lights, blossoms of fire and colour erupting in whistles and screams and crackling before they were quenched by the darkness. At the same time, in the distance he saw the first lickings of a flame as a fire was lit, a fire which burst into a chrysanthemum of golden light as someone splashed it with petrol. More fireworks went up. The sky splintered with sparks. Further along the valley a second blaze began, and there was a third, as though at an agreed time these beacons should be lit to unite the valley in celebration. It took the explosion of another volley of fireworks to light the sky before the bemused man who had stepped from his woodshed understood what was happening. It was the fifth of November. At six o'clock that evening, up and down the valley, the Guy Fawkes parties began . . .

So he could go home to Sussex after all! That glorious end-of-term feeling welled up in him again!

Home! Nothing need stop him, he'd leave nothing to incriminate him . . . The sky raced with explosions, the sparks and flares of rockets, and from near the fires which flamed across the valley there were the bright eruptions of Catherine wheels and Roman candles. Andrew busied himself. First, he picked up Phoebe's basket with its bundle of blankets and carried it into the woodshed, putting it down among the stacks of logs; he took Jennifer's washed-out watercolours there too, laying them on top of each other in the basket. Running to the car, he found the wellington boots he had packed away, and he put them on. His shoes were wet and muddy from scrambling about the woodland; returning to the woodshed, he tossed them inside, with the dog's basket and the paintings, and, after a moment's thought, he slipped out of the jacket he had put on for the drive south, took his keys from it, and slung it inside. With the deepening cover of night, the blackness of it enhanced by the fireworks, he could see nothing in the shed now. Again he went down the hill a little way, to the car, coming back with the torch he needed in the pitch darkness where the dead things hung on their hooks, beaming its pool of light below the badger's snout, under the swan's wide black feet, through the tangled fur of the dog and past the girl's boots. There, in a far corner, where he had first seen them weeks before, he picked out that assortment of paint pots and brushes, bottles of turpentine, and a couple of tins of fuel . . . Leaning past the body of the girl, so that he brushed one of her hands with his face, he took these tins of fuel and stood back. The movement of his head had set the girl swinging. The hook under her chin creaked in the rafters, for it was a long time since it had accommodated a dead thing; the hand which his face had touched now moved in the torchlight, indeed, had it not been that the kennel-maid's boots hung heavy in mid-air, she could have been realistically alive, her arms quite natural and casual by her sides, her face upturned as though she were fascinated by some tiny thing, perhaps the cocoon of a rare moth she had spotted on the rafters. The single runnel of blood was drying on her throat. Andrew wrested his stare from the whiteness of her taut skin. He inspected her fingers to see that she wore no rings, there were no keys in her pockets, she wore no watch. He set the torch down on the logs so that its beam lit the gloom of the woodshed. His head began to drum with the industry of the flies, they settled on his face, those which were gorged on the feast he had provided for them, they buzzed from their meal and the repositories of their eggs to the blond hair of their benefactor. Ignoring them, he unscrewed the top of one of the cans and sniffed its contents. Paraffin? The can was full. He splashed it over the driest of the logs, hearing its cheerful glugging in the throat of the can, admiring the golden lights of the fuel as it caught the beam from the torch. When it was empty, he opened and sniffed another can, pouring the paraffin on to the basket, the blankets, his abandoned jacket and shoes, pausing to feel that there was still plenty left. Precariously, he stepped higher on a big trunk of the silver birch and bent his head against the rafters. From there, it was easy to saturate the four dead things. The flies were not pleased. As he poured the fuel into the badger's corrupted anus until it overflowed and trickled through the coarse grey bristles, the flies rose in a cloud from the corpse. When he poured the amber fluid down the throat of the swan, hearing it run into all the secret channels of its gullet, a swarm of flies fled in disgust. He doused the bird's feathers. What was left of Phoebe's face gleamed wet as he drenched it, the liquid ran deep through the dog's coat and dripped from its hanging snout. Still there was fuel in the can, sloshing noisily as the level dropped. Stretching up, he tipped it into the girl's hair. She drank it, between bruised lips, swallowing drunken flies. It filled her mouth. He poured fuel into her shirt. When her clothes stank of paraffin, he stepped down to the floor again and emptied the can into her boots.

The inside of the shrine was heavy with the perfume. It maddened the flies. It obliterated the stench of the dead things.

Standing at the open door, he glanced away to the bonfires in the further darkness. People were dancing about them, holding flaming torches. There was the fizzing of sparklers as children whirled them round and round and round, the exhilarating whoosh of rockets which burst into sparks before cascading in glorious colours back to earth, all the wonderful paraphernalia of an event which the children loved, a celebration whose focus was the cremation of the effigy of a man . . . Poor kids! thought Andrew Pinkney. Is that what you call a bonfire? With a dummy made out of laddered tights stuffed with newspaper, an old gardening jacket, a plastic mask bought from a novelty store? A spineless rag-doll which the first flames will shrivel to nothing? You poor little bastards! Now, if you'd come over to this side of the valley, to Cockerel Cottage, you'd see a real witch burning . . .!

He struck a match and tossed it into the woodshed.

He was driven backwards by an explosion of flame. The floor of the shed seemed to launch a single blast of fire which filled every inch of the space, from wall to wall, right up to the rafters, so that the little outhouse became a capsule of intense white heat. The force of the flame was not dissipated by burning into the night sky, none of the heat was wasted as it was wasted from those other fires. Imprisoned by the confines of the woodshed, the blast fed on itself. One solid ball of fire swelled to fill the room, and then it raged more powerfully to escape. Andrew threw up his arms to protect his face from the heat, a sledgehammer of heat and brilliant white light which struck him from the open door, he saw the basket writhe and disappear while shreds of the blankets and his jacket spun up and around in the turmoil of flame. The logs, carefully stacked so that the air could move freely among them, flared fast as their bark curled and frizzled like frying bacon, and this became the unquenchable bed of the blaze to enflame everything above it. In a second, the four dead things were four torches, their shapes still quite separate and clearly defined, the white flames running over them and through them to find more of the fuel they craved. A pall of stinking black smoke rolled from the door, the girl's boots melted and dripping to burst into orange flames. The badger was a bubble of fire which broke there and then with a tearing of swollen flesh. It fell from its hook and was gone. The swan revelled in this new moment of glory, holding its head up to let the fire devour its wings, hanging white and holy, like a martyred saint. It dropped from its hook. The dog was nothing, blistered and shrivelled, a dead thing which slithered off the hook.

Only the girl remained. And what a Guy Fawkes she was! Without her boots, now that they were gone in a smother of black smoke, she was embraced by the fire. Her clothes slipped from her and blew about the woodshed like demented bats, the cinders of rags tossed by the heat. Only for a moment her exposed skin was as white as Andrew had once seen it . . . then it was as black as he had smeared it. The transformation was uncanny, so that he walked dumbly closer to the fire to watch it more intently, to stand in the full blast of the heat and gape with astonishment . . . Yes, it was the same trick! The trick of Hallowe'en played again on Guy Fawkes Night! First she was white, long and smooth and white as he'd undressed her in the firelight, and then she was black, distorted and writhing and black as he'd daubed her with wet soot! But this time, her skin bubbled. Flies struggled from her mouth, only to ignite into brilliant golden sparks. Hundreds of them, thousands of them burst from her into their individual pinprick of fire which then was gone for ever, like the distant implosion of a dying star . . . The flames sprang to her and fell away, recoiling with pieces of blackened stuff. She was a torch. She shivered with a coat of white fire. It covered her black body. And when her face and hair became one inseparable mass, when she exhaled a long plume of flame from between her lipless teeth, she slipped from her hook, consumed by the insatiable flames. Gone. The kennel-maid, the little witch-bitch, the woodwitch was gone.

Still the woodshed blazed. There was a great deal of timber, heated to such a pitch by the constraints of the fire which turned back on itself and fed itself to a greater frenzy, so that there was nothing the furnace could not consume. The rafters burned through. All the slates of the dilapidated roof crashed down. No longer confined, the fire roared up towards the black sky with a torrent of sparks. Across the valley, there were people who glanced over to see this blaze which was funnelled higher than theirs, people who admired it and wondered what kind of a Guy had been burned on it. Their effigies were gone. Nothing was left but a few cinders. And soon, as the logs of birch and oak and rowan continued to burn, folding themselves inwards as the stacks collapsed to engulf everything which had fallen among them, nothing remained of the four unlikely Guys which had hung on their hooks in the woodshed. Nothing. The four dead things were gone. Claws and bone, nails and even teeth . . . Nothing was left in the core of that fire.

In a daze at the dazzle, his nostrils scorched by the blast and by the diminishing stench, Andrew Pinkney stepped back from the relics of the shrine of the stinkhorn.

*

He sat in his car and watched the fire die down. It subsided, contained within the stone walls, but still it burned fiercely, wasting none of its energy, concentrating its heat inward and gorging on itself. Cocooned in the darkness, he only heard the random crackle of distant fireworks. The brightness of the flames was the only light, for the mountainside and its blanket of the forest rose sheer before him, merging into a blue-black sky. He saw the glow of the fire diminish, until he knew that nothing but a few embers were bedding down and beginning to cool. Then he started the car.

As ever, there was a smooth wave of shallow water running across the river bridge. In the beam of his head-lamps, it slid like silk, an inch or two deep. Glad of the wellington boots, he got out of the car and opened the gate, drove forward a little and stopped on the bridge while he walked back to shut the gate again. He paused there, with the water whispering past the wheels of the car, he stood in the water and felt its gentle pressure on his boots. Taking off his glasses, he closed his eyes and rubbed them with his fingertips. The blaze continued to burn inside his head, a flickering orb of fire in the dark cavern of his mind . . . And what else? There was something else. Screwing his eyes more tightly shut, he found that the image of the burning woodshed and its four torches became focused into the single white column of the stinkhorn. Yes, it was still there . . . How long would he be haunted? Would he ever shake off the ghost of the woodwitch?

He opened his eyes. High on the hillside, a fading pinpoint of light marked the end of the fire. Indeed, as he watched, it vanished, swallowed by the enveloping darkness of the night. The spark disappeared. And the effect of its disappearance was to obliterate every trace of his visit to Cockerel Cottage. If his mind were a slate on which a record of his stay had been inscribed, then it was wiped clean and blank by the sudden extinction of that spark. There was only blackness where the cottage, the woodshed, the dead things had been . . . But when he sat in the car and ran his tongue around his lips, he could still taste the final kisses of the kennel-maid. From his pocket he took a clean white handkerchief, wiping his mouth over and over and over again, until the handkerchief was smeared with blood. Once more he squeezed shut his eyes . . . There shimmered the spectre of the stinkhorn. So he would carry it home with him after all.

He slammed the car door. From the shadows of the trees, disturbed by the sudden sound, the heron beat heavily towards the bridge. The big grey bird flapped upstream and was illuminated briefly by the headlamps. There, it jinked and swerved before it was gone into the darkness, for it was enmeshed in a nightmare it could never throw off, haunted by a ghost it would never exorcise.

STEPHEN GREGORY

THE CORMORANT

From the moment of its arrival at the cottage in the Welsh mountains one drizzling October afternoon, the cormorant's malignant presence creates turmoil and spreads fear. As blizzards shroud the mountains in snow, the cormorant's evil power takes shape, hunting and haunting the family into fear and frenzy . . .

'A considerable delight . . . assured and restrained . . . The quality of prose is particularly impressive, as too is his economy of expression'

Time Out

'Promising and bizarre with some excellent set pieces'

The Times

'Extraordinarily disturbing but brilliant and utterly absorbing'

Western Mail

'I liked it. Intelligent and well-written with a natural feel for the avian vandal of the title which brings to mind the poetry of Ted Hughes'

Iain Banks, author of The Wasp Factory

SOMERSET MAUGHAM AWARD WINNER
WELSH ARTS COUNCIL BOOK AWARD WINNER

sceptre